# HOTT FLASH
## The Adventures of a 50-Year-Old Superhero

### Julie Ray

BALBOA PRESS
A DIVISION OF HAY HOUSE

Copyright © 2013 Julie Ray.

All rights reserved. No part of this book may be used or reproduced by any means, graphic, electronic, or mechanical, including photocopying, recording, taping or by any information storage retrieval system without the written permission of the publisher except in the case of brief quotations embodied in critical articles and reviews.

Balboa Press books may be ordered through booksellers or by contacting:

Balboa Press
A Division of Hay House
1663 Liberty Drive
Bloomington, IN 47403
www.balboapress.com
1 (877) 407-4847

Because of the dynamic nature of the Internet, any web addresses or links contained in this book may have changed since publication and may no longer be valid. The views expressed in this work are solely those of the author and do not necessarily reflect the views of the publisher, and the publisher hereby disclaims any responsibility for them.

The author of this book does not dispense medical advice or prescribe the use of any technique as a form of treatment for physical, emotional, or medical problems without the advice of a physician, either directly or indirectly. The intent of the author is only to offer information of a general nature to help you in your quest for emotional and spiritual well-being. In the event you use any of the information in this book for yourself, which is your constitutional right, the author and the publisher assume no responsibility for your actions.

Cover pictures by Julie Ray.

Printed in the United States of America.

ISBN: 978-1-4525-8435-5 (sc)
ISBN: 978-1-4525-8437-9 (hc)
ISBN: 978-1-4525-8436-2 (e)

Library of Congress Control Number: 2013918412

Balboa Press rev. date: 10/31/2013

This book is dedicated to my amazing, loving, beautiful mom, Linda. Thank you for teaching me the true meaning of "girl power," for instilling in me the love of books and animals, for being my biggest cheerleader, for reading my words, and for being the inspiration for the character, Ella Malone. (*Mean it!*)

# And Many More Thanks

Thanks to my cool aunt, Ann, for reading my words over and over while on her own vacation, for always being quick to laugh, for being there for my family, and for being the inspiration for the character, Tammy.

Thanks to my brilliant brother, Ron, for being brave enough to read a story about a woman with menopause, for never giving up, for being the inspiration for the character, Michael, and for being one of the most creative people I know. He created the spectacular cover of this book, which is better than I could have ever imagined.

Thanks to my wonderful boyfriend, Garick, for his support of anything I do (no matter how crazy!), for putting up with the good, the bad, and the ugly me during the writing process, and for being my "Superman."

Thanks to my powerful, angelic, scary-smart friend, Alexa, for her guidance and for making me believe that *I can do it*.

Thanks to my magical, talented, fantascular friend, Candie, for cracking a joke when needed and for being my friend for all of these years.

Thanks to my trail-blazing, fierce friend, Shelly, for being my "gurl."

Thanks to my friend, Renee, for her infectious laughter and constant encouragement.

Thanks to my friend, Robert, for his unending support for me and mine.

Thanks to my friend, Martha, for always being there through the years and the miles.

Thanks to my friend, Robynn, for never calling me, or my ideas kooky.

Thanks to my friends, Georgie, Rosemarie, Rebecca, Nina, Shari, Shereata, Helen, Tammy, Rochelle, Pam, Betty, Lesa, and Kat, for their support.

Thanks to Jessica and Mieke for their patience, persistence, and TLC.

Thanks to Dr. Sands and staff for keeping me on my feet.

Thanks to Sandra for keeping me on my rocker.

Thanks to Fran Drescher, Jessica Simpson, and Mally Roncal, for supporting women of all ages, for loving animals, for staying true to themselves, and for becoming successful businesswomen without sacrificing their integrity.

Thanks to Kim Harrison, Patricia Briggs, Vicki Pettersson, Jeaniene Frost, Charlaine Harris, MaryJanice Davidson, and Janet Evanovich, for writing the books that I love to read.

Thanks to HRH Collection, BentleyBlonde, Kandee Johnson, and LisaLisaD1, for making the YouTube videos that I love to watch.

Thanks to Joss Whedon, for Buffy, Willow, River, Zoe, Kaylee, and Echo.

Thanks to the movie *Red*, for showing what I've known for years—that you can be cool and kick butt at any age!

Thanks to my Angel, Elizabeth, for watching over me.

Thanks to my Angel, Jack, for being the sweetest soul I will ever know.

Thanks to my mom's cat, Monkey, for being the inspiration for the character, Monkey.

And finally, thanks to my cat, Cindy, for her quiet support.
*Hmm . . . Cindy is a really good character name . . .*

# Preface

THE MAIN CHARACTER OF THIS story, Ella Malone, came to me back in 2007. My mom had been struggling with a very gruesome menopause for ten years and was having a hard time staying positive and upbeat. I wanted to make her happy but felt helpless, until one day, out of nowhere, the idea of making a joke out of menopausal side effects—hot flashes, and the like—came to me. Then the idea of turning those side effects into superpowers popped into my head. My mom burst into laughter when I told her my ideas. At that moment, Ella Malone was born. I started writing Hott Flash in 2010 and finished in 2012.

I am so excited to finally be able to share Ella's story. I hope that you enjoy reading this book as much as my mom did.

# Hello!

THEY SAY THAT WITH AGE comes wisdom. Well, it's more like with age comes aches, pains, fatigue, memory loss, weight gain, increased gas, decreased bladder control, and—oh yes—my favorite: *The Ma'am*. The Ma'am is what many women fear the most. One day you're a Miss, then maybe you're a Mrs., or a Ms., but the dreaded day comes when someone much younger than you calls you Ma'am. You have now become the old lady in the room.

My name is Isabella Malone (Ella for short), and thanks to the cute and perky little checker at the grocery store earlier today, *I have become* the old lady in the room. You might be saying to yourself, "Wow! This lady sounds like she got up on the wrong side of the bed!" More like the wrong side of the *hill*! You see, I'll be turning fifty tomorrow, and I'm looking forward to it about as much as I am to my annual women's wellness exam.

Where have all the years gone? Just last week, I was twenty and having the time of my life, with my only concern being what to wear on my big date . . .

Fifty . . . Darn.

# And Away We Go

It's the morning of May 5 and I open my eyes—hey, I'm alive! I'm fifty, but I'm alive! Can I move? Yes. Do I still have all my original parts? Yes. (At least all of the important ones!)

*Whew! I made it to another milestone.*

I decide that I should probably get out of bed and start my day. I don't have anywhere I need to go, since I've been *retired*—I really can't stand that word because it makes me feel so old—for the past five or so months. My ex and I sold our business after the divorce, and I just haven't found anything else I want to do now to make money. I have the house to myself since my husband, Pete, or "Big Pete" as everyone calls him, decided that he wanted to trade me in for a newer model and left unexpectedly last year.

At first, I felt lost because so much of my identity was tied to my kids and my husband. When my kids flew the coop, I had Pete to comfort me and make me feel safe. Then he left and a feeling of insecurity came over me that took forever to get rid of. Without my friends and family, I'm not sure how I would have ended up. Thankfully, I found out that I am a whole person with hopes and dreams. For the first time in my adult life, I'm able to take care of *my* needs and wants. I discovered things about myself that I'm not sure I would've been able to as a wife.

I look at Pete's leaving as an unexpected gift. I got myself, and he got a twenty-eight-year-old bartender-slash-actress. I think I got the better deal!

I get out of bed, and while washing my hair in the shower, I think back more on my life.

I came from a modest background. My parents taught me that you have to work hard *and* smart for what you want in life. They didn't have the money to help pay for my college, so I managed, with the help of a partial scholarship and a full-time job, to earn my business degree.

I met Pete during my junior year of college. He was everything I never knew I wanted in a man. He was this big hulk of a guy who, of course, was on the football team. We dated for two years, and after the NFL drafted him right after graduation, we got married. We lived in several big cities over the next few years, and along the way, I became pregnant with my daughter, Maggie.

Maggie is twenty-six now and lives about a half an hour away from me in Houston. She owns a very successful beauty spa in the upscale neighborhood of River Oaks. She's also a very talented feng shui consultant and does consultations on the side. She says that she does what she does so that she can help people feel good about themselves and their surroundings. What a good girl!

My son, Michael, is twenty-four. He lives in Houston too. At twenty-three, he invented a device that has brought him top recognition in the world of science. He has since invented and developed things that have gone up in space and have helped our military. Despite all of this, he's a down-to-earth young man with a great sense of humor and an amazing sense of honor to the community.

He donates a lot of his money to The Muscular Dystrophy Association. This is because when he and Maggie were little kids, we encouraged them to watch the Jerry Lewis Telethon every year, to show them how fortunate they were to have their health and that it's everyone's duty to help others. My kids started collecting coins for Jerry's Kids back then and have continued to this day. I love my kids. (Smile.)

I step out of the shower and start toweling off, and that's when suddenly something doesn't feel right. I should say that my *face* doesn't feel right. I reach up to touch my chin . . . *What the heck?!* I run to the mirror, and to my utter horror, I see that I have a beard! A thick mass of quill-like, inch-long auburn hair is running from ear to ear!

*Oh my gosh! What's going on? A beard! I know I didn't wake up with one, and I sure as heck didn't go to sleep with one. Am I crazy? No, I don't think so, although I am carrying on a pretty long conversation with myself and for a brief time I used to wear gaucho pants . . . But this is real!*

I start to feel faint. I don't know what to do!

I call my doctor's office. While the phone is ringing, I try to get a hold of myself.

The receptionist answers the phone and says, "Clark's Clinic. How may I help you?"

"Is Dr. Clark available for a quick question?" I ask.

"Dr. Clark's with a patient. Would you like to leave a message?"

*Ummm . . . what to say?* "Could you have him call Ella Malone as soon as he can please?"

"I will give him the message. It looks like it will be about an hour before he has free time."

"Thank you so much," I say and then hang up. *Click.*

*Okay, an hour. Get dressed, eat, and try to forget about the forest growing on your chin.*

The phone rings forty-five minutes later. I jump to answer it. "Hello?"

"Hi, Mom, it's Maggie. Happy birthday!"

"Thank you, honey, but can I call you back in a bit?"

"Sure, are you all right?"

"Oh yes, I was just in the middle of something."

"Okay. Well, see you at dinner tonight. Love you."

"You too." *Click.*

The phone rings again. "Happy birthday, Mom!"

"Hi, Michael, sweetheart. Can I call you back later?"

"Is everything okay?" he asks.

"Everything is fine. Just in the middle of something."

"Okay, love you. 'Bye, Mom."

"Love you too, Michael." *Click.*

The phone rings. Thankfully, it's Dr. Clark.

"Oh Dr. Clark, thank you for returning my call! I've had something very strange happen to me today."

"What seems to be the problem?" says Dr. Clark in his most official-sounding doctor voice.

"Well," I say, "I went into the shower today, a normal woman. I came out with a beard!"

"What?" he says.

I explain what happened. He says, "Well, you know, Mrs. Malone, at your age, extreme facial hair is normal, due to the onset of meno—"

"Don't say it!" I say, not wanting to hear how his sentence ended.

"I would suggest that if you're uncomfortable with your facial hair, then maybe you should look into electrolysis," he says. It's clear that he wants to move away from this call and to his next patient with *real* health concerns.

"What about how quickly the hair showed up? It's not normal?" I say, looking at my reflection in the mirror. I realize with a start that I bear an uncanny resemblance to my crazy Uncle Otto.

"That hair was probably always there, Isabella. You just didn't notice it until today. I need to get back to my other patients. You take care now." *Click.*

Oh boy . . .

All right. I need to do something. Scissors! I'll cut as much off as I can, then call my daughter and beg her to make a house call with her electrolysis machine. (Thankfully, she has one.)

I go find a pair of scissors and position myself in front of the bathroom mirror. I open the scissors and then close them on a few hairs. The scissors can't cut through them! It's like trying to cut steel cables with a plastic spoon!

*What in the world is going on here? Have I completely lost my mind and just don't know it?*

I pick up the phone and call Maggie.

"Hi, Mom."

"How did you know it's me?" I ask, feeling stranger and stranger by the minute.

"Caller ID, Mom. Are you sure you're okay?" she asks, sounding worried.

"As a matter-of-fact, no. Is there any way that you could come to the house as soon as possible and bring your electrolysis machine with you?"

"What the—"

I cut her off and say, "You'll find out when you get here." *Click.*

# It Started in the Shower

MAGGIE ARRIVES TWO HOURS LATER with her equipment in tow.

I answer the door with a towel in front of my face.

"Okay, Mom, what's with all the secrecy?" I step aside to let her come in then remove the towel. She starts laughing. *Not* the response I expected. "You look like Uncle Otto! Good joke. Now why am I really here?"

I take her hand and put it on my beard. She stops laughing.

"Pull it," I say.

She gives it a tug and jumps back with her green eyes as wide as saucers. *"Mom, what's going on? That feels and looks . . ."*

"Real?" I say.

"Yes," she squeaks out.

"It *is* real! I went into the shower chin-hair free but came out of the shower with a full, prickly beard. Dr. Clark told me that I probably already had it but that I just didn't notice it until now."

"Well, did he *see* it?' she asks, staring at my chin nest.

"No, it was over the phone. I really don't want to go out looking like this. It's bad enough that I'm an old lady today. Now I'm a *bearded* old lady!" I start crying. I can't help it.

"Let's get you to your bed, then I'm going to take care of this craziness," she says, leading me into my bedroom.

I lie down, and a few minutes later, she comes in with her machine in tow.

"Okay, just relax," she says while flipping a switch. She has the instrument in her hand and is going toward my chin with a look of fierce determination. As soon as she touches my face, I get scared and tense up. I've never had this machine used on me, and I'm jumpy anyway today.

All of the sudden, she stops and turns the machine off. I look at her. She looks at me and then puts a mirror in front of my face. I take it from her because she's got it too close and I can't see a damn thing. I hold the mirror farther away and look to find a beard-free me.

"It just sucked right up into your skin as soon as I touched you!" My daughter looks perplexed and excited all at once. "Tell me again. When did the hair show up?"

"It showed up during my shower," I say.

"Okay, maybe we should retrace your steps. The hair is gone, but I want to make sure this won't happen to you again. Would you mind taking another shower?" she says, already on her way to the bathroom.

"All right," I say, pulling out a tank top and a pair of shorts.

Into the shower I go. I'm so happy to be beard free, and the water feels so nice on my face. Then I feel it—a strangeness in my face!

"It's coming back!" yells Maggie.

"Oh no! I was so happy just now," I say.

Maggie already has her machine ready to use on me. As she touches it to my face, I jump, and *poof!* The hair retracts again. "Fascinating. Mom, it seems that when you're relaxed, the hair comes out, but when you're tense, it retracts."

"Well, I was pretty much tense all morning after I discovered the hair on my chinny chin chin. Why didn't it go away then?" I ask, feeling a little angry and not expecting her to have an answer.

"I believe that it's because you weren't focused. As soon as I turned on my machine, it had your undivided attention, so your tension had a focus, giving it more power. Same as when it appeared, you were in the shower focusing on taking a shower." She looks very pleased with herself. "I'd like to try one more thing if you're up to it."

"What is it?" I ask, feeling utterly strange.

"I'd like for you to close your eyes and think about something that makes you feel happy and relaxed. Concentrate hard, Mom."

I close my eyes and think about a comfy recliner, a good book, and a cat curled up on my lap.

"Here it comes again. Okay, hold on . . ."

The next thing I know, I hear a *snap* and feel a sting on my wrist.

"What the . . ." I open my eyes and see Maggie standing there while triumphantly holding a rubber band.

Between the two of us, we determine that I have to figure out how to stay focused and stressed to keep the hair away, until we find out what the heck is going on. As the day has been progressing, a feeling of anger has been slowly creeping into the background of my mind, so I don't think that I will have to worry about the stress. My daughter recommends keeping a rubber band on my wrist, so that I can have a focus. (I stick a handful of them in my purse just to be safe.)

Maggie has to get back to work, and I assure her that I'll be all right for the next hour by myself, until I have to pick up my parents at the airport.

My parents are flying in from Sedona, Arizona, for my big birthday. They moved there from Wyoming when I was away at college. They said they liked the "vibe" of Sedona after going there once on vacation.

They are quite a pair! My mother, Jade, is seventy years old but looks and acts my age. She's a very talented artist who paints, does pottery, and makes jewelry. Then there's my seventy-three-year-old father, Tom. He makes jewelry too, and he's a musician who has a weekly gig playing his violin at the local Elks Lodge. They were childhood sweethearts who, to this day, are each other's best friends.

I arrive at the airport and spot my parents right away. My mother is wearing a turquoise blouse with red pants that are almost the same shade of red as her hair. My father is a little over six feet tall with a full head of white hair. They are standing next to a group of people and being their usual friendly selves. I can tell that my father probably just told a joke, because he has a look of satisfaction on his face that he gets when people laugh when he wants them to. He must be pretty satisfied by all the laughing that is going on. My parents seem to draw people to them, which shows that they were obviously born to be an artist and a musician.

*I am so lucky to have them as parents.*

*Snap! Snap!* goes the rubber band after I get that feeling in my chin.

I pull up to the curb, park, and get out. My father immediately engulfs me in a big bear hug. His blue eyes are twinkling, and I reach up to give him a kiss on the cheek. *Snap!*

"How's my girl?" he asks. *Ahh, parents! No matter how old you are, you're still their baby.*

"Fine, Pop. How was the flight?"

"Oh fine, fine. Hit a little turbulence, but nothing worth getting upset over."

Just then, I smell my mother's perfume. I think that it's more essential oil than perfume, because it's a pleasant combination of lavender and vanilla. *Snap!*

"Hi, Mom," I say, turning around to receive her hug that I knew was coming.

"Hello, sweetheart. How are you?" she asks, looking at me rather intently.

"I'm fine, Mom. Do I look like I'm not?" I ask, looking into her big green eyes.

"Oh no, my dear. You look fine," she says still looking at me hard.

"Okay. Well, let's get you both loaded up, so that we can go," I say, picking up her suitcase and heading toward my car.

We get loaded up and drive toward my house. My father begins a detailed story of their plane ride here, and my mom is looking at me intently out of the corner of her eye.

We arrive at my house about a half an hour later. We get everything into the house, and my parents settle into the guest room.

I go back to my bedroom to see how I look, because my mother's behavior made me worry that something else strange had happened to my face. I look in the mirror and see what I've seen my whole life, more or less. Dark auburn hair that goes a few inches past my shoulders. (I just can't bring myself to cut my hair just because I'm over forty.) Green eyes just like my mom's. And long fingers like my pops.

I'm five foot nine, so I'm a little on the tall side. My mom is five foot ten, so I had no choice but to be the size I am. I was always slouching when I was younger, because I was always teased about my height, but as I grew older, I made peace with the fact that I'd never be a dainty woman.

Just then, there is a knock on my bedroom door. "Come in," I say, and my mom steps in with a concerned look on her face.

"Mom, what's wrong?" I say with a feeling of dread.

"Ella, I need to ask you something that might sound a little crazy."

"What is it?"

"Did something strange happen to you today? And I need honesty."

I open my mouth to say no and then decide that I will be honest—even if I upset her and make her think that I've lost my mind.

"Mom, today I went into the shower a normal person, then came out of the shower with a full beard."

I wait for her reaction.

"It has begun," she says, looking very serious.

"What has begun?" I say, wondering why she wasn't looking for the nearest psychiatrist in the phonebook.

"The Change. The Change has begun, and your life will never be the same."

# The Change . . .

"**Y**OU MEAN I'M IN *MENOPAUSE*?" I ask, fearing the answer.

"Well, yes and no. I think that you should sit down, because what I'm about to tell you might really disturb you," my mom says, leading me to the bed and closing the bedroom door for privacy. I sit and look up at her expectantly.

"We have something in our family that is passed from mother to daughter, and it comes into power at age fifty. It's kind of like menopause with a kick." She stops for a minute and seems to search for words. "I don't know when or how it started, because back in my mother's day, things like periods and menopause weren't even discussed.

"A few months after her fiftieth birthday, my mother told me to expect a change to happen to me when I turned fifty. She also went on and on about a bearded lady, but by that time she was on medication from her psychiatrist, so I ignored that. I wish that I hadn't . . ."

She sits down on the edge of the bed. "You see, not long after she turned fifty, your Grandma Garnet was institutionalized for two years. Back then; doctors were really in the dark about menopause. They usually put women in the mental hospital when it hit, because the extreme mood swings and other things that happen during that time mimic insanity.

"I went to visit her a few times, but she was so heavily medicated that I didn't think that she knew who I was. When she was released from the asylum, she seemed broken. She never smiled and she barely spoke to anyone.

"A few months after her release, on the morning of my thirty-second birthday, my mother surprised me by calling me on the telephone. We chatted for a while about nothing in particular, and she actually sounded like her old self. At the end of our conversation, she said to me, 'I feel wonderful today. Good-bye Jade. I love you.'

"I'm told that later that evening, she just . . . disappeared."

"What Gifts did you receive on your fiftieth birthday?" I ask hesitantly. I'm almost afraid to hear what my fate might be.

She continued as if she didn't hear me. "A few months after my mother disappeared, I received a letter with no return address that had a postal stamp from a small town in the country of India. All that it said was, 'Be prepared for The Change of Fifty. You will acquire unusual abilities at this point in your life. Don't be scared. Try to embrace these Gifts, and use them to help mankind. You cannot find someone who does not want to be found.' I knew that this was from her, and I knew that she didn't want to be found, especially by my father, who would have had her committed again . . . Since she was still sounding crazy, I never told anyone of this. I kept the letter, and every once in awhile, I tried to make myself believe that she wasn't crazy, but sadly I couldn't—until I turned fifty."

"Wow, what a story. I always assumed that Grandma was dead, since no one ever spoke of her, and anytime I would ask you about her, you would change the subject. Which you're good at, by the way. So Grandpa went to his grave believing that she had run off and probably died alone somewhere out in the world. Did he try to find her after she left?"

"No, he didn't."

"Do you think that he witnessed any of her 'Gifts'?"

"Yes, I do. I believe that is why he had her committed."

"This is unbelievable," I say with tears in my eyes. "So once again, what Gifts do you have?"

*"Had*—not have," she says. "On the way to the airport this morning, I felt like something was ripped from my body. I had to run to the restroom as soon as we got our bags checked and give myself a once-over to see what happened. Then I noticed that I no longer had the underlying feeling of anger that I woke up with on my fiftieth birthday, and have felt every day to a certain degree, until today. I then realized that you turned fifty today. That's how I knew that possibly *my* Change was over and the torch—sorry—had been passed on to you."

"But why didn't you warn me, Mom?"

"Would you have believed me if I had told you before today?"

I thought about it for a minute. "No, probably not."

Just then, there was a knock on the door.

"You girls okay in there?" my father asks.

"Fine, dear, just talking," my mother says. "We'll be out in a bit."

"Okay, well, I'm going to go for a little walk and stretch my legs then," my father says.

My mom opens the door, plants a big kiss on him, and says, "See you when you get back."

She closes the door, turns to me, and says, "Now where were we . . ."

# You've Gotta Be Kidding!

"Let me get this straight," I interrupt. "Not only do I get all of the horrible side effects of menopause, but I should expect to get some additional crazy Gifts of The Change as well?"

"Honey, the thing is, the side effects are mainly typical ones you would get with menopause, but some are greatly amplified—like your beard."

"Well, shit," I say. "This is just getting better and better."

I realize that my mother seems to be having an episode of sorts, because she's got her hand over her mouth and her eyes are watering.

I touch her arm. "Mom, oh my gosh, what's wrong?"

She takes her hand from her mouth, and I realize that she is laughing.

*I sure as hell don't see anything funny at this point.*

"I'm sorry, honey. It's just that you never cuss, and when you did just now, it took me by surprise!"

"I cussed? What did I say?"

"Well, you said, 'shit,'" she says, trying to keep a straight face.

"Shit, I said, 'shit'?" I ask mortified. I don't cuss, even when I hurt myself. I tried cussing a few times in the past, but it never took.

"It's okay, Ella. It just struck me as funny, because it happened to me as well. When The Change hit me, I said things that'd make a sailor blush. Your father took it in stride though. He just chalked it up to my hormones and sometimes would just chuckle when I let something off-color fly. He and I found that if you can't find humor in things, they will just get you down."

"So I guess Pop knows then?" I ask.

"Oh no. I never told him. He only knew that I went through the *regular* change. No matter how understanding a man your father is, he could never handle the truth.

"Honestly, I don't think that *any* man could. All you have to do is say, 'Female problems,' and a man looks like he wants to cover his ears and run away crying. They'd wet their pants and faint if they knew the details. Sweetheart, we should probably continue this conversation later. If I'm still back here when your father gets back from his walk, he's going to start asking questions." My mom stands up.

"But Mom, *I've* got questions. You said that you felt like something was ripped from your body today. Does this mean that you're over The Change?"

"Yes, I believe it does," she says, smiling.

"The Change starts at age fifty, but I don't know how long it lasts. I don't know if it lasts until it's passed on to a daughter or if it would go away on its own, after the menopause cycle has passed. I had noticed that my Gifts were becoming weaker after ten years and continued to get weaker and weaker, until last month, when they went away completely. For the last month, I still had a feeling of underlying anger, or angst if you will, but that feeling went away when you became active."

"Okay, so I can plan on having a completely messed-up life for what—Maggie is twenty-six, so . . . Holy hell, the next twenty four years!"

I'm getting hysterical now. I've tried to be calm, mature, levelheaded, but come on! There's only so much a person can take.

"Honey, the anger gradually gets stronger, but then it gradually recedes until you hardly feel anything, and who knows? It might be easier on you."

"I just can't believe this. I don't know if I can deal with this."

"Well, Ella, you *have* to deal with this, because you have no choice," she says, looking me straight in the eyes.

"Mom—again—what kind of Gifts did you have?"

My father picks that exact moment to knock on the door.

# Happy Birthday to Me

MY MOTHER AND I NEVER get to finish our conversation, because there is so much to do in preparation for my birthday party coming up tonight.

My family knows that there is no way to throw me a surprise party, so the next best thing is to keep me out of the loop during the planning.

I have no idea where my party is being held, or who is coming, and I am kind of feeling a little angry about not having any control over things.

*Ella! How dare you be angry with your family! That's not like you at all. Snap out of it and appreciate what's being done for you!*

It's time to leave, and I don't want to get in the car.

A few minutes later, I am pleased to see that we have pulled up in front of my favorite Italian restaurant. That is the last pleasant feeling I have for the rest of the evening.

My birthday party turns out to be incredibly trying and stressful, instead of fun and nurturing. I don't have to snap myself with the rubber band the rest of the party, because I am so angry and upset by the turn my life has taken. The guests at my party help with the anger too by saying things like, "You look great for your age." And the younger ones would say, "I hope I look as good as you do when I get to be your age."

I know that they are trying to be nice. Hell, *I've* even said the same thing to someone before. However, when you're on the receiving end—not so great.

*Ahhh!*

Maggie keeps trying to get me alone to see how I am doing, but we never have a chance to talk. I tell her that I'll call her the next day. All I want to do all evening is grab my mother and take her someplace private, so that I can get the rest of my questions answered.

The party wraps up around eleven o'clock. By the time we get back to my house, I am so exhausted that when my parents say that they are going to bed, I don't even try.

# Another Day, Another Dollar (I Wish!)

THE NEXT MORNING, I WAKE up expecting to have grown another head or something, but everything seems to be in order.

I touch my face and no beard—score one for me!

I wonder why I don't have a beard since I've been sleeping, and obviously resting, but then I notice that I feel slightly restless. Kind of like I'd love to have someone push my buttons today so that I could punch 'em.

*Really, Ella? You, who rescues stray animals, helps the needy, and even helped an old lady (who was probably the age I am now) cross the street when you were a kid—you're wanting to hurt another human being physically?*

*Yes, I do,* I tell myself. I'd love to have that young boy who's a checker at the grocery store, who *never* acknowledges my presence when he's ringing me up, do that to me today. He's always so busy putting the lightest things like bread on the bottom of the bag and then putting things like milk jugs on top, even when I have asked nicely—repeatedly—that he not do that.

I've always let it slide because I didn't want to make a scene—I have always done everything I could to avoid confrontation, in every part of my life. Well, not anymore! I feel like I can take the world by the balls and make it mine. I feel so empowered, so alive . . . so . . . hot!

What the hell?

# We're Having a Heat Wave

As I'm having a full-blown conversation with myself (maybe I *am* bonkers), I've been getting dressed, and then *boom!* I feel like I've stepped into hell!

It's like I'm burning up from the inside out!

I've heard of people dying from spontaneous combustion—is this it? Does my life end at fifty and a day?

*Wait a minute. You're not dying; you're experiencing a hot flash dingbat!*

"Well, blow me down!" to quote Popeye.

My clothes feel like they're smothering me. I can't breathe. I'm just miserable! Help!

I want to tear off my clothes, but keep them on because my parents are here.

I go to my bathroom and splash my face with cold water, then I head to the kitchen in search of ice.

I find my mother cooking and my father sitting at the table and reading the newspaper. "It's gonna be another scorcher today," says my father.

"Tell me about it," I say, entering the room.

"How's my girl this morning?"

"Hot. Burning up from the inside," I say, opening the doors of the refrigerator and wedging myself inside it as much as I can. The cool air envelopes me and I start to feel slightly better.

"Oh, you must be having a power surge—I mean hot flash," she says, looking at me.

My father starts to fidget in his chair and says, "I'm going to the study so you girls can talk about your *Special Lady Time*. Yell when breakfast is ready." He kisses my mother on the cheek and leaves.

My mom turns to me and says, "See what I mean?!"

"We're really the stronger sex, aren't we?" I say to her.

"Oh yes, dear, we most certainly are."

I think about this for a while as I'm standing in front of the open fridge. When the food is ready, and my pop is back, I just eat, smile, and decide to let us all eat breakfast in peace, without any reference to my "Special Lady Time." After the dishes have been cleared and my pop has gone outside to "see the world," as he puts it, I corner my mother.

"Okay, what abilities did you have?"

# Jade's Change

"Well, thankfully your father had gotten up and left early on the morning of my fiftieth birthday to go take care of some last-minute errands. I decided that I was going to go for a run, since I hadn't done so in ages.

"I was just coming up to my house, when all of a sudden, I felt like a match had been struck in the middle of my soul. I felt like I was being burned alive! I was so scared that I rushed inside to see if I really was on fire. Thankfully I wasn't. I tried everything to cool down and finally ended up soaking in a cold bath.

"Your father found me there and remarked that he was happy to see that I was pampering myself. I told him what happened and that this was cold water. He turned a slight shade of pink, and said, 'Well, it *is* your fiftieth birthday today. Isn't this when you ladies usually start your Special Time?'

"It felt like a bus had hit me. I sat there after he left, thinking, *I'm old! I'm ancient! Dear Lord! It's the change of life!*

"I had started to cool down, and as I was toweling off after my bath, I felt something *move* under my right armpit. I raised my arm to see what was happening, and when I turned my head to look under there, I saw a lump! I reached out to touch it, and to my surprise, a few drops of water came out of it! I ran to a mirror and raised my arm again, but this time, a big jet of water shot out and hit the mirror! Needless to say, I was shocked. I started raising my arm and putting it down several times, and I noticed that sometimes I would raise my arm and nothing would happen. Other times, Old Faithful! I discovered that if I raised my arm and then lowered my shoulder a bit, it would put pressure on the lump, therefore squeezing the water out of it. I then inspected my left arm, but thankfully no lump.

"I was trying to think what my next step would be when *bam!* I heard my husband say again in my head, 'Well, it *is* your fiftieth birthday today.'

"Oh my goodness—the letter!

"I ran to my jewelry box and pulled out the last connection to my mother I had and read. 'Be prepared for The Change of Fifty.'

"Then I said, 'Well, shit.'"

# The Reaction

I AM SHAKING SO HARD FROM trying to keep from laughing. I know that my mother just shared something with me that she'd never told anyone else, but come on, a squirting armpit! Then I lose all control, and the laughter comes out full force.

"I'm so sorry for laughing," I say, trying to get control of myself.

"Umm . . . (I stifle a giggle) . . . can you show me your trick?" I snort, and start laughing again.

"No, Ella, I cannot show you my 'trick.' I don't have any Gifts left since you became active. Haven't you been paying atten—Ow! What was that?" she says, raising her hand quickly to her cheek.

"What was what? Are you okay?" I ask, sobering up.

My mother has a strange expression as she touches her cheek, and then she looks like she has a hold of something and pulls.

"What in the world?" she says, looking at something in her hand.

I look at her open hand and see blood, and what looks like a one-inch porcupine quill.

"Where did that come from? How did that happen? I don't understand."

"I think that *I* do," she says, looking at me with a slight bit of fear in her eyes.

"I believe that you shot me with one of your chin hairs."

*"I what?"*

"Think about it, Ella. You say that your beard comes out when you're happy. Well, I didn't want to alarm you, but when you were giggling, I saw a few hairs start to come out of your chin. When you were laughing uncontrollably at me, I was shot in the cheek. So I think that it's safe to assume that this is yours," she says, handing me the disgusting thing.

I reach out to take it. It's thick and hard—in fact, it doesn't bend. *Gross! This thing came out of me.* As I look at it resting innocently in my hand, my brain shuts down. "I'm going for a run," I say, as I head for the door.

I don't wait for her response.

I leave the house, and run to the public park a block away. I run several times around the track before I allow myself to think about the nightmare that my life has become. Visions of insane asylums and circus freak shows dance through my head. I stop to catch my breath for a minute, and remember that I'm still holding that horrible chin hair! I run over to a trashcan by the public restrooms, throw that icky thing away, and start running around the track again. I find that no matter how hard I run, I can't run away from my thoughts.

A half an hour later, I return home and find my mother on the front porch. "I've decided to stay a few extra days. Your father will be going back tomorrow morning since he has a gig at the VFW, but I'm staying until you can get control of yourself. I don't want you ending up like your grandmother."

By the look on her face, I know better than to argue with her.

# The Next Day

I TAKE MY FATHER TO THE airport by myself, because I feel guilty about spending most of his visit holed up in my bedroom with my mother.

"I'm sorry for keeping Mom from going home with you, Pop. I just really need her experience right now," I say, looking at him out of the corner of my eye.

"That's okay, my dear, I understand. From what little I know, your 'Special Lady Time' can be a challenge. When your mother was going through it, she became very different, almost secretive, like she was hiding something from me. In fact, for a few minutes, I thought that she was running around on me. Then common sense kicked in, and I realized that she was going through a hard time. I knew that I just needed to love, trust, and support her. She didn't have her mother to talk to, so I'm happy that she can be there for you."

What a sweet man . . . *Snap!* (Thank goodness I still have a rubber band on my wrist.)

We spend the rest of the time traveling to the airport laughing. Pop pulls out all of his funny stories to keep me entertained.

I drop him off at the curb and jump out of the car to give him a hug. "I love you, Pop," I say, not wanting to let him go.

"I love you too, Ella Bella." *Snap! Snap!*

I leave the airport and head toward home.

When I get back to my neighborhood, I turn on to my street and see that there are two other cars in my driveway.

*Oh, it's my kids!*

I walk in and find my kids and my mother sitting in the front room. I don't know what they were talking about, but they all stop talking when I walk in.

My mother stands up and leads me to a chair. "This is an intervention for you, Ella, dear," she says, settling into her chair.

"A *what?*" I say, realizing that my own mother might be the one who incurs the wrath of my ever-building feeling of anger.

"Stay put, Ella. You are dealing with an extraordinary situation, and you have two extraordinary kids who want to help you."

Maggie clears her throat and says, "I've been worried about you since you had me come over to help you with your *ummm . . .* beard. I knew that you were upset, so I knew not to push you. I called Michael and told him the situation that you're in. He *is* a rocket scientist, among other things, you know. Anyway, since then, Grandma has filled us in on what you're going through. Don't get mad at her. She's worried about you, and since she lives so far away, she wanted to know that you weren't alone during this challenging time. Wow, you've got an interesting life ahead of you."

"More like an *amazing* life ahead of you!" chimes in Michael. "I've been doing some thinking about the hair and how it shot out as a projectile. The tarantula has what's known as urticating—hooked or barbed hairs on it. When it's on the defensive, it uses its legs to flick these hairs at its attacker. The porcupine quill is very hard and will become dislodged during an attack, giving the impression that the quills are being shot at the attacker. I've only had a few days to do research on how this could happen and had hoped to find a species capable of this. From the standard medical viewpoint, when a woman reaches a certain age, her hormone imbalances can cause facial hair. Okay, there is facial hair, but why does it come and go, depending on the subject's—I'm sorry—on *Mom's* feelings? I was perplexed until I started looking at it from a quantum-physics angle.

"Everything is energy. Our thoughts can create great physiological changes in our bodies. If you're happy, your body is relaxed. If we throw all logic away, we could look at it like this: When your body relaxes, this could possibly cause a hair follicle to open up enough to allow a thick hair that was growing under the surface to break through. If you're startled, the hair follicle would constrict, possibly causing a contraction of the hair. If you're stressed, the hair follicle might possibly stay too small to allow the hair to come back out.

"As far as you shooting Grandma with one, I had her replay the conversation that the two of you were having, as well as your mental state. She said that you were relaxing as she was telling you her story and a few hairs appeared. When you were trying to hold back your laughter, the hair retracted. When you started *really* laughing—*at her*—the force of the energy brought on by your laughter caused one to break loose. It flew directly at her, I think because she had your full attention at the time.

"Just think: if we could figure out a way to produce the same results at will, you could have an incredible new self-defense mechanism!"

*I need a drink.*

# Experimenting with Chin Hair

THE NEXT FEW DAYS ARE spent trying to get control of my chin-hair shooting abilities, or as my son labels it, CHUD, which stands for, chin-hair urticating defense. He says that there really isn't an official term for what I do, but he wants to label it.

*Good grief.*

We buy a big piece of Styrofoam that is an inch thick, paint a big red target on it, and set it up in the family room. We can't risk having a neighbor witness me using my Gifts. My kids and mother take turns doing everything they can to get me to laugh so that I can try to shoot the target. We aren't able to recreate what happened with my mother. The whole situation is so ridiculous that I just can't focus.

My son comes up with the theory that anger seems to be my friend lately. When asked what makes me angry, I blurt out, "Your father!"

*So much for thinking that I had moved on from my divorce anger.*

"We need to find a picture of Dad. Do you still have one, or have you burned them all in effigy?" Michael jokes.

We put the experiment on hold while we all dig through boxes in the attic. We need to find a picture of Pete that is big enough for me to see from a few feet. We finally find one and Maggie decides to make extra copies of it on my color copier so I won't ruin the original. (I know that I don't care, but my kids do, so I keep my mouth shut.) Michael takes a copy and sticks it to the target. I focus on Pete, and all of the things that I still wanted to tell him—yell at him—while looking his picture right in the eye.

"Now let it out!" Michael yells.

I open my mouth, and pure anger comes out.

"Damn you Pete for cheating on me! Damn you for ruining this family!"

I go on and on about what a turd Pete is.

I realize that as I let it out, I feel great! I feel powerful! I feel like anger is my friend. I feel . . . a hand on my shoulder, and then I hear my mother's voice saying, "Okay, Ella, relax, honey. My goodness, you're so worked up that you're skin is getting hot!"

I stop my ranting and take in the scene before me. The face in the picture is completely covered in my CHUD! Gross, but surprisingly satisfying.

My mother and kids are looking at me with slightly wary expressions on their faces. I realize that they are a little bit afraid of me.

"Mom, oh my gosh! Your eyes turned black right before the hairs popped up and then out. I know this sounds crazy, but I think that I saw smoke coming from your hands!" says Maggie, while staying a few feet away from me.

"Don't be silly," I say. "I'm just a simple girl with simple skills. The only thing going on with me is the fact that I've got crazy chin hair and uncontrollable hot flashes."

Well, I *did* notice that my hands and forearms were hotter than normal when my mother touched my shoulder, but it was probably just the anger, which seems to have settled gently into my body like it was always a part of me.

My son has been quietly taking notes on his iPad, and when he looks up at me, it's like I am a big question without an answer. "Mom, you are definitely a mystery. It seems as though when you unleashed your pent-up anger towards Dad, it caused his picture to be your focus. You don't need to laugh hard to shoot CHUD, you just need to look at Dad's picture. I don't know what to think, but I *do* know not to mention any of this to my colleagues. They would have you imprisoned in a lab for the rest of your life."

My mother says, "That's why I never told a soul . . . until I had to."

# Experiment Over

WE DECIDE TO CALL IT a day. I apologize to them all for the foul language that flew out of my mouth. I also apologize to my children for the awful things that I said about their father. They all assure me that it didn't upset them. I think that they might've been so stunned by what I was *doing,* that they didn't pay much attention to what I was *saying.*

(Thank goodness!)

After the kids leave, my mother and I settle in to watch a rerun marathon of *The Nanny* on cable. (Fran Drescher is a brilliant comedic actress!) About an hour later, I decide that I could go for some chocolate cake. I could *really* go for some chocolate cake! I stopped eating desserts years ago in hopes of losing some weight, so there were no sweets in the house.

I grab my keys during a commercial. I tell my mom that I am running to the grocery store and that I'll be right back.

She stops me and asks if I'd pick up a few things for her as well, so I have to make a list.

By this time, it's dark outside, so I dig around in my purse trying to find my glasses. No such luck, so I figure that I'd be okay driving a few miles half blind.

*I need cake!*

I climb into my white Range Rover. (It was a divorce present to myself.) After wrestling with the seat belt for a few minutes, I am finally ready to leave my driveway. *Has it always been so frustrating trying to get out of the house?*

I arrive at the grocery store a few minutes later and decide to park at the far end of the lot, by the side street, so that I'm far enough away from the inconsiderate people who ding my car with their doors, or their shopping carts.

After a few minutes, I've found my beautiful cake and everything on my mom's list, so things are looking good. Just a few more minutes until I can sink my teeth into a big, juicy, moist—

"Excuse me, but this line is closed. Our computer is having issues, so if you wouldn't mind moving to the other line."

It's the girl who *ma'amed* me the other day. I move to the other line, which turns out to be the *only* line in the store.

I'm waiting and waiting. The anger is building and building.

It's finally my turn, and after I pay, I turn my head and see that the person responsible for loading my bags is none other than the little jackass who puts the bread on the bottom.

"Please make sure to put the cake on top," I say as sweetly as possible. He doesn't even acknowledge my existence. He puts the cake in first, and then loads the big container of vanilla ice cream on top.

*Okay, Ella, relax, breathe, and walk away. It's not worth it. Just go home and eat your cake.*

I make it out the door and am at my car fumbling for my keys when I hear a raised, angry sounding voice coming from the side alley of the store.

*Just keep moving. It's probably a drunk who's talking to himself.*

I put my precious cargo in the back seat, close the door, and am just about to open the driver door when I distinctly hear a woman's voice shout, "Stay away from me!"

I can't ignore that!

I creep toward the alley, staying in the shadows. I figure that if it's nothing serious, I'll leave, but if someone needs help, I'll call the police.

I get to where I can see two people—a man and a woman—standing under a flickering streetlight. The man looks to be a little under six feet tall, with very broad shoulders, and has a neck as thick as a tree trunk. The woman looks like a strong breeze could blow her away.

There is a car parked at an odd angle with both doors open, and they are standing in front of it.

"Get in the car!" the man shouts, grabbing the woman's arm.

"You're drunk, and you're hurting me! Please let me go," she says while struggling against his hold.

As soon as I hear "drunk," I call 9-1-1 and whisper the address and details.

"I didn't pay for dinner and a movie just to go home with blue balls!" he says.

He did *not* just say that!

He starts dragging her toward the open car door. I'm scared for her but also getting really angry. I can't just stand there, so I jump out of the shadows and yell, "Let her go!"

I surprise the man so much that he lets her go and reels around to face me.

*Oh no. What have I gotten myself into?*

"What did you say, *bitch?*"

"I said, 'Let her go!' And who the hell are you calling a bitch?"

My anger is starting to overpower my fear at this point. Suddenly, my chin starts itching, and my hands are starting to get warm. *Weird.*

"You need to stay the hell out my business, lady! Why don't you leave before you get hurt?"

"Are you threatening me?" I ask, feeling a comfortable feeling settling in over me. *Hello, Anger, my dear friend.* "I know you can't be so stupid as to threaten me! All I want to do is get home so I can eat my chocolate cake. Then I hear you over here making an ass out of yourself and abusing this poor woman! I suggest you take your drunk self home and leave this woman alone before I call the police!"

*Ha ha. I already called them, you rotten turd.*

"Listen, Granny, I am fed up with your damn mouth. I think you need to be taught how to shut it!"

He starts walking toward me, but I'm not scared. I am so angry that I'm seeing black. He called me *Granny*!

"You just stop right there. The police are on the way, you drunk bastard. How *dare* you call me Granny! I'm only fifty years old! I'm still in the prime of my life, and I don't need a rotten, mangy, no-good piece of shit stink like you—"

"My face!" someone screams.

I continue my stream of profanity—*it feels so good*—and see the man clawing at his face and wobbling around like he's on fire.

"My face! My face!" the man screams in agony.

I stand there in shock just staring at him and trying to see what is wrong with his face. With the help of the streetlight that has finally decided to stop flickering and stay on, I see that his face is covered in my CHUD. And he is still trying to come at me!

He doesn't seem to have much control over himself since he is drunk and injured. I'm standing my ground, planning my next move and feeling happy. *Happy?!* When he gets within a few feet of me, I kick him as high and as hard as I can.

*Wow! Those six weeks of kickboxing sure paid off!*

My lucky strike lands in the middle of his stomach, which causes him to fall back toward the car. As he is falling, he tries to twist away from the car, but that just completely throws his balance off and causes him to fall face first into the car's bumper. He lands on the pavement with a thud, and then silence.

I look down at his motionless body and don't feel guilty at all when I smile. Seeing that big dumb fool sprawled out on the ground is just what I need to lift my spirits.

"Is he dead?" the woman asks.

I stop smiling.

"I don't know," I say, fighting the urge to poke him with a stick just to see. Instead, I choose to use my foot to nudge him. He whimpers quietly. *Hee hee!*

"No, he's not dead," I say, still staring down at the big buffoon.

"Oh, wow! Thank you!" she says.

I turn to look at her, and she grabs me in a big bear hug. She's pretty strong for being so petite. I am caught off guard and I just stand there.

She lets go of me and says, "Oh my goodness, you saved me!" She looks like she's fighting the urge to hug me again. "My name is Jane. What's yours?" she asks, extending her hand toward me.

*Oh shit! She's gonna grab me again. Oh, wait! She only wants to shake my hand!*

Don't get me wrong: I love hugs. But right now, I just want to get home and eat my cake.

*Manners, Ella.*

I shake her hand and say, "My name is Ella. I'm just glad that I could help."

Just then, the police show up. Jane didn't see me use my CHUD on him since thankfully the streetlight flickered on and off at just the right times. She thinks that he was so drunk that he turned crazy. She *did* see me kick him, but that's okay. Nothing to worry about. The police ask me about the things on his face. I say that I have no idea what they are and that maybe, when he fell face first on the pavement, he landed in something.

I ask if I can please go home, and they ask if I want to file a complaint against him. I say no, but I tell them to check his blood-alcohol count.

The woman says that she is going to file assault charges on him. Apparently, it was their first date, and they had met online.

"He seemed so nice on the phone," she says as she is getting into the police car.

*Good grief.*

The policeman tells me that I am free to go, so I walk to my car and drive home.

When I get home, my mother asks what took me so long.

All I say is, "I'll explain after I've had my cake," as I'm hacking off a giant piece. The ice cream has started to melt, but I plop it on the plate too. I sit down at the kitchen table and start eating.

*Ahhhhhh . . . Cake . . .*

# Cake Makes Everything Better

After I finish my cake and ice cream and wash it down with a big glass of milk, I get up from the table and head toward the living room.

I feel so much better. All of the earlier tension is gone. I feel like my old self again, except for that tiny little piece of anger in the background now. It's not uncomfortable. In fact, it actually feels strangely comforting, like it's my shield against the world.

I sit down next to my mom and begin to tell her about my grocery store incident. I can tell that she is slightly alarmed, but when I tell her about my "on the mark" CHUD and my kick to the drunk guy's midsection, she leans forward in her seat. It looks as though she is fighting a smile.

"Okay, Mom, you look like you're enjoying this story. What gives?"

"Think about it, Ella. You saved that girl."

"*Jane.* Her name was Jane," I interject.

"You saved Jane from a very dangerous situation. Granted, you could've gotten badly injured, or worse, in the process, but you didn't. You stepped in and saved the day—or night in this case. It must've felt wonderful."

I guess that since the cake was the main focus for most of my night, I didn't stop to think about how the incident made me feel. I know that I felt a little scared, and then angry, but then relief that I could go home. But now that my tummy is full, I can look back and see that I did a pretty amazing thing tonight. But . . .

"I wasn't relaxed, and I wasn't laughing when I shot the drunk guy with my CHUD, so how did I do it? I was angry, so very angry. I remember seeing black, if that makes any sense. Then my hands became hot and my chin felt itchy. Then I started yelling at him, and then he's clawing at his face. I'm confused, though. My CHUD flies out when I see a picture of Pete, but I didn't have a picture. My CHUD comes out when I'm happy, and I wasn't happy until *after* I shot the drunk guy with my CHUD," I say, reflecting on the fight.

After a few minutes of thoughtful thinking, my mother says. "I've noticed that you were smiling and relaxed while you were eating your dessert a few minutes ago, and I didn't see any hair. I wonder why. Have you been angry or scared since you got home?"

"No," I say. "Well, I guess you could say that I was angry. I *am* angry. What I mean is that when I yelled at that stupid picture of Pete, I felt this different kind of anger creep in. I've felt this underlying anger ever since."

*"Aha!"* she says, "That's how I felt when I woke up on my fiftieth birthday!

The anger just settled into my being like it was a part of me."

"So maybe since I feel constant anger, my body reacts the way it did with the snap of the rubber band. I was cussing at the drunk guy when I shot him, so maybe expressed anger has the same effect that expressed happiness does," I say, feeling like a light bulb just went off in my head.

"That could very well be it. I'm so proud of you. You were that woman's hero tonight."

I let the words settle in, and . . . I kinda liked them.

# A Star Is Born

I AWAKE THE NEXT MORNING FEELING amazing! I no longer feel like a useless old lady. In fact, I feel like a badass! *More cussing, Ella. You're a changed woman. Yes! Changed for the better!*

I decide that I've got a pretty good handle on my new Gift. I tell my mother that I think that I'm going to be okay and that she should go home and be with Pop.

"Are you sure?" my mother asks.

"Yes, I'm very sure," I say, smiling.

I'm already wondering if I'll get to "save" someone else sometime soon.

We spend the rest of the day avoiding the elephant in the room and choose to have a normal, relaxing day together before she flies home tomorrow.

We decide to do some shopping and then lunch. I live in Clear Lake, Texas, which is about halfway between Houston and Galveston. It is such a wonderful area, full of things to do and see. We decide to go to the nutrition store across from NASA Space Center that I frequent, to see what new healthy goodies are in this week. As we drive into the parking lot, I see a for lease sign in the window of a retail space not far down from where we are headed.

*Hmmm . . . I have a lot of free time on my hands since selling the Tex-Mex restaurant that Pete and I owned. I wonder . . .*

I'm mulling over the idea of opening my own business as my mother and I look around the nutrition store. Then I spot a display for "Sea Salt for your bath." I am immediately drawn to it.

Since starting with the power surges, I get hot, then sweaty, and then icky feeling. The idea of a nice, cool, therapeutic bath sounds divine.

I strike up a conversation with the owner of the store, Helen, and she says that there is actually a thing called "a salt flotation tank."

I ask her what a salt flotation tank is.

She says, "It's an enclosed bath of sorts that has a few inches of water so saturated with salt that you float. Besides being very relaxing mentally, it takes the pressure off of your spine, making it very relaxing physically as well. It's also a great way to rid your body of toxins."

"What do you mean by 'enclosed bath'?" I ask.

"Well, it's a big box with a door on it that you can close and cut off the outside world. Stimulus reduction, if you will. This really helps the person inside achieve the ability to completely relax," she says, smiling.

"That's brilliant! I want to float. Every woman of a certain age should float!" I am so excited that I can't contain myself.

We end up buying a few items and then head to lunch at my favorite Southwest restaurant.

# It Started with a Google

As soon as we sit down to at the table, I pull out my iPhone and Google "salt flotation tank."

"It says here that there is one flotation center in Houston, but it's on the other side of town," I say with my eyes glued to the screen. "I don't want to make that drive. I need one close to me, so that I can float when I need to."

I click on another page and find the company that sells the tanks. I read about how they are fine to have in a home but that people are making good money opening the flotation centers.

*Kapow! I've been so bored—well, other than all of the crazy Change things that have happened lately—I need this tank. It sounds like heaven on earth, and since it's so expensive, the logical thing to do would be to use it to make money.*

"Mom, I'm opening a salt flotation center," I say excitedly.

"That sounds wonderful, my dear, but are you sure that you can handle The Change *and* opening a new business all at the same time?"

"I'm very sure. I helped Maggie with ideas when she was starting up her spa business, and I was good at it. This will be a piece of cake!" I say, smiling.

I decide to wait until my mother leaves before diving into the new business. As soon as I drop her off at the airport the next day, I am on the phone with my Realtor, telling her about the space that I'm interested in. Within a few hours, my Realtor and I meet at the space by the nutrition store. When we see the inside of the space, I see that the layout is very awkward and would require a lot of extra work. Luckily, my Realtor had the foresight to bring a list with a few other available spaces that she thought that I might like. I ended up finding the perfect space in League City, which is close to where I live and close to I-45, making it the perfect location.

Thankfully, I have the money needed to start another business, so all I have to do is make a few phone calls, fill out some paperwork, and *presto!*—I am a business owner.

I have been putting money into savings since I was age sixteen, having invested wisely since I was in college, and with the recent large amount of money I made from the sale of our business, I have a pretty big nest egg. I have worked hard for many years, and I really don't have to work anymore if I don't want to. It's just that I can't stand the thought of being in that house all alone (except for my cat) day after day, year after year . . .

*Focus, Ella.*

Now I have plenty of things to keep me busy, like working with a contractor on how I want the build-out to look, what colors I want to use, and so on.

Oh yes, I also need a name for my business.

I can't get my license without a name.

*Hmmm,* let's see . . . Float Your Boat? No! I'd have sailors coming in looking for supplies. Float Store? Too boring. Float For Fun? Good grief! I stop this train of thought and picture what it must feel like to float in a tank. I imagine it being blissfully peaceful. Floating Bliss, Flotation Bliss, Flotational Bliss. (Is that even a word?) Okay, think about it. What is a flotation tank? It's basically a salt bath. I will also be selling salt products . . . My business is salt. How about just Salt? Short, sweet, and to the point. How about SALT in all caps? That's perfect!

It's almost 9:30 p.m., and I realize that I haven't felt strange all day. *Yay!* I guess having something to occupy my mind helped. I'm just getting ready for bed when, all of the sudden, I feel like I'm on fire!

*Shit. Looks like I'll be camping out in a cold bath for a while.*

I can't wait 'til the salt tank arrives. It seems like the answer to everything.

I turn on the cold water and watch the tub fill.

# Caught Black Handed

THE NEXT DAY, I WAKE up feeling particularly crabby. I didn't have a restful sleep because I had a frustrating dream about my ex, *and* I kept waking up from the "surges."

I get out of bed. When I reach for the covers to straighten things up, I notice strange marks on the sheets where I was lying. I stop and see that they are dark, brownish-black handprints!

*What in the world?*

I honestly don't know what to do with this new discovery, so I decide to pull the sheet off the bed. I remove the sheet and discover the same handprints on the mattress. I'm having a harder time wrapping my head around this issue than I did with the chin hair!

*Was I filthy and I just didn't realize it before I got into bed? No, I took a bath before I went to bed. It looks like the sheet and bed were burnt. Don't think that, Ella. That's crazy thinking. Well, I remember smelling smoke and feeling like my hands were on fire on the day that I was target practicing with my family . . .*

*When I have my power surges, it feels like I'm on fire. Maybe I came close to spontaneously combusting while I was asleep.*

*Ahhhh! This is too scary to think about!*

## Cleaning Usually Helps

I DECIDE THAT I NEED A bit of normalcy. So after taking my morning shower, I put the sheets in the washing machine and go about my day.

I'm in the middle of dusting an end table when I'm hit with a feeling of intense fear. I know that yesterday I was ready to take on the world, but after the handprints, I don't know. Maybe I should call my mom. Maybe she experienced the same thing during her Change and can help me get a grip.

They say that knowledge is power, and I need all the power I can get.

As soon as my mother answers the phone, I start crying!

"Ella? What's wrong?" my mother asks, sounding worried.

"I woke up this morning and found black, burnt-looking handprints on my sheets. I don't want to be a badass! I want my old life back!" I sob.

"Ella, calm down. Now tell me again what you found."

"I found black handprints on my sheets that look like they were branded on. I'm assuming that they're mine. If they're not, then we have a whole haunting thing to contend with now," I say, trying to stop crying.

"Oh dear, I wonder what could've caused this to happen," she mused out loud.

"You mean you never had this happen to you?"

"Well, no, this isn't something that I've ever experienced, although I *have* experienced the mood swings like you seem to be dealing with."

"Mood swings? I think that it's perfectly okay for me to be crying on the phone with my mother after what I woke up to," I say, feeling the anger that had settled in so nicely and comfortably a few days ago start to surface again.

"See, mood swing. It's all in your head. Suck it up, and stop crying. I had horrible things happen to me, but I didn't cry about them."

"Did you just tell me to 'suck it up'?!" I say feeling a whole lot of anger building.

All of the sudden, I notice that my hands are getting hotter and hotter.

*How dare my mother speak to me that way! She's supposed to be supportive and loving, not mean and bitchy.* Then I smell smoke and I look at my hands. On the hand that is holding the phone, I see smoke rising. I hold out my other hand, and I can see what looks like waves of heat hovering above my hand.

"I'm on fire!" I yell into the phone.

"Ella, oh my goodness! What's happening?"

I explain what I see, and she says, "Oh, I'm so sorry, dear. This is my fault."

"Your fault?" I ask.

"I remembered smelling smoke and then feeling how hot your hands had gotten when you were so angry that time when you were doing target practice. I thought that we could nip this thing in the bud and see if getting angry today would produce results. Then we could work on controlling this new Gift too. I'm so sorry for the things I said to you! I just wanted to help you, so I thought that by saying things that weren't so nice, we could . . . Oh, I feel so useless being so far away from you!"

As soon as I realize that she was just trying to help in her own backward kind of way, I start to calm down.

"Well, I have flying chin hair, and apparently now I can heat up leftovers with my bare hands."

*Silence . . .*

*"Bwa ha ha ha!"* We both erupt into insane laughter.

"Oh . . . my . . . stars!" my mom says in between laughter.

Meanwhile, my laughter has turned into a bad mishmash of laughter and hiccups.

"I . . . *hee hee* . . . don't know . . . *hick* . . . why this is so funny . . . *ha ha!*"

I remember that all of my life my parents tried to find the humor in things, and I realize that it was a coping mechanism that has saved us all many a time. And boy, is this one of those times!

We finally get control of ourselves.

"Wow, I guess I need to figure out how to control this new Gift," I say, while looking at my hands in wonder—and a slight bit of fear.

"We know that it's caused by anger, so we need to keep you calm," Mom says.

"Right," I say, feeling confused. "Let's see. My CHUD came out when I was happy and relaxed, but once the constant underlying anger settled in, it was no longer an issue. Then I had to worry about laughing at someone and hitting them with it. We realized that the constant anger helped that but that if I really focused on someone, and became really angry, I could shoot the CHUD at them.

"So what's to keep my hands from heating up if I have a power surge or get really angry at someone at the bank, instead of some drunk guy roughing up a girl?"

"I don't know, Ella, but we'll get this all straightened out. Who knows? Maybe there is something you can use your hot hands for instead of just as a microwave."

We both start laughing again and say our good-byes.

# Testing One, Two, Seven

I DECIDE TO GO WITH THE good feeling I have after laughing with my mother and go for a walk at the park.

I get on the track and my mind starts to wander as I start walking. *Okay, I can control my CHUD, so surely I can learn to control my hot hands. Think, Ella. It happened during a particularly bad night of surges and unsettling dreams of my ex. I guess that's what brought it out in me.*

*So I burned during my sleep, and I burned again when my mother said awful things to me. The last time this happened I was upset, freaked out, and staring at a picture of my ex. Maybe that's it. I need to look at his picture and see if it will happen again on cue. I should probably call Michael and Maggie, but this is just too much to have to deal with their reactions too. I think that since I'm not feeling overwhelmed, I should try to deal with this on my own and then amaze and astound them when (if) I can learn to control this.*

After an hour of walking and musing, I head home. I decide to check the mailbox on the way. I reach my hand into the box, pull out the mail, and to my disdain, see a letter addressed to my ex on top of the pile. *Son of a . . . ! Why is he getting mail here again? I am so angry at that moron, two-timing jerk face! He had to go and ruin my good mood!*

I'm standing and fuming by the mailbox, staring at his letter in my hand, when all of the sudden, it starts smoking.

"Shit!" I say, and I drop the letter like it's a snake.

At that moment, I hear a noise. I look to my right and discover that the neighbor boy, Sam, is looking over the fence at me with his mouth and eyes wide open.

*Damn it, Ella, why did you let yourself get so worked up? You're on a public street and you just got caught being a weirdo. What am I going to do? Say it was a letter with a match in it and somehow it ignited? No, I'm taking the chicken's way out and act like nothing happened.*

I pick up the blackened envelope, look over at Sam, smile, and wave. His eyes widen even farther, and then he quickly ducks his head down to try to hide. A few seconds later, I hear a door slam.

That'll teach *him* for spying on people.

I decide to call the post office to nip this little *ex*press mail problem in the bud.

I find out that after a period of time, mail forwarding stops and you can't do it again on the same person. So now I have to get word to my ex that he needs to check with all of his contacts and make sure that they all have his new address. *Aaahhh!*

# I Need Some Mary Time

I HAVEN'T SPOKEN WITH MY BEST friend, Mary (who happens to be Big Pete's sister) in the few days since my party. She was a grade behind Pete and me in school when we all met, and we became instant friends. We have managed to stay friends, through good times and bad. (I can't blame her for her brother; in fact, she thinks he's a jerk for what he did to me as well.) Mary is a little shorter than I am, with curly brown hair and big blue eyes. She looks sweet and innocent until she opens her mouth, and then *kapow!* Out come the swear words. At my birthday party, she overheard the younger girl telling me that I looked good for my age, and later she took me aside and said, "Who the *bleep* does she think she is, saying such *bleep*ing *bleep* to you! I'm gonna have a little talk with her." I barely saved my neighbor's twenty-one-year-old daughter from the butt chewing of her life. Mary tells it like it is, cusses like a sailor, and I wouldn't have her any other way.

"Hey, lady!" I say, when she answers the phone.

"Hey, Ella, long time no hear! What the *bleep* you been up to?"

"Well, I *uh (developed strange abilities on my birthday)* . . . I'm starting a new business. Yes, I'm starting a new business and I'm really excited about it." I proceed to explain what a salt flotation tank is and then tell her about Pete's letter.

"Why can't that rat bastard ever take care of his business? He probably accidentally on purpose forgot to update his address on a few contacts, just so he can have an excuse to come by," Mary says, as I hear strange sounds in the background on her end.

"What's going on at your place, and what do you mean, 'so he can have an excuse to come by'?"

"Well," Mary says, "he and his little Lolita broke up, and he's been in a mood ever since. I think he misses the attention, so I would assume that he will start sniffing around your place soon. The sounds you're hearing are my three new cats I rescued last week. They are so damn cute. I figured since it's just my crusty ass living here, why not have some furry friends? When they get to playing, they are so funny! In fact, I almost pissed myself the other day watching them."

Leave it Mary to interject so much profanity into talking about cute little cats! Mary has lived alone for about seven years now, since kicking her horrible husband out, and she's happier now than I've seen her in years. Living alone instead of living with someone who is unkind is so much better for the soul.

*Wait. Hold on. Did she say Pete broke up with his girl*fiend*? (And yes, I meant 'fiend'.)*

"So Mary, what's this about Pete being single again?"

"Oh yeah, Miss Prissy Pants wanted to get married and have kids, and Pete's too old for that shit, so when she gave him an ultimatum, he did what he does best—he left. Now, anytime he calls me, which is a lot more often than when he was with *her*, he asks about you. Like, 'So how's Ella doing?' or 'Have you spoken with Ella lately?' He knows he messed up when he left you. Why is it that a man can't see a good thing standing right in front of him, but he'll notice a twenty-year-old with fake boobs standing *behind* him?"

"Probably for the same reason they never ask for help when they're lost, but they will take up all of your time asking you where the mustard is or where their keys are," I say, pondering the puzzle that is man.

I feel my hands heating up, so I bring the conversation to an end.

"Well, I need to get going. I've got lots of things to do to get this business up and running. I'll talk to you soon, Mary," I say, looking warily at my hands.

"Okay, I'll talk to you later El." *Click.*

I've been fuming since hearing about Pete's breakup. He broke up with me for her, and now it was for nothing. Since my hands still feel warm, I decide to experiment. I need a picture of Pete. The last picture of him was so riddled with CHUD that you couldn't see his face. *Ha!* I remember that we had made copies of his picture on my color copier and that they were in a drawer in the kitchen. I find the copies in the drawer, and when I pick one up—*poof!* It goes up in flames. Actual flames! They shoot out of the palm of my hand! Flames about the size of lighter flames, but it's interesting that it only happened on the hand I was holding the picture with. Maybe I can use this ability for something useful other than in the kitchen. *Hee hee.*

# Another One Bites the Dust

I DECIDE TO MAKE THE GARAGE my training station so that if things get out of control I won't destroy any furniture. (I can't believe that I had my CHUD practice in the family room! Thankfully, no damage was done.)

I move my car and clear out all flammable fluids, and then I bring in a metal bucket, a jug of water, and a fire extinguisher—just in case.

I go back to the drawer to get another picture of Pete. I make the mistake of looking at his smiling face. *Woosh!* It burns in my hand.

"Well, shit," I say out loud. I go put the burning picture in my kitchen sink along with the one that I burned before and pull another picture of my ex from the drawer. *What a waste of ink!* This time, I immediately turn the picture over and head to the garage. I manage to tack the picture up while looking at it out of the corner of my eyes and not focusing on it. I stand back, look at his smiley, smarmy face, and small flames shoot out of *both* hands. I look down at my hands and focus on breathing and calming down. The flames die down. I then get the idea to try for flames out of one hand without holding his picture. So I close my eyes and ball one hand into a fist.

*I am so glad that my kids turned me on to paranormal/ fantasy books, because without Kim Harrison and some of the other amazing authors out there, I wouldn't have a clue how to act or react to my life right now. I see now that all of the fiction books that I have read over the years have really been training manuals of sorts. If you can enjoy and open up your imagination to a story about witches, vampires, pixies, and a couple of demons thrown into the mix, then you can pretty much wrap your brain around* anything *that comes your way!*

I hold out my open hand, palm up. I open my eyes, look at Pete's face, and *voila!* It works.

Then I wonder if I could possibly have the flames if I am angry enough at someone other than my ex, so I turn my back on Pete (the flames die down) and think for a minute. *Ah ha!* That low life I fought by the grocery store. He could get the juices flowing. I think about him and how he spoke to me. I feel my hands get warm, then warmer, but no flames. *Hmmm . . .*

I turn around and *poof!* Flames.

I try this a few more times, thinking of everyone who has ever angered me, including Pete, but the flames only come when I look at that face.

Okay, I can get hot hands with the waves of heat coming off of them if I get angry enough, like when my mother tried to help me by being ugly to me on the phone, but it takes looking at Pete's name or face to bring on the flames. Damn that Pete!

I store this piece of information in the back of my brain and get the idea to practice using my CHUD. I feel that I've pretty much mastered it—you just get angry, focus, and let 'em fly! It's so much fun watching a hair hit Pete right between the eyes! I start playing around making funny designs on his face, like on the old games with the faces that have magnet flecks and you use the magnet "pen" to create beards and mustaches. Ha! Funny!

I grab the last five copies in the drawer so that I can create special looks for Pete on pictures that aren't all torn up. I use my phone and take pictures of the ones that turn out particularly funny. Hey! You never know when you're going to need a good laugh.

It's at this point that I realize that when I'm concentrating on using my CHUD, my hands only heat up but don't burst into flames when I look at Pete's picture. Interesting. Maybe because I'm thinking about how funny his face looks with CHUD all over it and I'm not as angry . . .

I stop thinking about my CHUD and just look at his picture. Flames! I start focusing on my CHUD and no flames, just a little bit of heat. *Well, how about that!*

I practice until I am sure that I have it all under control.

After awhile, I decide that it's time to call it a day. I go back into the house, glance at a clock, and realize that I was in the garage for almost three hours. I guess that it was time well spent, because I certainly don't want to hurt anyone with my hands. The only way that I can make sure that this won't happen is if I take The Change, and all that it entails, seriously.

All that practicing honing my skills has left me a little tired, so I feed Monkey, pop in a DVD of *The Nanny* (I didn't get to watch much of the marathon when my mother was here), get myself some leftover chicken salad from the refrigerator, and recline in my favorite chair.

# Good Morning, Clear Lake, Texas!

I WAKE WITH A START AND find that I had fallen asleep in my chair. I look at a clock and see that it's eleven o'clock. *Wow, I took a nice nap. I should probably go to my bed, so that I don't throw my back out with the lack of support. Wait a minute. It's light outside. It's not 11 p.m.; it's 11 a.m.!*

*I've slept for roughly sixteen hours! Does my back feel okay after being in that chair all that time? Yes, it does. Do I feel alert from all the sleep, or am I groggy for oversleeping? I feel great!*

I don't think that I have felt this great in a long time. I start tidying up the mess I made last night and discover that the arthritis pain that I have woken up with every morning for the past four years is gone. I can walk, not hobble around like I usually do every morning for the first few hours.

*This is amazing. Maybe I should sleep for sixteen hours every night!*

# Mirror, Mirror on the Wall . . .

AFTER SKIPPING AROUND THE HOUSE for a few laps (because I could), I skip into the bathroom to freshen up for the day. I pick up my toothbrush, look in the mirror, and then proceed to drop my toothbrush and scream like the little boy did in the movie *Home Alone*.

What I see is someone who looks like me, but better. I look like I am glowing from within, and my skin is firm and dewy. Over the last decade, my skin had really started to get dry and lackluster, thanks to the aging process. I had resigned myself to the fact that I needed to make peace with my aging skin.

Wow! I don't have as many wrinkles—just a few small lines at the corners of my eyes that I've had forever.

"This is unreal!" I shout as I lean forward to inspect my face a little closer. I then realize that the gray roots that needed a little touch-up (I was going to color my hair the morning of my birthday, but with all that happened that day, I forgot) are gone! In fact, my hair looks full and shiny like when I was in my early thirties. "Wow!" I say while running my fingers through my luxurious hair. I just can't believe this is happening, but a funny thought hits me. I have yet to question my sanity during this. I guess that after you find out that you can roast marshmallows with your bare hands, anything else seems acceptable.

Even though I'm not questioning that this is happening, I'm still a little leery of taking a shower. Remember what happened to me on my birthday? I look at myself in the mirror another time and realize that I'm up close to the mirror and it's not blurry. My eyes! Even my eyes seem younger.

I'm still trying to wrap my head around this new discovery when I take off my shirt and slept-in bra and discover that my boobs are where I left them at age thirty! They are full, and firm, and amazing! I'm so overwhelmed! *Oh, I feel woozy . . . so dizzy . . . Why is the room spinning?*

The next thing I know, my phone is ringing and I'm lying on my back in my bathroom. *What happened? Why am I on my bathroom floor? Wait a minute. I remember now. I must've fainted from the new boobs!* I sit up, and the world is still a little off-kilter, so I sit for a minute and recount what has just happened to me—*before* I fainted.

I reach up and touch my face, then my hair, then my boobs. I can't believe that this is happening. I look to my right and see that my cat, Monkey, is sitting on the edge of the bathtub and staring at me with her big green eyes.

"Monkey, can you believe this? This is like a dream come true! Don't I look so young?"

Monkey just stares at me and blinks.

## But Wait! There's More!

I SLOWLY STAND UP AND EXPECT to feel some aches and pains all over from falling down on the tile floor, but I don't. *Amazing.*

I stay strong with my decision to forgo a shower—if I still look like this tomorrow, then I will certainly consider risking a shower—and enter my walk-in closet. I look in the mirror on the back of the door one more time at my superb boobies (they are too perky to be called breasts) and then bend over to remove my pants.

*What the—? Something's wrong. I didn't have to struggle to get out of my pants. Did I go to sleep wearing my baggy pants?* No, I was wearing my regular pants that usually end up being too tight at the end of the day. I look up from the pants in my hand, see myself in the mirror, and . . .

I wake up for the second time on the floor. This time, I'm not as confused as the last time. This time, I know *exactly* what made me faint.

I stand up to admire what can only be called a miracle. The skin from my boobies on down is now as smooth and as firm as my face has become, which means that my once soft and dimply thighs and bottom that no amount of exercise could help are now as tight and as firm as they were in my early thirties!

# I Feel Pretty!

I SPEND THE NEXT FORTY-FIVE MINUTES posing and staring at my new bottom. It is almost mesmerizing. I think about all of the times when I was too self-conscious to wear a skirt or shorts that didn't come to at least my knees. The many pool parties I was invited to that I was too afraid to take off my cover-up. Of course, most of the other women at those things who were my age kept theirs on too, but the younger women always stripped down and seemed to enjoy being in their own bodies.

Whoever said that "youth is wasted on the young" was so very right. But now I have the chance to live without body-image issues—at least until I go to sleep or take a shower. I'm still worried that this new Change isn't permanent.

My phone starts ringing again. I decide that I should probably get out of the closet and start what looks to be a wonderful day.

(The phone call turns out to be my doctor's office calling to check up on me. I tell the nurse that I'm feeling quite fine now and ask her to tell Dr. Clark thank-you for his concern.)

# Retail Therapy

TODAY IS GOING TO BE about fun, girlie stuff and not about serious, life-changing special Gifts kind of stuff. (Except for the Gift of renewed youth that I will cherish every day for the rest of my life, no matter how long the Gift lasts.)

I decide that shopping would qualify as "fun, girlie stuff." After digging in my closet and finding a sundress that sort of fits me, and that is so old that the writing on the tag has long ago faded, I head to T.J. Maxx for a few hours of "therapy." What good is being young again if I have to wear the baggy clothes hanging in my closet? Since my body has gotten firm again, I have lost several inches of unwanted fat, which makes all of my clothes useless. Well, except for maybe a few T-shirts, sweatshirts, and sweatpants. I can always keep them to use when I'm just hanging around the house or when I'm cleaning. I guess I don't need a whole new wardrobe, but I *do* need some new clothes. If I go around wearing baggy clothes, I won't look very professional, and that won't work for me. I've always tried to make myself look presentable and put together. Don't get me wrong, I love to be comfortable, and my outfit of choice would be a T-shirt and a pair of shorts, but when I'm out in public, considering that I've been a business owner for many years, I want to put my best foot forward. *Okay, Ella, now that you have talked yourself out of feeling guilty about buying new clothes, you need to get to shopping!*

I enter the store and head toward the women's clothing section. I know that I'm no longer the size that I was, which was a size twelve, so I take a shirt and a pair of slacks that are a size ten to the changing rooms. The young, twentysomething salesgirl hands me my plastic number two sign, and I head back to find an empty room.

I lock the door, turn toward the mirror, and gasp. I never thought that I could look this good in these horrible fluorescent lights. *Thank you, young hormones, for giving me back the glowing skin that I once had!*

"Are you okay back there?" the salesgirl calls out.

"I'm fine, thank you. It's just that I've recently lost some weight, and I always surprise myself when I look in a mirror."

"Good for you!" The salesgirl sounds like she is right outside my door. "I've been working on losing some weight myself. How much did you lose?"

"I honestly don't know. I just know that my clothes no longer fit," I say.

"Well, what size were you before?"

"I was a size twelve," I say while buttoning the shirt.

"Oh well. I'm starting out a bit bigger than you. I'm a size eighteen, but my goal is to get down to at least a size six by Christmas."

*Lose twelve sizes in seven months? The optimism of the young.*

I zip the zipper of the slacks and stand back to see what the outfit looks like on me. It looks baggy.

I open the door, and the salesgirl steps back to look at me. "Hmm . . . I think you need to go about two sizes smaller than what you have on. What size do you have on?"

"A ten."

"Congratulations, 'cuz I'm pretty sure you're a size eight now!"

"Really? You think so? Gosh, I haven't been a size eight since I was in my thirties," I say incredulously.

"You say that like it was a long time ago! How old are you now? Thirty-one? Thirty-two?"

"Oh no! I'm . . ." *If you tell this young girl that you're fifty, you're going to have another fainting person on your hands.* "Thirty-five. I'm thirty-five," I say, waiting for her reaction.

"Well, you sure do look good for your age!"

Are you kidding me? When was thirty-five considered old? I guess it can happen at any age if the person telling you that you look good for your age is very young and very clueless. I can't believe the manners of kids today. They are so . . . *Holy crap! She thought that I was in my early thirties. I shouldn't be angry—I should be hugging her!*

"Thank you, dear, *err* . . . dude," I say, feeling very off-kilter. Note to self: must get some pointers from Maggie on how people from her generation speak.

She looks at me with her head cocked to the side like a dog that just heard a sharp sound. Then she smiles and walks back to her station.

I'm just pulling my sundress over my head when there is a knock on my dressing room door. "Someone's in here," I say.

"It's me, Becky from a few minutes ago."

*"Umm,* hi, Becky. Do you need this room? I was just leaving to go look for something else to try on."

"Oh no, I have something for you to try on."

I open the door, and she's standing there holding a dress and smiling. "I thought that you should try this on. It's by Jessica Simpson, and we just got it in last night."

"Jessica Simpson? I can't wear Jessica Simpson! My *daughter* wears Jessica Simpson," I say, wondering why she would even *think* to bring me something that is worn by kids.

"Jessica Simpson is timeless. Her clothing can be worn by teenagers, people my age, people your age, and even *some* people in their forties can pull it off if they still look good by that age."

Still . . . she didn't think that she had said anything wrong.

"Just please try it on. It's a size eight, and I know that it will look awesome on you."

"Okay," I say grudgingly while taking it from her.

The dress was yummy. It was one of those stylish asymmetrical dresses that are sleeveless on one side and have a long sleeve on the other. It was made of a sheer fabric that was thankfully lined. It was a beautiful, swirly mixture of the colors lime green, sapphire blue, cranberry, and cream. "Here goes nothing!" I say.

"Did you say something?" Becky asked.

"I said that this dress is amazing." I unzip the zipper and pull the dress over my head. I arrange it in all the places that it wanted to stick to the ACE bandage I had to use because none of my bras fit. (I just can't make myself go braless, even with my new perky boobies!) I zip it up, turn around, and oh, my stars! I look amazing! I look—I look . . .

Uh oh, the room is spinning! I've been through this enough to know that I need to sit right down before I fall on the floor and they find me with my dress up over my head. Besides using the ACE bandage in place of my bra, I had to use safety pins on my panties to make the waist smaller, to keep them from falling down. (I can't make myself go commando either.) Yikes! This is a sight that I hope to never show anyone.

"Are you okay in there?" Becky asks.

"I'm fine—just got a little light headed. *Ummm* . . . I guess the shock of seeing myself as a size eight finally hit me. I'm okay though."

I decide that I should go out so she can see me.

Becky squeals and says, "I was right! You look *a-ma-zing!* Hold on a minute. I'll be right back." She walks around the corner.

A few minutes later, while I am staring at myself in the mirror, Becky comes up behind me and says, "Okay, so I've asked Carrie to take over the changing room so that I can help you pick out a new summer wardrobe. We should probably get you some new bras and panties too, because the bra that you've got on now isn't flattering your figure *at all*."

"Oh no, that's okay. I don't want to take up any more of your time," I say, embarrassed by the attention *and* her keen eye.

"I insist. We're pretty slow right now, and it's my lunch break coming up anyway. Who can think of a better way to lose weight than by skipping lunch and burning calories from shopping?" Becky asks me over her shoulder as she's heading back out into the store.

Three hours, six huge shopping bags, and $823 later, I leave T.J. Maxx and Becky, with a smile on my face and enough clothes and accessories to last me through the summer.

# Time to Myself

I DIDN'T WANT THE HAPPY FEELING to end, so I stayed in my house for a few days, just trying on my new clothes, bagging up my old clothes to donate to Purple Heart in case my newest Gift was permanent, and dancing through the house—because I *could*! I also wanted to experiment with the new makeup from Mally Beauty that I purchased during this time from QVC. I was flipping through channels late one night and came across this beautiful, exuberant woman who was talking about how even women aged forty and over should feel beautiful. Her products are designed for women of all ages. She was using models who were in their twenties, thirties, forties, fifties, and sixties, and they all looked happy and beautiful. She demonstrated how to apply each product, and it looked easy enough, so I bought all-new makeup to go with the all-new me. I knew that sooner or later, I was going to have to address my other Gifts again and speak with my family, but for now, I just wanted to feel young and carefree.

# Time to Tell the Kids

A FEW DAYS HAVE PASSED, AND Maggie calls to see if I want to have lunch with her today. I thought it best that I prepare her over the phone, because this is more of a transformation than my Uncle Otto beard, and I don't want her to faint and hurt herself.

"Yes, Maggie, lunch would be nice. Could you meet me at the house at one o'clock?"

"Sure, Mom, no problem. Is everything okay? You sound different."

"No, everything is fine—in fact it's great actually. *Mmmm* . . . I need to show you my latest Gifts."

"Wait—what?" Maggie says. "You've had more things happen to you since we last spoke?"

"Well, yes," I say. "I wanted to get a handle on them before I dragged you and Michael into my craziness. Your grandmother helped me through the first one, and Monkey tried to help me through the second one. I don't want to alarm you before you get behind the wheel of a car, so all I'm going to say is that I can defrost a freezer with my bare hands."

Pause.

"Huh?" Maggie says.

"That's okay. Once I show you, you will get a better understanding. The second thing that happened is something that will amaze and astound you. I slept for sixteen hours last night, and when I woke up, my face and body look like they did when I was in my thirties."

Pause to let it sink in . . .

"What?! Mom, I don't understand."

"That's okay, honey, you will when you see me. I'm going to call your brother to see if he can come at one also. Please be careful driving. See you soon. Love you," I say, admiring my reflection in my compact mirror.

"I love you too, Mom," Maggie says, still sounding confused.

*Click.*

I call Michael and try to explain to him what has happened. When I stop talking, all I hear is silence.

"Michael, honey, can you come to my house today at one o'clock?" I ask, wondering if he's still on the line.

After a few seconds, he says, "Yes."

*Click.*

I decide that I should probably wear something that's a little baggy on me, so as not to completely overwhelm them when they see me. I head to my closet to see what I have. The other day when I was going through my clothes, I decided to keep a few old comfortable tees and sweatpants to lounge around in. I change into an old yellow T-shirt and some navy blue sweatpants. I also wash off my makeup.

I look at myself in the mirror. You can still see a difference, but at least it's not so obvious.

The doorbell rings at one o'clock on the dot, and when I open the door a crack, I see my kids standing on the porch, looking scared.

"Hello, my children!" I say, opening the door wide and stepping out of the way so that they can come in. I stand there for a few seconds, and I realize that neither of them is moving. They're just standing there like statues with their mouths hanging open.

"Please come inside, you two. You're gonna catch flies with those mouths," I say, gently guiding them through the doorway. I get them both in the house, and all of the sudden, Maggie yells, "Holy shit! Holy shit! *Hooooly* shit!"

Michael silently walks to the bar by the kitchen.

"Isn't it amazing?!" I ask, doing a twirl.

"Mom, what did you *do*?!" Maggie asks.

"What do you mean, what did I do?"

"I mean I can't believe that this happened overnight. Are you sure you didn't visit a plastic surgeon on the sly?"

"No, I didn't. I woke up this way. It's taken a bit to get used to, but I'm so excited I can't stand it. I even feel as young as I look," I say, doing a cartwheel in the living room.

Michael has since returned from the bar with a shot glass of I-don't-know-what in his left hand. He starts walking around me, poking at me here and pinching me there.

"Michael, I'm not one of your test subjects. Quit poking at me!"

"It's amazing. You look twenty years younger!" he says, still circling me. He pauses to down the shot.

"I know. I feel wonderful! Maggie, I need to show you something amazing that I can't show Michael. Come with me to my bedroom." I want her to see my new boobies and perky bottom in my new smaller underwear! She follows me to the bedroom, and I say as I am removing my shirt, "I was so overwhelmed when I saw what I looked like this morning that I . . ."

*Thump!* Maggie faints.

When she comes to, she just stares up at my concerned face and proceeds to faint again. Luckily, she was already lying on the floor.

When she comes to a second time, I have a ski mask on, thinking that it will soften the blow, but it does the opposite—she screams.

"Oh my goodness, Maggie! I thought that this mask would make things easier for you by covering my face. I didn't even *think* that it would scare you too. I'm so sorry!" I take off the mask and help her to her feet.

"Mom, I just can't believe it. It's like you went back in time, but the rest of us didn't. This is absolutely amazing. This is so . . . Oh my goodness, I want this to happen to *me*! Except maybe shave off *ten* years instead of twenty, because I wouldn't want to look like a ten-year-old. It would put a serious crimp in my dating life."

*She's trying to joke around. That's a good sign. It means that she's okay—no permanent damage from her ding-dong mother.*

"Maggie, I feel so wonderful, and I wish that both you and Michael could feel as good as I do. I guess that something good had to come from The Change. Let's go back out to see Michael."

We head back to the living room, and I can feel Maggie's eyes on me the whole way.

We find Michael reclining on my recliner. He has another drink in his hand (he never drinks) and a thoughtful look on his face.

"I think that I've got it figured out," Michael says with a slight slur. "Mom has hit menopause, a mega menopause if you will, and so her hormones are all askew. I've been researching menopause, and it looks as though your Gifts are amplified symptoms. We know that hormones control us through our entire lives, and they are responsible for a lot going on in our bodies. Around the age of forty, a woman's estrogen levels start to drastically decline, which causes changes in your hair, skin, and weight. It seems as though the opposite has happened, and that Mom's hormones are reacting like they were before the decline—almost like she's going through puberty. It's really quite remarkable. Imagine what this could mean to the scientific world . . ."

Two angry women stare at him.

"I mean, *if* we were assured that Mom wasn't going to be held prisoner by the government and dissected, and I had your permission, but I don't. And since I don't want to see you cut up into itty-bitty pieces . . ." He giggles. "Mom, I love you too much to dissect—" *Hiccup!* "Oh, my! I do believe that I am inebriated! So this is what it feels like . . ."

Silence.

Michael has passed out in the chair.

"Let's just let him sleep," I say to Maggie while taking his drink out of his hand and turning off the light.

Michael works from home a lot, so I didn't think that a day, and possibly a night, spent at his mom's house would mess up his schedule too much.

Maggie and I go to the kitchen and settle in at the table with iced tea, sandwiches, and pastries for lunch.

"Mom, I have to tell you that I am completely blown away by all that's happened to you. If you hadn't shown me, I wouldn't have believed a word. In fact, I'd probably be looking to put you in a mental hospital for psychiatric evaluation."

"I know, sweetie. It has been so hard for me to keep it together mentally in order to accept everything. I'm so glad that you can see what I see. If I didn't have you two and your grandmother to see for yourselves that it's really happening to me, I would be in a mental institution right now of my own accord," I say, taking a big bite of pastry. *Mmmm . . . pastry.*

"Do you think that all of this will happen to *me* when I turn fifty?" Maggie asks me with wide eyes that look slightly scared.

"I don't know. There doesn't seem to be any rhyme or reason to how it works. We know that your great grandmother had it, but we don't know to what extent or for how long. Your grandmother lost hers when I became 'active,' and so far, all I know is that she was able to squirt water from her armpits."

*"Ewww!"* we both say in unison.

"I wonder if she doesn't want to tell me about her Gifts because she's afraid of scaring me," I say, pondering this new thought. "I just wish that I knew what to expect. I'm almost afraid to go to sleep now, because of what may happen next. Of course, this last Gift really was a *GIFT!*" I look down the front of my shirt.

"Mom, you are so crazy! In a good way," Maggie quickly interjects. "I sure do hope that if I end up with The Change happening to me that I get the age-reversal thing. If we could only bottle that Gift and sell it . . ." she says wistfully.

"I think that this is pretty much a self-contained Gift, although I could lick your cheek and see if my saliva would do anything to your skin," I say, giggling.

"Mom, gross! That sounds like an experiment that Michael would do to you if given the chance. Although I guess it wouldn't hurt to try," she says looking at me expectantly.

"Really, Maggie?"

She's still looking at me—waiting for me to lick her face.

"Okay, if we're going to do this, let's do it in a more ladylike manor. I will spit in a bowl, and we can use a cotton swab to smear a little on your hand. I don't want to take a chance and have my saliva disfigure you or something," I say, looking in a cabinet for a small bowl.

Maggie has already produced a Q-tip from her purse and is sitting there looking like a kid on Christmas morning.

I delicately spit in the bowl and take the Q-tip from her hand.

"Are you sure?" I ask, feeling both excited and scared. I would feel horrible if my saliva injured my beautiful daughter.

*If I can produce fire from my hands, then what must my system look like on the inside?*

"Mom?" Maggie is trying to bring me back from my thoughts.

"I'm sorry. Give me y . . ."

She shoves her hand under my nose before I can even complete the sentence.

"Here goes nothing—I hope." I rub a small amount on the back of her left hand. She's right-handed, so I don't want to risk injuring her dominant hand. We both stare at her hand for a solid five minutes.

"Do you feel anything?" I ask every minute.

"No, nothing at all. No change in texture or elasticity," she says, looking heartbroken.

"I'm sorry," I say while rinsing out the bowl.

"That's okay, Mom. I had a feeling that it wouldn't work, but I had to try."

I realize that the day is getting away from me. It is nearly three o'clock and I need to meet with my builder, Javier, to see how things are going down at the salt spa.

"Wow, I need to get over to the building to meet with Javier for our weekly visit. Do you want to come with me?" I ask while cleaning up the crumbs I left on the table (and my shirt) from the sandwich and tasty pastry I had eaten during our visit.

"No, I should get back to work now. My best girl is on maternity leave, so we're shorthanded. Thank you for the invite though. How about I stop by day after tomorrow?"

"Sounds good, Maggie. Don't work too hard," I say while walking her to the front door.

We pass Michael, and he moves a little in the chair. He mumbles, "Menopause."

Maggie and I cover our mouths to stifle our giggles.

# You Could've Heard a Nail Drop

I HEAD ON OVER TO MY new business (*Yay!*) and walk through the front door that's been propped open to let the sawdust and strong fumes air out. I step into what will be the waiting area, remove my sunglasses, and say loudly (the drills and saws are quite loud), "Javier, are you here?"

One by one, power tools start shutting off and the men using them are laying down their tools and staring at me.

"Hey, guys, why are you all stopping? Let's get moving," Javier says, coming from the back of the building. He sees me, stops dead in his tracks, and stares at me wide-eyed.

I look around, and everyone is staring at me like I've grown two heads. Out of the corner of my eye, I see movement. I look, and one of the men is doing the sign of the cross. Then one of them says, "A dios mio!" Another says, "El diablo!" And then from the back of the room I hear, "Cubachabra!"

They look absolutely terrified—of me!

I start fumbling for my compact, thinking that maybe some new Gift has popped up, and I really *do* have two heads! I look in the mirror and see what they see: the face of a thirty-year-old woman who looked fifty just last week. *Ohhh*, I forgot. In my haste to get to this meeting on time, I have forgotten the obvious.

Meanwhile, Javier is just standing there open mouthed.

*Quick, Ella, think of something to say, or else you're going to scare off the best builders in town.*

"Oh, my! I'm so embarrassed. I had some work done last week. You know, a face lift, chemical peel, liposuction, those kind of things."

Javier finally finds his voice and says, "Doesn't that kind of work take weeks to heal?"

"Oh no," I say. "With all of the advances in plastic surgery, they can fix you from head to toe, and you can be back to work in a week."

*I hope he buys this.*

"Well, wow! Whoever did this to you is an artist. Not that you looked bad before, it's just that you look so young," he says while reaching out as if to touch my face. He catches himself and puts his hand down.

"Anyway, I guess we should start going over the things that have been done this week. I think you will be pleased," he says while showing me to one of the back offices. "Get back to work, guys," he says as we leave the room, and the power tools start turning back on.

Javier leads me to what will be my private office at the back of the building, and I gasp when he opens the door.

"Holy shit!" I say without thinking. "Oh my goodness, Javier! I'm so sorry. I don't know what has gotten into me lately. I didn't mean to cuss around you. It's not professional at all."

"Don't worry about it. What you said is rated G compared to what I hear on a daily basis. Well, what do you think about your new office?" he asks while motioning with his hand like a game-show hostess.

Although the room isn't painted, the flooring and furniture aren't in yet, and the sheetrock hasn't been hung yet, I can tell from how it is laid out, and with just having the walls framed, that it is going to be amazing.

"This is absolutely perfect, Javier. You gave me exactly what I asked for," I say, walking around the room.

I had wanted a nice-sized office so that I could spread out and get my work done at an office away from home. I've never liked mixing personal life with professional life.

The room is located at the back left side of the entire business space, which puts my office in the wealth area, according to Maggie. She helped plan how to build things feng shui friendly. I was very happy to get that help, because I have seen how using feng shui in my home has helped me tremendously. So why not apply it to my business?

The room is thirteen feet wide by fifteen feet deep with two big windows on the right wall to let in lots of light. At the back of my office, I have a private Relax Room (will explain in a minute), and I had them build two columns to separate my desk area from my seating area.

We walk through another door and end up in my own private float room. I don't want to have to book an appointment to float, so having my own makes sense.

So far, the plumbing isn't in for the shower, toilet, or sink yet, but the built-in vanity area has been framed out. I think of my private office as my own "Bat Cave," and I can't wait!

The whole business space has been divided in half. On the left side, starting at the front of the building, are three float rooms (each with its own shower, toilet, sink, and vanity area), then my float room, then my office. On the right side, starting at the front of the building, we have the waiting area (which will have couches, tables, and chairs) and then a kitchen with a long granite bar. We will be serving smoothies and other healthy goodies. After that, we have a restroom, and three Relax Rooms. These Relax Rooms will each have a recliner and a wall full of shelves from floor to ceiling. The shelves will hold twenty-four Himalayan salt lamps per room. The salt lamps are very healing and relaxing and can be used in conjunction with the salt tank for a super-duper relaxation combo.

We are finished with the tour, and as we're walking toward the front of the building, we hear a loud *clank*! We look to our right just in time to see that someone has bumped the ladder of the man who is nailing a two-by-four up near the twelve-foot ceiling. The ladder starts to move, and the man on it is just about to fall.

"Look out!" I yell, and shoot several CHUD at the loose sleeve of his flailing arm. I just want to hold him up there so he can get his footing, so I think that by "nailing" him to the wall, he can have a chance. The CHUD hit its mark, and his arm jerks toward the wall.

*I can't believe it! I did it! Oh, my hell! I did it—in front of witnesses!*

Thankfully, everyone had been looking up at him—the guy who called me "el diablo," so no one actually saw me do it. After he gets the ladder settled and composes himself, he pulls the CHUD out of his sleeve and the wall. I see him looking at them in his hand for a minute before he brings them down to show everyone.

"These are strange," Javier says while looking at one of the CHUD. "I've never seen nails like this before, and by the way, who did this? Who has a nail gun? You just saved your coworker from serious injury!"

The room is silent, and then everyone turns toward me.

*Oh no! Think, Ella! Look for a nail gun that's not being used.*

Luckily, there is a nail gun lying on a workbench just a few feet away from me. "Oh my goodness. I guess I saw him start to fall and grabbed the first thing I could find to try to help him," I say, hoping that they believe me.

Javier walks over to the nail gun and starts looking at the nails that were in it.

"Hmm . . . These nails don't look anything like the nails that were in his sleeve. Odd . . ."

"Well, I had better be getting back home. Thank you all for your wonderful work," I say while backing toward the door.

*Just a few more feet and you're home free.*

Suddenly, a hand grabs my shoulder and I scream. I turn around and find that it's the worker that I "nailed."

"Please excuse me, but I would like to thank you for saving me, Mrs. Malone."

*Not what I expected to hear.* "Oh, you're welcome . . ."

"Pablo," he says, taking my hand and shaking it.

"You're welcome, Pablo. I'm just glad that I could help," I say back to him.

"Good-bye, everyone!" I say, waving and walking out the door.

*Wow, Ella! You just helped save another person. You are amazing! You are a champion! You are . . . tired!*

Saving people sure does take a lot out of me.

I decide to go home and regroup after the saving of Pablo. Well, I guess I didn't really save his life or anything. I just helped him to be able to find his footing, which he probably would've done without my help. Gosh, I really hope that no one saw that it was me who shot the "nail" at his sleeve. I really don't want to be dissected and experimented on by the government.

# Sanctuary

After a quick stop at the bakery for some sweets, I head back to the sanctuary of my home to check on my son. I need to see if I've caused him any permanent mental damage by showing him my latest Gift.

When I arrive home, I find him awake but still in the chair. He looks startled when he sees me.

"I was hoping that it was just a dream," he says quietly.

"No. It's all real," I say while sitting on a chair next to his. I take a deep breath. "So Michael, I have something else to show you."

He looks at me and says, "I'm afraid to ask, but what is it?"

"I'll need to show you. It's pretty amazing. Do you feel up to seeing it?" Might as well get it all out there in the open.

"Go ahead. Show me," he says looking like he did when he was a little boy sitting in the dentist's chair.

"We need to go to the garage for this one," I say, getting up from the chair. He follows my lead.

When we walk into the garage, I lead Michael to a lawn chair and motion for him to sit down. There will be no fainting on concrete.

I walk over to the pile of pictures of Pete where I added the CHUD beards and, without looking, pick one up to show Michael. When I hold it in front of his face, he bursts into laughter.

"*Haaahaaaha!* I thought that you were going to show me something really bizarre!" He giggles and snorts. "I was actually *scared*. That's good, Mom. You really got me." He laughs again.

"Actually, that's not it. I thought that I would give you a good laugh—loosen you up a bit before I show you what I really want to show you." I look at him hopefully.

He sits there silently.

"Okay then. Let's do this," he says, suddenly serious.

I hand the picture of Pete to Michael.

"Now show me the picture," I tell him.

He turns the picture over, and holds it up in front of me. *Whoosh!* Flames.

Michael's eyes become huge and he says, "Well, shit! I wasn't prepared for that at *all*."

I can't help myself—I start laughing. Then *he* starts laughing. We laugh for a good five minutes, and then we get control of ourselves.

Michael is the first of us to speak.

"You're like a superhero. We should call you . . . Let me think . . . Ms. Menopause. No that's dumb. *Hmmm* . . . I've got it! Hott Flash! But Hott is spelled with two T's. You know . . . because you have the flames coming out of your two hands and . . ." He trails off because he finally notices me staring daggers at him.

"First of all, I'm *not* a superhero. Second, never call me Hott Flash again. I don't care if it's spelled with *three* T's.

It's embarrassing," I say, trying to control the heat building up in my hands.

"I'm sorry, Mom. I was just caught up in the moment. I will never call you Hott Flash again. But you have to admit it's kind of clever." He looks at me hopefully. By the look on my face, he knows that I don't find it clever at all.

"Anyway!" Michael says changing the subject. "I *thought* I saw smoke coming from your hands that day we were helping you with your CHUD! This is amazing. Scientifically impossible, but amazing."

We spend the next few hours in the garage with me doing my fire-and-CHUD tricks. Every once in a while, Michael shouts, "Amazing!" but most of the time he just sits there silently with a slight smile on his face. Suddenly, he snaps his fingers. He pulls out his iPhone and begins taking pictures of Pete's bearded pictures, and then he shoots a video of my flaming hands.

"I think it might be less of a shock to Maggie's already rattled system if she sees the pictures and videos first," he says.

I agree with him.

Michael has to return to work, so we go back into the house in search of his car keys. After he finds them in the recliner, and I'm satisfied that he is completely sober, we say our good-byes. He leaves with a strange little smile on his face.

I close the front door and walk to the kitchen. My eyes come to rest longingly on the goodies that I bought at the bakery . . .

When I finish the last bite of a chocolate-covered cake doughnut, I do a Google search for Chupacabra, because I have no idea what that means. If someone is calling me that, I need to know if I should be insulted.

I click on one of many links and learn that a Chupacabra is the Hispanic version of Bigfoot or the Loch Ness monster. Apparently, this "monster" kills farm animals and then drains them of their blood . . . Huh? *Bwaa haaa haaa!* Oh, I needed another good laugh!

I'm sorry that I scared the man, but still . . .

Now that my question has been answered, and I'm all laughed out, I fill Monkey's food bowl, give her fresh water, and pop in a video of *The Nanny*. I settle into my favorite chair, start to devour a big piece of cake that I now have no worries about eating, and Monkey shows up on cue to warm my lap.

Just as I'm nodding off, my phone rings. "Hello?" I answer sleepily.

"Hi, Mom, it's Maggie. Michael came over when I got home from work. He showed me some pictures and a video," she says. And then silence.

"How do you feel after seeing that?" I ask.

More silence.

"I feel like I'm a very lucky girl to have you as a mom," she says.

"You're not scared or freaked out?" I ask incredulously.

"No, Mom, I'm not scared. I mean it's definitely hard to look at you now because you look like you're close to my age, but in the big scheme of things, your Gifts are miracles. I'm sure one of these days your fiery hands are gonna come in handy. At the moment, I can't think of what your new looks could come in handy for, but I'm sure there's an upside."

I think for a minute. *Aha!* "Along with my thirty-year-old looks, I also *feel* like I'm in my thirties again. Remember that cartwheel I did the other day? There is no way I could've done that before."

"Well, there you go—the upside!" I can hear the smile in her voice.

We chat for a few more minutes. She asks me questions about my Gifts. I ask her if she's sure she's okay, and she assures me that she is. I guess that her brain has finally allowed her to accept everything like mine has.

We've both had long days, so we say our good-byes. My eyes start to close before I can even set the phone down.

# Rip Van Malone

I WAKE WITH A START. OH no! Déjà vu! How long have I been sleeping? I look outside, and it looks like the sun is coming up. I went to sleep early afternoon, and now it's the next morning!

What time is it? The clock shows that it's seven o'clock. Seven o'clock in the *morning*? Oh, my hell! I can't believe that I slept all day and night again. What's wrong with me? Oh no! What's *wrong* with me?

I run to the bathroom mirror and do a full head-to-toe inspection of myself. Nothing seems to have changed, thank goodness, except for what looks to be a big blob of paint on the back of my head that I must've gotten when I met with Javier.

"Oh shit! I have to take a *bleep*ing shower!" I say this out loud, and I am absolutely mortified that I used that word!

I turn and notice that Monkey is sitting in her usual spot on the edge of the tub. Her big green eyes are open wide, and she looks as mortified as I feel.

I really don't want to take a shower because of my fear of losing my newfound youth, but I can't go around with a dirty body and paint in my hair.

I turn on the shower faucet and slowly disrobe in front of the mirror. I turn from side to side, admiring the new young me in wonder. I know. I know. I shouldn't worry so much about my outside—it's the inside of a person that counts.

But wow! It sure is something to go from looking fifty to looking thirtyish overnight!

Finished with admiring myself, I gingerly step into the shower. I start washing my hair. All of the sudden, I panic, so I quickly step out of the shower to look in the mirror again. It has gotten fogged up from leaving the hot water running for so long.

I hesitantly reach my hand up to wipe at the mirror with a towel, and I see that my hand is shaking.

*Stop it, Ella. Get a hold of yourself. Beauty is only skin-deep!* I know all of this, yet the vain part of me that I keep buried under my emotional basement has risen from its grave and is making itself at home in my emotional master suite!

I shake my head a few times to clear my head and decide that I should just wipe the mirror quickly, like ripping off a Band-Aid, so that the pain of what I see only lasts for an instant.

Swipe, swipe, swipe. Before me, I see a young, vibrant woman with rich, thick, shiny auburn hair and big, sparkly, green eyes. There is no beard this time, just a smile from ear to ear.

I get back in the shower and finish what I started. A few minutes later, I step out of the shower with a bounce in my step. Monkey has resumed her position on the tub and is now looking at me expectantly.

"Yes, Monkey, I'm going to feed you now," I say as I head to the kitchen.

"I am so sorry that you had to wait so long to get fed today," I say as I fill her food bowl. Monkey looks up at me and then walks over to her bowl.

I go back to the bathroom to finish getting ready for the day. As I pass by a window, I stop in my tracks.

"What in the world?" I say out loud. I realize that it has gotten darker since before I started my shower. "What's going on here? Why is it getting darker outside?" I start to panic, because I am so completely confused at this point.

I open my cell phone to call my mother, and I look at the display.

When I woke up, it was seven o'clock p.m., *not* a.m.! The date is still the same as when I went to sleep, which means that I only napped for a few hours, and not a few days!

Well, this is certainly not something that I'm going to be sharing with anyone. In fact, I'm embarrassed that Monkey knows.

# Catching Up with Mom

LATER THAT EVENING I DIAL my parents' number. I want to tell my mother about what happened today at SALT.

My mother picks up on the second ring. "Hello, Ella. How's my daughter today?" she asks with a smile in her voice.

"I'm fine. Actually, I'm great! So much has happened since we last spoke." I proceed to tell her about my CHUD that kept Pablo from falling off a high ladder.

"Oh, my! Are you sure that none of them saw you actually shoot him with your 'nail'?" my mother asks.

"I'm fairly certain, Mom. Anyway, they were so distracted by my appearance that I think that most of them were still in shock."

"What has happened to your appearance?" I can hear the alarm in my mother's voice.

How could I have forgotten to tell my mother about the greatest "Gift" of all?

"A lot can happen in a few days around here," I say, trying to figure out how to explain what I look like now.

I know! I'll send her a picture on her phone. *How did we ever survive as a society without the iPhone?*

"Give me just a minute. I'm going to take a few pictures and send them to you, because you'll have to see it to believe it. I woke up the other day looking twenty years younger!"

I thought that I should prepare her, because I really didn't want her to faint like Maggie and I did.

"You *what?!*" she asks.

"Please prepare yourself for what you're about to see, and for goodness' sake—sit down before you look at the pictures. I'm hanging up now so that I can get them taken and sent to you. Please call me when you get them."

I hang up and start taking pictures of my face and my body with clothes on. (I don't want to put her in the hospital!) I get them sent . . . I wait a few minutes . . . I wait a few more minutes . . . *I wonder why it's taking so long?* After another five minutes or so, the phone finally rings.

"Well, what do you think?" I ask.

"Ella! This is your father. I'm calling to let you know that something has happened to your mother and I have called 9-1-1."

"What happened?" I ask, fearing the worst.

"I need to be brief because I don't want to be on the phone if she needs me. Your mother and I were working on a puzzle together at the kitchen table when you called. Your mother excused herself and went to the bedroom to chat with you—you know, you two hens have gotten very secretive lately. Now where was I? Oh yes, after a little while, I called out to her to see if she was still on the phone. She didn't respond, so I called out to her again, thinking that maybe she didn't hear me the first time. Something didn't sit right with me, so I quickly got up from my chair to go check on her. I got to the bedroom and found her unconscious on the floor. I don't know what happened to her. She came to after a few minutes, but she was very disoriented and kept mumbling over and over again, "I can't believe it. I can't believe it."

"Oh Pop, I'm so sorry! How is she doing now?"

"Well, she's sitting up." He pulls the phone away from his mouth and says to my mother, "Hold on, my dear. Don't try it without my help! You need to take it easy until the ambulance gets here!"

I hear my mother in the background say, "Is that Ella? Let me talk to her please."

I hear fumbling and then, "Ella? Don't worry. I'm okay. I've been trying to convince your father to cancel the ambulance, but he is so determined." Then she says to Pop, "Is that the ambulance already?" She returns to me. "Honey, I need to hang up now, but I will call you when everything has calmed down. I love you!"

"I love you too, Mom! I'm so sorry this happened to you. I'll talk to you later." *Click.*

I hang up feeling like the world's worst daughter.

Around midnight, my mother calls and tells me that the ambulance technician insisted that she go in for a CAT scan to rule out any trauma. Nothing showed up on the scan, and she passed all of the other tests, so they released her from the ER. Thank goodness she wasn't hurt seriously. I would never have been able to forgive myself if she had been. I'm afraid that the only injury she sustained was mental. If there were a machine that measured emotional trauma, my mother would've been held indefinitely at the hospital!

# Catching Up with Mom—Take Two

THE NEXT MORNING, MY MOTHER calls to tell me that she is okay and to discuss my new Gift.

"Ella, I just can't get over how you look now! You look just like you did when you were in your thirties. In fact, your father saw the pictures when he picked up my phone and asked why you were sending me pictures from twenty years ago! I told him that we are working on compiling scrapbooks for the family."

"Good thinking, Mom. I don't know how I'm going to explain my looks to him when I come to visit you for Thanksgiving." I say while trying to think of an excuse. "I guess I'm going to have to tell him, along with everyone else, what I told Javier and the crew: that I've had some work done."

"Well, the story would be believable, since you *are* at that age."

"Mother!" I say, pretending to me insulted. "You know, if I were you, I don't think that I would be throwing stones! You're twenty years older than me!"

"I call a truce!" she says, laughing.

"Truce," I say, smiling.

"On that note, I had better get off now. I have to go to the store and buy scrap-booking supplies, since I told your father that that's what I'm working on. You know your father. He has a mind like a steel trap, and he will most certainly ask me how my project is going. I had better have something to show him."

"Okay, Mom, I love you."

"I love you too, Ella."

*Click.*

# Gotta Move My Body

I DECIDE THAT I SHOULD GET back in the habit of jogging every other day, so I go put on one of my new little short sets. I'm actually going out in public wearing shorts that don't go all the way down to my knees! I put on some sun block. (I still have to protect my skin—even if it *is* twenty years younger!) I grab my iPod, keys, sunglasses, and water bottle and head to the track. (It sure is convenient having a track just a block from my house!)

I get to the track, plug in my ear buds, and Journey's "Don't Stop Believing" gets me going.

As I'm jogging, I notice that I feel so completely good. Gone are the days of the soreness and pain that I used to have just getting out of bed.

I've been jogging for about a half an hour when I see out of the corner of my eye someone coming up on my left side. I move over to let them pass. This person stays next to me and doesn't pass. In fact, I think this person is saying something to me.

Without slowing down, I pull out my ear buds so that I can hear, and I look over at this person who wants to intrude upon my good mood. Damn! It's my nosey neighbor Edith from down the street. This woman has her nose in everyone in the neighborhood's business. In fact, Edith knew about Mr. Brown's wife leaving him before *he* did! She was on his doorstep with a casserole at the exact moment that he was reading his wife's good-bye letter.

"Oh my goodness, Ella! I could barely catch up with you! Do you have a rocket in your pocket?" she jokes.

I continue jogging, because the last thing I need to worry about is Edith spreading gossip about my new look.

"Hi, Edith. Sorry, but I can't slow down. I'm training for the Houston Marathon."

*Way to think on your feet!*

"I was just admiring your legs, Ella! All that runnin' you've been doin' sure has paid off! You look good, girl!"

Thank goodness I'm wearing oversized sunglasses, or else she'd be asking about my face!

"Thank you, Edith! I've been working hard!"

I speed up a little, hoping that she will get the hint and leave. No such luck. She stays by my side.

"Did you hear about the Rileys over on Carnation Court?"

I glance at her out of the corner of my eye and silently will her to go away.

She takes my silence as, "Yes, I would love to hear your horrible gossip about people's business that is not yours to share."

"Well, apparently the husband has a gamblin' addiction and has just recently lost his job, so they've been fightin' like cats and dogs every evening when the wife gets home from work."

I concentrate hard and think, *Shut up, and go away!*

"Well, I heard them loud an' clear one night, and he was sayin' . . . Oh, my. I do believe that I need to go and sit down. All of a sudden, I'm not feelin' too well," Edith says while slowing down.

I, on the other hand, am not slowing down.

"I guess I'll talk to you after you're finished with your run!" Edith says while coming to a dead stop in the middle of the track.

"Bye, Edith! I'll see you later!" I shout over my shoulder.

I look back and see her walk slowly over to one of the park benches to sit down.

*Did I do that? Is mind control one of my Gifts now? That would be really cool if it was!* I look back at her. *I hope she's not going to be sitting there waiting for me to come and finish our delightful conversation!*

I keep on jogging for another fifteen minutes and think really hard, *Go home, Edith!*

Nothing.

She's still there waiting to pounce on me and spew her gossip.

I make another lap, and she's still there. Obviously, mind control is *not* one of my Gifts.

Finally, after thirty minutes or so, I see her get up from the bench. She half-heartedly waves to me and then heads toward her house.

I give her a few minutes to get all the way home, and to get all the way inside her house. When I feel that the coast is clear, I head home too. I could have kept jogging for hours, but I really don't want to have to deal with any more nosey neighbors.

As I leave the park, I notice a little yellow and white VW Mini Bus parked across the street. *Cute!*

# Guess What I Did

When I get home, I realize that I haven't told my kids about the Pablo incident. I call Michael before I forget.

"Hi, Mom," he says, answering on the first ring.

"Hello, Michael. I'm surprised to have you answer so quickly. It usually goes to voice mail."

"You just caught me at a good time," he says with a chuckle.

"Well, I have a story to tell you if you have the time," I say.

"Sure, Mom. Is everything okay?" he asks, sounding concerned.

"Oh yes, Michael. Everything is fine. I just wanted to tell you about what happened the other day," I say. I then proceed to tell him about Pablo and the ladder, and my quick thinking that saved me from explaining myself. I also tell him about the reaction of the workers, and when I tell him about being called a "Chupacabra," Michael starts laughing harder than I've heard him laugh in a long time. "That is priceless! My mom, the Chupacabra! Have you told Maggie yet?"

"No, not yet."

"Hold on just a minute. I'm going to call her, and we'll make it a conference call because I have to hear you tell her what you told me."

I hear the phone ringing, and Maggie answers.

"Hi, Maggie. Michael and I have you on a conference call. Do you have a minute?"

"Sure, Mom, I have a minute. Is everything okay?"

"Yes, dear, everything is fine. I just want to tell you about my latest adventure."

When I get to the part about Chupacabra, she starts laughing as hard as Michael did.

Apparently, I'm the only one who didn't know what a Chupacabra is.

"Oh Mom, I sure did need that laugh! Today seems to be the day that all of the cranky people have decided to come in for spa treatments. Well, Carol is waving to me frantically from across the room, so that's my cue to go. Congratulations on being a hero again. I love you both. Bye."

After Maggie disconnects, Michael says, "I've been thinking more about your newest Gift. This is something that you can't really disguise from people who know you. Unlike your other Gifts, that aren't visible unless you use them, this Gift is always there. It's the new you, and I have to say it bothers me a bit not to see the face that has smiled at me for the past few years. I know, I know, it sounds silly, but I remember your face looking very close to what it does now when I was younger. Since then, your face has aged right along with mine . . . until now. To have you looking like you're close to my age is very disconcerting. You look like you're young enough to be my older sister! I can only imagine how Maggie must feel . . ."

"She assures me that she's okay with everything, but thinking about it, how *can* she be okay? I don't think that

*I* could handle it if one day my mother answered the door looking as young as me! Oh, poor Maggie! She's probably worried about *me* and all that *I'm* dealing with and doesn't want me to worry about *her*!" I feel like the world's worst mom.

"Well, I'm sure that in time it will get easier for us all to look at you, but there's a reason that I brought this subject up. Don't get upset with me, but I think that you need to consider going out of town for a few weeks."

"What?" I ask.

"Think about it. Grandma, Maggie, and I know what's going on with you, but the rest of the world isn't supposed to. What are you going to say to any of the neighbors who get a good look at you?"

I tell him about Edith accosting me at the track.

"See! If she had gotten a better look at you, you would've been in trouble. The excuse you gave to Javier is perfect. You need to go away for a few weeks, so it will lend credibility to your story."

"I hate to admit it, but it makes a lot of sense. I don't want to hide in my house for weeks, so if I go somewhere where nobody knows me, I can go out into the world and enjoy it, without fear of someone fainting from the sight of the new me." I'm thinking happy thoughts of wearing my new Jessica Simpson dress without fear of someone screaming, "Imposter! You're too old to be wearing that!"

*"Hmmm . . .* where should I go? I really want to go check on your grandmother and see how she's doing. She fainted the other evening when I sent her pictures of myself. I'd like to lay my eyes on her and see if she's doing okay after her

fall. I wish that I could go to Sedona and check on her, but I don't want to cause your grandfather to faint too!"

Michael was quiet for a minute.

"Michael, are you still there?"

"Yes, I was just thinking. You know, I don't approve of keeping something like this from your dad, but since you've decided to do that anyway, you can always check into a hotel in Sedona on the other side of town and see grandma on the sly."

"That's a good idea, Michael. Thank you. I guess I had better go and start making plans. I'll talk to you later, honey. I love you!"

"I love you too!"

*Click.*

The next call I make is to my mother, and she is thrilled with the plan.

I head off to take a shower before I call the airline. I'm not scared of the shower anymore, and my nose is very thankful of this.

# Are You Okay with This?

THE NEXT MORNING, I CALL Maggie and invite her over for coffee if she's got some free time.

"Hi, Mom."

"Hi, Maggie. I was calling to see if you had some time today to come over for a chat," I say expectantly.

"Oh Mom, I'm sorry! We are booked solid today, but I have a few minutes now for a quick chat."

"I'll be brief then." I decide to let the conversation regarding my new appearance, and the effect it has had on her, wait for now. "Michael suggested that I should leave town for a few weeks in order to lend credibility to my story about getting some work done, so I'm going to go spend some time in Sedona with Grandma."

"Does Grandpa know? Did you tell him too?"

"Oh no! He still doesn't know, so I plan on staying at a hotel on the other side of town."

"Sounds kinda sneaky to me," Maggie says.

"I agree with you, Maggie, but I really need to see my mom," I say, close to tears.

One minute I'm happy, and the next minute I'm sad or mad.

"I'm sorry. Of course, you would want your momma, especially since she's been through the same thing! When do you leave?" she asks.

"Day after tomorrow."

"Would you like to me to cat-sit Monkey while you're gone? The house seems empty since Jack left, and it would be nice to have another heartbeat around." Jack was Maggie's cat who'd passed away from feline leukemia last year. She knew that he was positive when she adopted him, but she didn't care.

"Every animal deserves a chance. Even if he only lives a month, I'm going to make sure that he knows every day of his life that he is loved," she said the day she brought him home. He ended up living three happy, love-filled years with my daughter. *What a good girl!*

"Oh, that would be wonderful! I didn't want to ask you, since you've been so busy with work, plus with Jack and all . . . I was planning on driving so that I could take Monkey with me since she doesn't do well flying, or staying at the kennel. She doesn't do well on long car rides *either*, so this makes things easier on us both! Now I can just fly out and rent a car. Thank you so much!"

"I'm happy to help!"

"I'm going to go check on flights now. I will call you when I get something set, and then we can plan on when I can take her to your house."

"Sounds good. I love you, Mom!"

"I love you too!"

*Click.*

# Monkey's Big Adventure

It's the next morning. Last night I was able to get a good deal on a nonstop flight leaving at eight o'clock today, so now I am on the way to Maggie's house to drop Miss Monkey off. Monkey wasn't happy *at all* this morning when I put her (shoved her) into her carrier, but she will just have to get over it. Knowing her, it will take from a few days—up to a week—before she will forgive me. Oh, the joys of being a cat parent!

I get to Maggie's place and she comes out to meet us. She stops short. Her eyes pop out when she sees me, but then I see her set her shoulders back like when she's determined to do something. She continues on out to the car. She looks happy to see me, and very happy to see Monkey.

"Hello to you both," says Maggie when she gets to us. "Sorry about the weird look I gave you. I'm still getting used to your new look."

"No need to apologize, my dear. I have that look on my face every time I catch my reflection in a mirror!"

She opens the front door, and we go in. I go to sit down on the couch in her living room. Next to the couch is a cat-climbing post that is taking up a lot of space along the wall.

"I thought you donated Jack's climbing post to a shelter," I say while opening up the carrier to release the beast.

"I did. I bought this one last night after work. I thought Monkey might be a little scared and out of sorts being in a new place, so I figured that this might help," Maggie says while watching Monkey slowly poke her head out the carrier.

"It's okay, Monkey," I say. "Come on out girl."

She gingerly steps out, looks at me, hisses, runs to the climbing post, and proceeds to climb to the very top. Up there, she finds the little cubby that was made for cats to hide in.

I walk over to her, but she has me on ignore.

"Good-bye, Monkey. Be a good girl while I'm gone. I love you, my little crusty cat!" I reach out to pet her, and surprisingly she lets me. She won't look at me though.

"You had better get going, Mom, or you're going to miss your flight," Maggie says as she heads to the door.

"You're right. Okay, here is her food. She gets some canned food in the morning and night and then some dry food to nibble on throughout the day."

"She's in good hands, Mom. Don't worry; I'll take good care of her."

"I know you will, and on that note, I will head out. I love you," I say, giving Maggie a big hug.

"I love you too, Mom. See you in a few weeks, and give Grandma my love."

"Will do," I say, feeling a lump in my throat.

I don't like leaving my kids for too long. I had said my good-byes to Michael last night when he stopped by with doughnuts. He sure does know how to make his mom happy!

# Sedona, Here I Come

I BOARD THE PLANE WITH A mixture of excitement and sadness. I'm excited by the thought of seeing my mother again but sad about leaving my children behind.

I find my row and see that I'm in the aisle seat. My window seat neighbor is already settled in. He looks to be in his mid to late forties and is reading a paper, which is code for "I have no desire to speak to you."

I pick up my carry-on, which is heavier than I remember, and start to fumble with it as I lift it up to put in the overhead compartment. A male voice behind me says, "Here, let me help you with that."

I turn around and see a very cute young man with dark-brown hair and the most beautiful hazel eyes that I have ever seen in my entire life, and he's smiling down at me. He looks a lot like Dave Annable from the sadly canceled TV series *Brothers and Sisters. Wow! He's cute!* I just stand there staring at up at him.

He takes my silence as a yes and takes my carry-on from me. He puts it in the overhead compartment with ease. I'm so used to being ignored by men lately that I don't know how to react! I find my manners and tell him, "Thank you." He continues on to the back of the plane, and then he turns around and smiles at me when he gets to his seat. I realize that I'm still standing there in the aisle like a moron!

I hear a man clear his throat behind me. I turn around and see a man who looks impatient. "I'm here," he says, indicating the middle seat.

"Excuse me," I say, moving out of the way. He says nothing.

After he sits down, I sit down, because people going to the back seats keep bumping me. One more bump, and someone is going to get a CHUD injury!

As the plane zooms down the runway, I feel a rush of adrenalin. After the rush of adrenalin, I feel a rush of sleepiness. When we level off and the ride becomes smooth, I lean my chair back to relax.

I'm enjoying a nice nap on the plane, when all of the sudden, I'm on fire! Oh no! Not a power surge *now*!

I reach up with my right arm to open my air vent. I am bringing it back down when I feel a strange feeling under my arm. It's like there's something under there. I look to my right and see that the two people that I'm sitting next to are asleep, so I turn toward them. I don't want anyone on the other side of the aisle seeing me mess with my armpit. I lift my arm to investigate what's going on under there and take a peek. There is a lump about the size of a grape! I take a look over my left shoulder to see if anyone is watching me from across the aisle, and find that everyone is either sleeping or reading. I turn to my right a little bit more, so that the light from the window can shine on it better. I lift my arm, and without thinking, I squeeze it.

Big mistake! A small but steady stream of water shoots out, hits the window, and splashes window-seat neighbor in the face! (He was unfortunate enough to be leaning toward the window as he slept.)

He snorts loudly as he wakes up. He starts wiping at his face with his hands while he looks around to see if he can figure out what just happened.

If the situation wasn't so incredibly embarrassing and horrifying,, it would be unbelievably funny! The look on his face is priceless! I can feel hysterical laughter creeping up on me.

*Don't laugh, Ella. It's not funny. Pull yourself together!*

He wakes up enough to have his wits about him, and then his eyes settle on me. I know that he knows that I saw something.

*Think, Ella, think. Okay, you spilled your drink on him . . . but you don't have a drink in front of you. Oh no! He's waiting!*

Just then, a child of maybe age two, who is sitting in the seat in front of Window Seat Neighbor, pops his head up and looks at us. He must've been awakened by the loud snort.

*Hee hee.*

An idea pops into my head. I'm not proud of myself for thinking of it, but desperate times call for desperate measures!

I turn to look at Window Seat and then put my left hand up to cover my right finger that is pointing at the little boy. Window Seat looks at the little boy and shakes his finger at him. The little boy's lower lip pops out, and he turns around and sits back down in his seat.

*I'm such a bad person!*

Window Seat climbs over Middle Row and me, and then heads in the direction of the restrooms. Middle Row looks at me with a scowl on his face. Too bad I didn't squirt *him* instead.

At this point, I realize that my power surge has subsided, and I feel a lot more comfortable. A few minutes later, Window Seat squeezes back in and uses the paper towels that he has brought back with him to clean the liquid off the window and seat. I look at him out of the corner of my eye and send him a silent apology.

About five minutes later, the stewardess tells us to bring our seats back to an upright position and to prepare for our final descent.

# The Beginning of an Awkward Situation

On my way to the baggage claim, I'm startled when a male voice behind me says, "Hello again!"

I miss a step, and the man comes around to my side. He falls into step with me. I turn briefly to look at him, and see that it's the young man who helped me with my carry-on bag!

*Does he expect a tip?*

"So do you live in Sedona?" he asks.

"No, I'm here visiting my parents," I say awkwardly.

*Why is he talking to me?*

"Me too!" he says excitedly. "How long are you staying?"

"I don't know," I say, wondering if I should just reach into my purse and give him a few dollars so he can be on his way.

"I'm here for three days for my mom's sixty-fifth birthday party."

"That's nice," I say as we arrive at the baggage claim.

I pick a place toward the back because I don't like people pushing and shoving while they try to be the first to grab their luggage.

"I'm Brendan, by the way," he says, extending his hand.

I release the handle of my carry-on that I've had a death grip on since the beginning of this conversation and shake his hand.

"I'm Ella," I say, feeling more confused as this conversation continues.

"Well, it was nice meeting you, Brendan. Thank you again for helping me with my bag earlier on the plane."

"It was my pleasure! I like rescuing pretty damsels in distress," he says with the most adorable smile.

*Wait a minute! Adorable smile? Damsels in distress? Pretty? What the hell?*

I feel my head cock to the side like Becky the salesgirl and ask him, "Are you calling *me* a damsel in distress?" I feel as if I'm in an alternate universe.

"Yes, a *pretty* damsel in distress," he says with the same adorable smile.

*Oh my goodness! I think he's actually flirting with me!*

All I can do is laugh. This whole situation is so embarassing and awkward, and *wrong*!

He looks slightly taken aback and asks, "Did I say something funny?"

I realize that I'm being rude. I get a hold of myself so I can stop laughing. "I'm sorry. No. You didn't say anything funny. In fact, you said all the right things, I haven't been considered a 'damsel' in many, many years," I say, giving him what I hope is a normal smile instead of that of an awkward teenager.

"Many, many years? You make it seem like you're an old woman!" he says while chuckling.

"If you only knew!"

*Did that come out of my mouth?*

"Knew what?"

"Uhhh . . . that the baggage is starting to come out of the baggage thingy."

*Smooth save, Ella!*

"How many suitcases do you have?" Brendan asks.

"I have two. Why?"

"I plan on finishing what I started and help you with all of your bags. Do they match that one?" he says, pointing to my carry-on.

"Yes, they do."

*What are you doing? Don't let him get your bags! The longer he stays with you, the harder it will be to get out of this mortifying situation!*

He sets his own leather duffle bag on the floor next to me and goes over the conveyer belt that the luggage rides around on. A few minutes later, he comes back with my suitcases and a smile.

"Thank you," I say, pulling my rental car paperwork out of my purse, preparing to leave as quickly as possible.

"It seems like you're in a hurry to go see your parents, so I wonder if you would be up to having a drink with me later on tonight. Around nine?" he asks hopefully. "I figure that should be plenty of time for a nice long dinner with our folks. Then around the time that they're getting tired and ready for bed, we can meet up for a drink and get to know each other better."

I'm standing there. He's looking at me expectantly, and I'm still standing there, frozen like a statue, holding my paperwork in my motionless hand.

*A boy that has got to be at least twenty years younger than you has just asked you out for a drink, which for that generation is a date. He's looking at you. Say something! Say something!*

"I *uhh* . . . just got out of a very long relationship, and I'm not really ready for drinks just yet. Sorry."

"Oh, I understand. Been there, done that! How about just a friendly cup of coffee in the light of day? Tomorrow around two if you don't have plans?"

He hands me his card. It reads, "Brendan O'Connor—Owner/Landscape Architect—Landscape Designs by B." I seem to attract men who are Irish. Maybe because I'm part Irish on my mother's side.

It also has contact information including an address in Clear Lake, Texas, just a few miles from my house.

It is a very small world!

I look up from the card, and he's giving me that smile again.

*Stop looking so adorably handsome! I'm a sick old woman for even thinking that! What should I say?*

*Oh, I know.*

"If I have time, I will call you. I can't guarantee that I will get a chance before you go back to Houston, but we'll see," I say, using the same line that I used on my kids when they were younger. It's my way of saying no without actually saying no.

For some reason, this seems to satisfy him.

I put his card in my purse, smile, and say, "It was very nice meeting you, Brendan. Thank you for all of your help today. Have a lovely time with your parents." I extend my hand. Maybe he will take the hint.

He takes it in his. *Ooh, it tingles!*

"Thank *you*, Ella, for making an airport enjoyable," Brendan says, smiling that smile. He releases my hand, turns, and walks away.

Would it be icky of me to say that I was a little sad to see him go?

About half an hour later, I'm in my rental car, headed to the hotel, and wondering what the hell just happened!

# Home, Sweet Temporary Home

I ARRIVE AT MY DESTINATION. SINCE I have to be away from home for so long, I thought that I should go all out and stay in one of the beautiful spa resort hotels that they have in Sedona.

I pull up to the front entrance of the resort and am immediately met by a concierge. I give him my name, and he arranges to have my luggage sent to my room ahead of me while I am checking in. How very nice!

I approach the front desk and am met with a smiling face. "Welcome to Sedona Resort and Spa. How may I assist you today?" a perky girl says from behind the counter.

I look behind me and realize that all of this warm and fuzzy behavior is for me!

"Hello. My name is Ella Malone, and I have a reservation for today," I say smiling back at her.

It's contagious!

"Okay, great. I see that you have reserved a Deluxe Guest Room for two weeks." She does some typing on her computer.

"Ms. Malone, unfortunately we have a little bit of an issue. Your room was double-booked. We seem to be pretty full at this time. How does an upgrade to a Jacuzzi Guest Suite at no additional charge sound?" she asks cheerfully.

"That sounds wonderful. Thank you!" I say, knowing that I just got a great deal.

We finish the transaction. She hands me the key and says, "Enjoy your stay. Oh, and by the way, I love your top!"

I look down at myself and remember that I have a whole new wardrobe that is full of fun and trendy things. I look back up and say, "Thank you! I got it at T.J. Maxx!"

*What do you know? I'm a fashionista, or a "Maxxinista" as they say in the T.J. Maxx commercials.*

I'm smiling when I enter the elevator that is taking me to my third-floor paradise.

I enter my suite and find my luggage waiting for me.

*Brendan . . .*

*Wait just one minute. Did you just think about that young man from the plane? He can't be much older than thirty—young enough to be your son! Stop it right now!*

I feel dirty from my thoughts, the flight, and the whole water squirting from my armpit ordeal. So after calling my mom, Michael, and Maggie ("Monkey is doing fine," she says) to let them know that I landed safely, I take a long, long shower.

Surprisingly, I am tired, so I decide that since I really don't have anything to do but unpack, I will take a short nap.

## Another Story to Tell

Five hours later, my room phone is ringing, and I'm trying to wake up enough to form a proper sentence.

"Hello?" I answer.

"Hello, Ella, it's your mother. I couldn't reach you on your cell phone, so I thought that I would try your room. Are you all right, honey? You sound strange."

"No, Mom, I'm just sleepy. Everything is fine."

"Okay, that's good. Is it okay if I come on up?"

"Come on up to what?" I ask feeling very confused.

"Come on up to your room. I'm in the lobby now. Didn't you say that you were on the third floor?"

"Oh yes, I'm sorry. My mind is fuzzy. Come on up," I say dragging myself out of the bed.

*Why am I so sleepy after I use a Gift, and why do my Gifts show up when I've been sleeping?!*

A few minutes later, there is a knock on my door.

I go to the door and open it a crack.

"Mom, I want you to close your eyes and let me lead you to the bed, so that you can gently sit down instead of falling down when you see me."

"Okay, I will. I don't want to have another fall either!" she says, reaching out her arm for me to take.

I lead her into the room, guide her to the bed, and help her sit down.

"Okay, open your eyes."

She opens her eyes, makes a squeak-like sound, and falls back on the bed.

"Mom!" I say, rushing to her side.

When I bend over her, she opens her eyes and says. "Gotcha!"

"Don't do that to me! You scared the hell—I mean heck—out of me! You have an odd sense of humor, lady!" I say, trying to settle my heart rate back down by deep breathing.

"I couldn't resist! Everything has gotten so serious lately and I just couldn't stand it any longer. I'm sorry, dear; I guess that now is not the time to joke around. On a brighter note, I didn't *really* pass out this time!"

"Well, thank goodness! My heart was doing some crazy flip-flops at the sight of you fainting! Anyway, enough about that. I want to know how you are doing. How is your hip? Pop said that you were lying on your side when he found you."

"I'm fine. I wish that everyone would stop fussing over me. I want to talk about *you!* Take a turn around and let me look at you!"

I give her a twirl, feeling like a little girl.

"My, my, it's incredible! The pictures didn't do the transformation justice. I'm glad that you sent them though, because I honestly don't know if I could've handled seeing you in person first."

"The thing is, besides looking this young on the outside, I feel this young on the inside! I went for a jog the other day and didn't feel any of the aches and pains that I have had almost every day since I was in my late thirties. Don't get me wrong. I was in pretty good shape for my age." (*Did I just say that?!*) "I used to go jogging at least every other day, and occasionally I would pop in a workout DVD at home. I honestly feel like I have a do-over on my life. I don't know if this Gift is permanent, or only temporary, but I want to make every day count!"

I look over at my mom, and she's smiling at me with so much love. I begin to feel sad, really sad, and guilty.

"Mom, I wish that this could've been one of your Gifts. I feel so guilty for having this wonderful, amazing thing happen to me while the rest of you only get to sit back and watch."

"Oh Ella, dear! Never for a minute feel guilty about having this miraculous transformation. If the roles were reversed, would you want me to feel guilty, or would you want me to enjoy every amazing minute? *And* you deserve this after the other Gifts that you've received." she says emphatically.

She stands up and puts her hands on my shoulders. "You deserve this!" she says, looking me square in the eyes.

"But you had to deal with The Change too!" I say, still unable to shake the guilt. "I don't know about your other Gifts, but I know that you had water squirt from your armpits for years, which by the way, I know exactly how that feels."

I think about the look on Window Seat's face and chuckle.

"What's so funny, and how do you know how it—oh! You got it too?"

"Yes, I sure did!"

We sit down, and I tell her about my flight, and how I woke up because of the power surge. And how I found the lump.

She has a faraway look on her face while I'm talking. She must be remembering finding *her* lump all those years ago. When I get to the part about accidentally squirting Window Seat in the face, her faraway look turns to horror.

"Oh my goodness! How horrible! How did you handle it? Did anyone see you?"

"Nobody saw me . . . that I know of. It was early in the morning and most of the passengers were either sleeping or reading."

I hesitate before telling her how I handled the situation. I'm not proud of putting the blame on a child, but I was in a situation that could have gotten a lot worse if I would have been further questioned. I was so shocked and nervous that I was afraid that I would lose control and accidentally shoot my CHUD, or produce smoke, or a flame, or develop a new crazy Gift that could land me on top of an examining table in a lab, waiting to be dissected!

"What happened next?" she asks, interrupting my thoughts.

I tell her about trying desperately to think of something that would prevent me from being questioned, and then I close my eyes. (I can't bear to see the look of disapproval on her face when I tell her.) I tell her what I did.

Silence . . . huh?

I open my eyes, and she is staring at me with a very strange look on her face. It looks as if she is trying to do an algebraic equation in her head. Then she bursts into laughter.

"I've got to hand it to you. You sure can think on your feet," she says, wiping tears of laughter from her eyes.

*This is not the reaction I expected. I thought for sure that I would get the disapproving look that I spent my whole life trying to avoid.*

She starts laughing again, and then she stops. She has that strange look on her face again.

"Ella, I have to ask. When you noticed the lump under your arm, why didn't you just go to the restroom?"

I slap myself in the forehead. *Why didn't I think of that?!*

"I don't know! Maybe because I was in shock from having water squirt from my armpit! A new Gift that I acquired in *public,* I might add!" I'm slightly annoyed at myself and at *her* for catching me acting like an idiot.

"I'm hungry," I say, changing the subject. "Do you feel like eating breakfast, or lunch, or whatever meal is appropriate at this time of day? What time is it anyway?"

"It's almost six o'clock, dear."

"It is? Oh, dam . . . *err* . . . darn! I slept the day away again! I seem to get very tired when I use one of my Gifts, and they appear during my sleep. I go to sleep every night worried about what new and unusual thing I might wake up with!"

"That's how it was for me too." My mom looks deep in thought.

"Are you sure you're okay?" I ask, worried that she never fully recovered from the shock I gave her a few nights ago.

"I'm fine. It's just going to take me some time getting used to seeing my daughter so young looking again. By the end of the trip, I bet I won't even notice," she says happily.

She looks at her watch again and says, "I'm afraid it's getting late, dear. Your father will be ready for dinner right about now. I've got some roast beef in the slow cooker that should just about be ready to eat. Do you mind if I come back tomorrow morning around nine o'clock, when he's out playing golf?"

"Sure, that would be great," I say, walking her to the door.

She turns to give me a hug.

"I love you so much, Ella! I'm glad to have you here."

"I love you too, Mom. It's good to *be* here!"

She leaves, and I go in search of the room service menu.

I order a cheeseburger, fries, and a piece of apple pie, with a chocolate malt to wash it down.

I know that I shouldn't be eating like this, but . . . I'm footloose and fancy-free. I need to splurge once in a while.

When I'm finished with my meal, I open up my sliding glass door and go out onto the balcony. I've got an amazing view of the red rocks. It's so different from Houston. Houston is flat. I love Houston, but there aren't any hills of any kind to look at. This view is a vacation for my eyes.

Speaking of my eyes, they are getting heavy. I can't believe I'm sleepy again. It must be a combination of getting a new Gift *while* traveling for several hours.

After the dishes have been removed from my room and my teeth are brushed, I crawl back into bed. I realize that when telling my mother about my day, I left out the part about meeting Brendan. It was just too embarrassing. *And* I realize that once again, my mother has managed to avoid telling me about her other Gifts.

*She will not change the subject on me again! I'm going to make her tell me tomorrow when I see her, and I won't take no for an answer!*

Yawn!

# A *What* Kind of Dream?!

I'm dreaming that I'm in a round room with gray, stone walls. I walk over to a mirrored dressing table that is across the room from me. I see that I'm wearing a long, corseted, pink, flowing dress. My hair is long and reaches almost to my waist. I'm also wearing a jeweled tiara. In the reflection of the mirror behind me, I see a window. I walk over to the window and see that there is no glass in it. It is open to the outside. I find that I am up high in this room. I panic and shout, "Please, somebody save me, for I am a damsel in distress!"

*Damsel*?

From down below, I hear, "Fear not, dear maiden. I will rescue you. Stand back, for I am going to scale this castle wall!"

*Castle*?

Just then, an arrow attached to a rope comes flying through the window. It finds its mark between the stones of the wall across from the window. I hear scraping and scuffling sounds and look down to see a dark-haired man climbing the rope. He finally makes it to the window, pulls himself in, bends over to dust his pants off, and with a flourish, stands up. He raises his hand as if to hail a cab.

"It is I, Prince Brendan, who has come to rescue you from the clutches of your evil stepmother!"

I think that this dream is a mishmash of several fairy tales all rolled into one!

*Brendan?!*

He walks toward me, takes me in his arms, dips me, and kisses me long and hard!

*This certainly isn't a* children's *fairy tale!*

He brings me back up and stares deep into my eyes. His hands that are still on my waist move around to my front and up toward the bow at the top of my dress. He slowly pulls the bow open. He starts unhooking the ribbon from the hooks of my corset. I'm afraid and excited at the same time! I must not be too afraid because my hands seem to have a mind of their own. They start to travel up along his hard, muscular back.

*Oh, my!*

When he has a few hooks undone, he says, "My god, you are so beautiful!" He then picks me up and lays me down on a big, four-poster bed that is draped in sheer-white material. He gets on the bed beside me and is holding himself up on his left elbow. He looks down at me and says, "I have wanted you since the moment I first saw you." and then he bends over and starts kissing the exposed areas of my chest. If I weren't already lying down, I'd be swooning!

I feel the passion building inside of me. Something that I haven't felt in a long time.

His lips are back on mine, and his body is as well! I feel his hand slowly traveling up my inner thigh! It's getting closer . . . and closer . . .

"Oh yes! Take me now!"

Just as his hand finds its mark, I'm startled by a loud buzzing sound. What is that?

# Oh No! It Was Just a Dream

IT'S THE ALARM CLOCK TELLING me to stop having fun and wake up!

"Oh no! It was just a dream!" I say dejectedly.

I remember every detail, right down to how his lips felt on mine. I squeeze my eyes shut in the hopes of getting back to the dream, and to finish what we started, but sadly, the moment has passed. I lie in bed savoring the feeling of his hands on my body for a few more minutes.

*It's been too long, Ella. If you don't use it, you'll lose it!*

"Well, I'm not going to use it with a boy who is young enough to be my son!"

I slap both of my hands over my mouth when I realize that I just said this part out loud.

*Note to self: Must work on internal dialogue skills. Can't have another close call like at the airport with Brendan.*

After much arguing with myself over when to keep my mouth *and* my legs shut, I (we) come to an agreement. I can use "it" with anyone I want to in my dreams—just not in real life. For the first time since The Change started, I'm actually looking forward to the next time I can get some sleep!

# Forget about the Dream

I FINALLY PULL MYSELF OUT OF bed and step into a cold shower. I do my hair and makeup, and then pick out an outfit. I start off by choosing a Louis Vuitton Monogram Canvas Neverfull MM bag. (Hello, my name is Ella Malone and I am a Louis Vuitton handbag addict! I don't have a huge LV collection, but I do own several. I rarely use them for fear of ruining them, but at the last minute, I decided to bring a few of them with me on this trip. What's the point of owning pretty things if you don't use them?) Next, I choose a pair of jeans and a cream-colored camisole top. I accent it with a chunky gold fashion chain. It was one of the many neat things that Becky helped me find. I'm slipping on my brown leather sandals when there is a knock on the door.

Nine o'clock on the dot.

"Good morning," I say, opening the door to my mother. She looks momentarily stunned when she sees me but then composes herself.

"Good morning, dear. Did you sleep well?"

I can feel heat rising in my face.

*Uh oh! Power surge! . . . Wait a minute! It's not a power surge. It's a blush! I'm blushing!*

"Are you okay, Ella? You look a little flushed."

I can't look her in the eyes.

"I'm fine, just maybe a little jetlagged," I say, hoping she believes me.

"Do you need to get some more sleep? Should I come back later?"

"Oh no. I'm fine. I just need to get moving my body, so my mind can wake up. Would you like to go down to breakfast?"

"I already ate breakfast with your father, so as to not raise any suspicions. I didn't want him thinking that I need to see a doctor because I don't feel like eating breakfast. I can certainly sit with you while you eat, and I can always make room for some tea and pastry!"

I get my sweet tooth from my mother.

We go downstairs and find our way to the restaurant. The hostess asks us if we would like to eat outside. In unison we say, "Yes, please!"

When we follow her out to the balcony, we both *ooh* and *ahh* over the view. The sun is shining on the red rocks, making them look surreal. We get settled in at our table, which is off to the side and away from the other customers, and then our waitress comes over to take our orders.

My mom orders a cup of tea and a blueberry muffin. Since I ate a horribly unhealthy dinner last night, I order an egg-white omelet, wheat toast, a bowl of fruit, and a green tea.

Our waitress smiles and says that she will be right back with our drinks. As she starts walking away, I stop her. "Excuse me, but I just thought of a few more things that I'd like to add to my order."

She gives me a big smile and asks, "What else can I get for you?"

"I'll have one of those yummy-looking banana nut muffins, and I think maybe I'll also have an apple Danish please," I say, feeling my mouth water. *There goes my attempt at a healthy breakfast.*

"Okay, got it. I'm going to go get your drinks now." With another big smile she turns and heads back indoors.

"What a beautiful view," my mom says, looking at the rocks.

"It is, isn't it?" I say, feeling happy that I can enjoy the view with her.

The excited/shameful feelings from the dream last night are fading away, and I'm feeling more like myself.

"So I'm here, and you can't run away, because I know you don't like to make a scene. What other Gifts did you have before I became active?" I ask, after a few minutes have passed. I hold my breath in anticipation.

Just then, our waitress returns with our drinks. Perfect timing! When she leaves, I stare at my mom and wait. She has the nerve to act like she doesn't see me staring at her.

"Come on! Why won't you tell me? If you have any words of wisdom that can help me with what I'm going through, you should tell me! It's not very nice making me go through this without any guidance on how to control my Gifts!"

My hands are heating up.

*Relax, Ella. Breathe . . . Think good thoughts . . . Brendan . . . What?! . . . Where did that come from?*

The good thing about my train of thought is that it has interrupted my anger, and my hands have returned to normal.

My mother takes a sip of her tea and says, "Ella, I had two Gifts. One, as you know, is the squirting water thing. I didn't have any of the other Gifts that you have developed, so that's why I haven't had any words of wisdom for you. I thought that by being here for you and supporting you, I was offering you at least a little bit of comfort."

She sounds like she's about to cry.

"I'm sorry! I didn't mean what I said. You've been a *big* help to me! Don't listen to me. One minute I'm nice; one minute I'm bitchy. I know that I would've fallen apart if it weren't for you and all of your love and support. I've just been frustrated that every time I ask you about your Gifts, you find a way to change the subject—just like you did now. Why won't you tell me?"

"I haven't wanted to tell you about my other Gift because I'm afraid that it will scare you."

"Scare me?" *Aha! I was right!*

"Yes, scare you," she says, looking me square in the face.

*She looks so serious! What could it be? How can it be scarier than having flames come out of my hands?!*

"I can handle whatever it is, Mom, just please tell me."

"I promise that I will tell you, but this is not the time nor the place."

"But!" I say, and as if right on cue, our waitress arrives with our food. I have no choice but to quit asking and eat my food, which looks divine!

We finish our breakfast together in semi-comfortable silence. When I finish stuffing the last bite of the yummy muffin into my mouth, I look up and see my mother staring at me.

"Well, it's good to see that at least *some* things haven't changed." That breaks the ice, and we both burst into laughter.

When we compose ourselves, my mom looks at her watch and says, "It's a little after eleven. What do you feel like doing?"

"Why we don't we go see some of the galleries?" I say, wiping at my mouth with a napkin.

"I know just the gallery to take you to," my mother says while taking her credit card out of her purse. "Don't even think about putting up a fight over who's paying the bill," she says, using that mother tone designed to put you in your place.

"Yes, ma'am!" I say, saluting her.

"You little rascal," she says, chuckling. She pays the bill and we leave the restaurant to go see the world.

# Out and About with Mom

WE DECIDE TO TAKE MY car, so that we can go around incognito. My mom gives me directions to our first destination. I find a place to park, and we walk about a half a block.

"We're here," Mom says as we come upon a brightly colored building.

I'm delighted to find that "here" is a jewelry gallery. I grew up with an appreciation of jewelry because of my parents. It's something that has stayed with me all of my life. In fact, I came *this close* to being named Emerald by my mother. *Thank you, Pops, for picking my name.*

We enter the building, and my mom leads the way to a tall case that is filled with some of the most amazing jewelry that I have ever seen.

"These are beautiful!" I exclaim. I am entranced. *These are so beautiful. These are . . . my mom's?*

I'm staring at a sign that reads, "Designed by Jade Borrelli."

I turn to my mother, and she has a big smile on her face.

"Why didn't you tell me?" I ask.

"Well, I just recently received the invitation to display them in here, and I thought that I would surprise you!"

"I am so proud of you!" I say, giving her a big hug.

"Thank you, Ella. I've worked really hard to be able to display my work in a gallery like this one. It's a dream come true."

We spend the next hour looking at each of her pieces and then move on to look at some of the other artists' work. After that, we decide to go on foot and explore the wonderful galleries and shops along the way.

We take a break for something to drink and a snack (a big piece of chocolate cake) at a little sidewalk café. After a few minutes, my mother looks at her watch and says. "Oh, my! It's almost one o'clock. I should be getting back home so that I can be there when your father gets home."

"I think you're being a bit paranoid, Mom! Dad won't think that you're up to no good if you're not home."

"You're right, but we've developed habits over the years, and any time our habits become disrupted, it makes your father very uncomfortable. He likes stability. Change sends him into a tailspin."

"Then we had better get you home!"

We get back to the resort and I park beside her car. We both get out and give each other a big hug.

"I had fun today. I'm sorry for making you upset though," I say, holding her tight.

"No need to apologize, my dear. You're going through a lot and it's a stressful time for you," she says, holding me tight.

"I love you, Mom."

"I love you too, Ella."

She drives out of the parking lot and on to make sure that my pop's life stays on schedule.

I get back to my hotel room. The alarm clock, which is my sworn enemy after what it did to me this morning, says that it's thirteen after one.

Suddenly, I think of Brendan and his invitation to coffee at two o'clock.

Should I? I mean, he said that it would be a "friendly" cup of coffee. Maybe I was so tired from traveling yesterday that he seemed dreamier than he really is. Maybe if I see him again today, he won't be so absolutely perfect. Maybe . . .

## You Know You Want To!

*He's so young! You're a dirty old lady! You should tear up his card and forget that you ever met him!*

"Why do I feel this way?" I ask out loud. It was as if a switch had been flipped while I was dreaming about him, and now I feel like a lovesick—and dare I say horny—teenager!

Over the past ten years, my libido has slowly been dwindling down to next to nothing.

Thanks to the anonymity of the Internet, I know that part of it was hormonal, but the other part was Pete.

He started becoming super critical of everything I did. At first, the criticism and sarcastic digs were about little things. He would say, "You missed this water spot on this glass, Ella. You must be slipping." He would say it like it was a joke. At first, I thought that he was just teasing me, but then the comments started getting personal.

"Looks like you're packing on a few extra pounds. You might think about exercising *more* and eating *less*!"

When he told me he was leaving me, my heart broke. I had known him for most of my life, and I couldn't imagine my life without him. Later, when I found out the real reason for his departure, Miss Actress Slash Bartender, I felt as though it was my fault. If I hadn't let myself gain that extra weight, and if I had felt like being intimate more often, he wouldn't have had to get what he needed elsewhere.

Later still, I realized that I was an idiot for blaming myself. If he had shown me kindness instead of criticism, I would have felt better about myself and would've felt like being closer to him physically.

This revelation has helped to lighten the blow of his absence a bit, but I still miss the man who was my best friend for decades.

*Pete, you asshole!*

I begin to feel my hands grow warm, so I rush into the bathroom to hold them under the cold tap water. Steam rises from my hands, and I look at myself in the mirror.

*Ella, what are you doing? Why don't you just go ahead and call Brendan? You probably have nothing to worry about! This romantic feeling is probably just one-sided anyway. He probably just wants to ask you if you can refer your friends to his landscape business. Okay. Stop lying to yourself, Ella. You're actually worried that this feeling is only one-sided and it will hurt you if he really does end up only wanting referrals for his business. Oh, just put on your big-girl panties and call him!*

*What's the worst that could happen?*

# Calling Brendan

THE EVIL CLOCK SAYS THAT it's now twenty-one after one. I pull the card from my purse and stare at it in my hand. I feel like a teenager who is about to call the boy she has a huge crush on.

*Breathe* . . . I take a deep breath . . . *Pick up the phone* . . . I pick up my cell phone . . . *Dial his number* . . . I dial his number with a shaky hand . . . *It's ringing!*

"Hello?"

It's him! It's Brendan! *Ahhh!* I don't know what to say!

"Hello?" he asks again.

*"Umm* . . . Hi, this is Ella. From the plane," I say hesitantly.

"Hi, Ella! I honestly didn't think that you would call! What a pleasant surprise!"

I can hear that smile in his voice.

"So *umm* . . . I was wondering if you still feel like getting a cup of coffee today. I know it's last minute, but . . ."

"That'd be great. There's a coffee shop that I always go to when I'm in town. It's called The Mean Bean. Have you heard of it?"

I actually *have* heard of it. My parents have been living in Sedona since I went off to college, and on one of my many trips out to visit them, I discovered The Mean Bean. It's one of those younger-generation places to hang out, but they sure do serve a mean cup of coffee.

"I have," I say.

"Great! So is two o'clock still a good time for you?" he asks.

I look at the clock; it now says that it's twenty-five after one.

"Yes, two o'clock is still good for me," I say, wondering how I am going to make it through coffee without acting like a fool.

"Okay. I will see you then," he says.

"See you then," I say.

*Click.*

I have thirty-five minutes. It will take me around fifteen minutes to get to the coffee house, so that means that I have a good fifteen minutes to freshen up, and five minutes for traffic, or anything else unexpected.

My outfit still looks fresh, so I use the time to brush my teeth and touch up my makeup. I don't know if I'll ever get used to seeing myself like this. I don't know how long it will last, but I'm going to make it count.

I fluff my hair, give myself a wink and a smile, and leave the room.

By the time I reach my rental car, my false sense of bravado has worn off. *What are you doing? This is going to blow up in your face!*

*Shut up and let me pretend to be young and carefree again.*

"I am so tired of playing it safe. If I make a fool of myself, I make a fool of myself," I say out loud. I start the car and turn on the radio to drown out my thoughts.

# Meeting Mr. Cutie Patootie

I ARRIVE AT MY DESTINATION WITH five minutes to spare. After a quick look at myself in the rearview mirror, I get out of the car. With wobbly legs, I enter the building.

I stand near the entrance for a few minutes to let my eyes adjust to the darker atmosphere of the coffee house. I look to my right, and *there he is!* My god! He looks better than I remember. *Gulp!*

He is coming toward me with that smile on his face. *Help!*

"Hi, Ella," he says when he gets to me.

"Hello, Brendan," I say.

Thankfully, my voice doesn't sound as terrified as I feel. I want to hug him, but instead I stick my hand out for a shake.

He grins, shakes my hand, and then we go over to the counter to order our coffee. I order two scones to take the edge off. When our coffees are handed to us, I start to reach into my purse for money to pay.

"No, this is on me. I invited you, so I'm going to pay," he says with a smile. Who can argue with that smile?!

He leads me to our table, quickly sets our drinks and my scones down, and then pulls out my chair.

*Wow! He's such a gentleman!*

After we get settled in, he asks, "So how are you doing today? Is your visit going well with your parents?" He's looking at me with those gorgeous hazel eyes.

"Yes, my mother and I had a nice time earlier today."

I tell him about my time with my mother and how she surprised me with her jewelry being displayed in the gallery. For obvious reasons, I don't tell him about the conversation that my mother and I had at breakfast.

"And you? How is your visit going with your parents? You leave tomorrow, right?" I ask.

"My visit has been great. My mom's birthday party is tomorrow night, so I will be heading back to Houston the next morning," he says. "Hey! How would you like to come with me to my mother's party? It'd be fun!"

*Did he just invite me to his mother's birthday party? His mother who is only fifteen years older than I am? Quick! Think of an excuse.*

"I'm sorry, but my pop and his band have a gig tomorrow night, and I already told him that I'd go." I feel guilty telling him a lie. It's really only a *partial* lie. My pop *does* have a gig, but I'm not going. I can't risk having him see me.

"I understand. Hey, that's pretty cool having your dad in a band. Does he sing or play an instrument?"

"What are we doing here?" I blurt out. I can't believe that I said that out loud. I can feel the heat begin to rise in my cheeks.

"Excuse me?"

*Oh shit. I have to speak again.*

"Umm . . . errr . . . What I mean is . . . I thought that this was just a 'friendly cup of coffee.' I'm confused." I'm thankful that I didn't say anything else embarrassing.

"I know that you said that you just got out of a long relationship, but I just can't help myself. You are just so adorably cute and funny." He smiles at me.

"You have a little crumb," he says as he reaches toward my face with his hand. He touches the side of my face and then his thumb starts rubbing my bottom lip.

*Oh, my . . . This feels nice. Wait a minute! I can't be enjoying this!*

I jump as if I've been shocked.

"I'm sorry. I was only trying to help," he says, looking as though he really *is* sorry to have caused me any discomfort.

*Why did I have to order those crumbly scones?*

"No. *I'm* sorry. You're a nice boy—er, guy—who is treating me like a gentleman would, and I'm just a crusty old lady who doesn't know how to take a compliment!" I feel tears of frustration well up in my eyes.

"Ella," he says, laying his hand gently over mine. "First of all, you're *not* an old lady. Second, you've obviously been through some emotional hard times from your last relationship. Don't be so hard on yourself."

"You are so calm, and collected, and wise," I say, composing myself.

He smiles at me.

*He's looking at me! I hope my Mally "bulletproof" makeup is keeping me from having raccoon eyes.*

I quit talking to myself and notice that his hand is still on top of mine. I also notice that it feels really good.

Just then, the song "Sweetest Sin" by Jessica Simpson starts playing. I never even noticed there was music playing in here until now.

*Oh no! This song is about having sex for the first time! Ahhh!*

I feel my cheeks blushing.

He's still smiling at me.

I'm looking (staring) at him in what probably looks to him like pure terror.

His smile gets bigger.

*Is he enjoying my discomfort?*

I cough and delicately move my hand out from under his.

"You know what you need?" Brendan asks.

*Yes! I need for you to take me in your arms and ravish me right on top of this table!*

"No," I say innocently. "What do I need?"

"You need to have some fun. Do you like to dance?" he asks with a twinkle in his eye.

I haven't been out dancing since . . . I can't remember the last time that I've been out dancing. I used to love to dance, but sadly, in the last decade, Pete and I stopped dancing together. Between our busy restaurant with the long hours and then his ever-increasing criticism, we stopped having fun a long time ago.

"I love to dance," I say without thinking.

"Good. Then tonight, after dinnertime—say nine o'clock—we are going to go out and paint the town red. What do you say?"

He speaks with such excitement that I get caught up in the moment and say, "Yes!"

"Great! I know this really fun place. You'll love it." He's telling me all about this dance club that is *the* place to go, but all I'm hearing is the voice in my head saying, *What in the bleeping hell are you doing, Isabella Marie Borelli?!*

When I'm really angry with myself, I use my full maiden name.

*You're playing with fire, you silly girl. You're going to get burned.*

*Oh yeah?* I tell myself. *Well, if I'm gonna get burned, I can put out the flames with my squirting armpit!*

I didn't have a decent comeback for myself.

"So what do you think?" he asks expectantly.

"I think that we are going to have lots of fun!" I say. I'm trying hard to ignore the voice in my head that is telling me to pull my head out of my hiney.

I suggest we meet at the club, but ever the gentleman, he insists on picking me up at my hotel. I figure that can't hurt anything, since he will be leaving town soon, but I *do* tell him that I will be waiting for him in the lobby. No need to add gas to the fire I'm playing with by having him come up to my room. I give him the name of my hotel, and he says that he knows exactly where it is. One of his high school buddies is the night manager.

We stay for another twenty minutes. He tells me about how great it is to be able to see his niece and nephew again. It turns out that Brendan has an older sister who lives in Sedona with her husband and two kids. Brendan's face lights up when he talks about them. I can tell how much he loves his family.

*What a good boy. Ooh . . . Ick! Don't think that way, Ella. Oh yes. Do think that way, or else you're going to get yourself into a big pile of trouble.*

*Shush! He's still talking. Pay attention.*

I finish the last bite of my scone and thoroughly wipe my face with a napkin. No need to have a repeat of the rogue crumb incident.

"Are you ready to go?" he asks me.

*No! I just want to stare at you for the next day or two.*

"I guess so," I say, trying not to sound disappointed.

We clean up after ourselves and walk outside. He turns to me and asks, "Are you okay?"

"Okay?" I ask.

"With us hanging out and going out dancing tonight. You sure you're up to it? I don't want to push you if you're not ready," he says with a serious look on his face.

"I'm fine. You know us girls. One minute we're up; one minute we're down."

That's an understatement!

"Alright. Until tonight then." Brendan steps toward me.

"Until tonight," I say, sticking out my hand.

He chuckles and shakes it.

The drive back to the hotel is filled with me arguing with myself over accepting a date. I don't know who will win the argument because I tune out after a few minutes.

When I get back to my hotel room, I change into shorts and a tank top and decide to spend the next few hours going for a jog outside. It's easier to control my thoughts when I'm jogging, and right now, I don't want to think about anything but moving where my legs take me.

My brain is on overload and needs a rest. I don't want to explode in a fiery ball of CHUD!

# You Can't Run from Your Thoughts

I CALL THE CONCIERGE DESK AND ask if there are any good jogging trails nearby. I am told that there are several to choose from that are right next to the resort. They have a map that I can take with me. It has all of the trails marked. The resort is located away from the city and is rather secluded, so I'm sure that I won't encounter too many people out on the trails.

I go down to pick up the trail map, and the concierge hands me one. "Just be mindful of where you're going," he says. "We are surrounded by miles and miles of desert, so you need to pay close attention to where you're going. If you ever feel like you're going the wrong way, look for the cairns."

He sees the confused look on my face and explains. "A cairn is one of the ways that hikers mark the trails. It is two or more rocks stacked on top of each other to form a sort of sign. They are designed to stand out in their surroundings so that someone who is looking for them can spot them."

"Well, you learn something new every day!" I say happily. How interesting.

I locate the vending machines and buy two bottles of water and some granola bars to take with me. I'm glad that I remembered my iPod and fanny pack. Maggie gives me grief over the fanny pack because she thinks it's outdated. Meanwhile, I see runners running along while *carrying* their water. I don't want to carry my water. Too cumbersome. My pack has a holster on each side that securely holds a bottle of water and a zippered pouch on the front that can hold snacks, sun block, wet wipes, and anything else I decide I can't live without at the time. It's also waterproof, which comes in handy during our rainy Houston winters.

I put on my sunglasses and iPod and wave to the concierge on my way out into the wild.

I decide on a ten-mile run because (a) I can now and (b) I need plenty of time to clear my head.

I start out the trip just fine. I'm listening to music that gets me moving and looking at the most amazing scenery, when out of the blue my brain starts doing its thing.

*Just less than five hours until I get to see Brendan again!*

*Stop that thinking! You have no business spending time with him. But he's so cute and dreamy, and kind, and funny, and . . .*

Why do I feel this way? I feel like a teenager with hormones flying all over the place. I remember Michael talking about how my hormones must be going in reverse since my body did its thing, so I guess it makes sense. Those damn hormones will get you every time. My body must be *so* confused! One minute my hormones are dwindling down to next to nothing because of my age, and then *kaboom!* My body gets a big infusion of hormones that I've been deficient in for years, all in the time span of about sixteen hours!

I sure don't remember feeling this way when I was in my thirties, but it's been twenty years since then. Twenty years!

*That's enough, Ella. Look around you. Enjoy your surroundings. Be present. Life is good! You've got a twenty-year do-over. Yes, and I've also got a twentysomething that I want to do over and over again! Yikes! Did I just think that?!*

I decide to take my own advice and concentrate on my surroundings.

I turn up the sound on my iPod. I sing along with Hilary Duff to "Why Not" at the top of my lungs, as I go jogging merrily along.

(Okay, I can hear the confusion out there. Hilary Duff? I'm a fifty-year-old woman and I like Hilary Duff? Yes, I do. Thanks to an open mind, and a persistent daughter who also loves this kind of music, I have discovered that I love tween pop. It's so happy, upbeat, and catchy. I will admit that some tween songs are a little young for me, but most of them I really enjoy. If you get a chance, listen to "Why Not" by Hilary Duff, "Party in the USA" by Miley Cyrus, or "Stronger" by Brittney Spears, and you'll see what I'm talking about.)

After a half hour or so, I stop for a drink of water and a snack. I also rub some sunscreen on my face and shoulders, because I don't want this beautiful skin to burn.

Boy, this dry desert air sure is hard to get used to. The humidity back home in Houston is thick enough to drink most of the time.

While I'm stopped, I happen to notice a pile of rocks at the edge of the trail. It's a small pile, with three rocks stacked on top of each other. "It's a cairn. I found a cairn! How do they get them to stay like that?" I ask out loud.

"Oh, I see." Upon closer inspection, I see that a small strand of metal is sticking up slightly from the top rock. I guess they attach these rocks together, and to the ground with a metal spike since this is a man-made trail.

"Smart!" I say as I dig my phone out of my fanny pack to take a few pictures.

After a few minutes, I hit the trail. The miles and time fly by, and I find myself back where I started at the beginning of the trail. Along the way, I notice several of the cairn rock signs and stop long enough to take pictures of them too because they are all so very different from one another.

All in all, I had a pretty good time.

# Back to Reality

I GET BACK TO MY ROOM, and the evil clock tells me that it's almost six o'clock. It's a good thing I didn't stop to take pictures of every cairn, or I'd be running late for my very important date.

I start stripping off my clothes along the way to the bathroom and turn on the water for a nice relaxing shower.

My mind turns to Brendan. *That's okay. There's no harm in thinking about him. Thinking about those eyes, that smile, that dream!*

The water feels so good running down my body. I stand still for a long while just enjoying the sensation. *Mmmm... Brendan!*

Just then, I hear my cell phone ring. Out of habit, I grab a towel and rush to answer it.

"Hello?"

"Hi, Ella, this is Brendan." *Woosh!* My cheeks start burning, and my heart starts pounding. *Holy Shit! He knows what I was thinking about in the shower!*

"Are you okay? You sound out of breath."

*Ahhh! Be cool, Ella. Don't act like a ding-dong. Act like the woman that you are: a practical, sensible, intelligent woman.*

"I'm fine. I was just taking a shower." *Oh... my... god! A shower?! You told him that you were taking a shower? You idiot!*

"So you were taking a shower, were you?" I hear him smiling through the phone.

"I *uhh* . . . I . . ."

Brendan starts laughing. "I was just calling to see if we're still on for nine, but it sounds like I caught you at an interesting time. Why don't I go, so you can finish what you started?"

*He* does *know!*

"Uhh . . . Good-bye," I say. *Click.*

I throw my phone on the bed and cover it with a pillow. For some weird reason this makes me feel a little bit better.

I get back into the shower, but this time it's all business. I wash my hair, I shave my legs and underarms (luckily, I don't find any lumps under there this time), and wash my body in record time. I'm just finishing blow-drying my hair when my cell phone rings again. This time I think to check caller ID. Thankfully, it's my mom.

"Hi, Mom!" I say, answering the phone.

"Hello, dear. I just wanted to call you and tell you that I had a wonderful time with you today."

"I did too, and once again, I'm so proud of you for getting your pieces accepted by the gallery!" I say, holding the phone with my left cheek and my left shoulder, so that I can start rolling my semidry hair with Velcro rollers. This is one of the many helpful tricks I have learned from Maggie. I get my hair almost dry and then put big Velcro rollers in it. It makes my hair turn out nice and smooth without having to use a lot of heat on it. I usually let my hair air dry, but on special occasions like tonight, I want it to look smooth and sexy!

"I hope that you're staying busy and aren't too bored there by yourself. Do you have any big plans for tonight?" she asks innocently.

*Whoosh!* There go the cheeks. Why have I started blushing all of the sudden? I stopped blushing when I was seventeen or so. Why now?

"I *uhh* . . . I think I'm going to go down to the restaurant they have here in the resort and have dinner. Breakfast was so good that I figure they will serve a good dinner too."

*Growl!* My stomach tells me that this is a lie, and that I haven't had anything to eat since the two granola bars I ate along the trail, and I don't really have time for dinner if I want to look good for my date. This primping is all still new to me, so it takes a while to get my makeup and hair the way I want it. It's usually a trial-and-error kind of thing.

"Well, I won't keep you, my dear. Go have a wonderful time. I wish that your father and I could join you."

"Me too, Mom, I love you."

"I love you too, Ella." *Click.*

After twenty minutes, I finally get my hair and makeup just right. I walk to the closet and open it, knowing exactly what I'm going to wear. The Jessica Simpson dream dress. I carefully pull it over my head, get it zipped up, and survey my work.

*Damn, girl. You look good!*

*Why, thank you.*

I add a few gold bangles, my diamond stud earrings, gold high heels, and an LV White Monogram Multicolore Canvas Pochette that I've owned for years but have never worn, to the ensemble. As an afterthought, I choose a white cardigan to carry in case I get cold. Now I am good to go.

I don't care how dorky I sounded on the phone, or how big of an ass I'm probably going to make of myself tonight, I know I feel good and look good. I'm going to enjoy myself tonight, come hell or high water!

Look out, Brendan. I'm on my way!

I blow myself a kiss in the mirror and head out for my date with destiny.

*Or disaster.*

*Shut up!*

# Remember to Breathe

I STEP INTO THE ELEVATOR. As soon as the elevator door closes, my self-confidence disappears. My phone shows that it is ten minutes to nine. I have ten minutes before he gets here. What should I do? Should I go sit down? Should I stand by the lobby door? I feel so awkward. I'm still trying to figure out what to do with myself when the elevator door opens.

I take a deep breath, walk out into the lobby, and pause.

That's when I see him. He is sitting in a chair across the lobby and facing the elevators. He stands when he sees me, and I can see his smile from across the room.

*Okay, Ella, be cool, be calm, be graceful.* I wave and walk toward him on legs that are having a hard time moving.

*Don't trip. Don't trip. Don't trip. Oh, my! He looks so handsome! Don't trip. Don't trip. Don't trip . . .*

*You made it!*

Brendan reaches out his hand and takes mine. "I want to hug you right now, but I know how fond you are of shaking hands," he says as I'm about to swoon. "You look beautiful, Ella. I feel honored to have you by my side."

"You look beautiful . . . er . . . handsome as well."

*Snap out of it, Ella. Let him know that you have a brain buried somewhere under those cobwebs.*

*Look at him! How can I possibly get through an evening with a man that looks like this and not make a fool of myself?*

*Man indeed! Gray sports jacket over a white, button-up shirt, black slacks, and nice shiny dress shoes.*

"Are you ready for some fun?" he asks.

I find my voice again and say, "Yes, I am!"

We step out into the night air, and I shiver slightly. "It's amazing how it can be so hot during the day and then become so cold at night," I say as we approach the car.

*Really, Ella? You're talking about the weather?*

"It surprises me every time I come back home to visit. Are you going to be warm enough?" he asks while holding the car door open for me.

"Yes. Thank you for asking." I show him my cardigan as I'm getting in the car.

We're both sitting in the car, and a wonderful smell fills my nose. It's a combination of clean clothes and male. He smells so good! I try really hard not to be obvious when I take in a few deep sniffs.

"Are you sure you're going to be warm enough tonight? It sounds like you have a little bit of a sniffle," he says, looking at me sideways. He should be a detective on the vice squad, because his powers of observation are unbelievably perceptive!

"No, I'm fine. I'm plenty warm, thank you," I say, trying not to sound as embarrassed as I feel.

We drive in silence for a minute or two when, *"Gurgle growl!"* comes from my stomach. I am mortified.

"Sorry! I guess my tummy wants to add to the conversation!" I say, finding the humor that has always gotten me through tough times.

"You have such a way with words," he says with a chuckle. "They have really good bar food at this place. We can get your tummy filled up and full of enough fuel to dance all night." He turns and smiles at me.

I smile back.

# A Whole New World

WE PULL UP IN FRONT of the nightclub and the valet opens the door for me. Brendan has managed to get around to my side. He takes my hand to help me out. He continues to hold my hand when we bypass the long line of people waiting to get in.

"My friend owns this place," he explains.

We enter the club, and my eyes and ears are pleasantly surprised when I discover that this is one of those swing dance places. I've heard these have been popping up all over and are wildly popular.

"This is great!" I yell above the music. "Not at all what I expected!"

He smiles. "I'm glad you like it!"

We are greeted by a hostess who shows us to a big booth toward the back of the room. Brendan pulls out my chair for me.

"Thank you," I say as I sit. I don't have to yell this time. This booth is against a wall and has curved walls on each side. It is very cozy. The designer did a good job in keeping with the theme of this place.

We have menus on the table, so I pick mine up and start to look. "I am so embarrassed about my stomach! It's not like me to skip a meal," I say.

"I have to admit that I didn't eat much today either," he says while picking up his menu.

When the waitress comes, I order two crab cakes, calamari, a small side salad, and a piece of apple pie. Brendan orders hamburger sliders, french fries, and cheesecake.

"So . . ." he says.

"So . . ." I say.

We both start laughing in unison.

"So tell me about yourself. What do you do for a living? Do you love what you do? What are your hobbies?" Brendan asks.

Oh boy. I have to pay close attention to what comes out of my mouth.

"Well, I recently started a relaxation center, featuring a salt flotation tank."

"That sounds interesting. What is that?"

I go on for a few minutes about what it is and how it works.

"It's not open yet, but hopefully in another month or so it will be ready. (I leave out the part where my new business is just a few miles from where his business is.) As far as hobbies, I like to jog and read, but not at the same time," I say, attempting a joke.

He laughs, and I relax a bit more. Something about that smile and that laugh . . .

"I like to jog and read too. What kind of books do you like to read?" he asks.

"Urban fantasy. Some of my favorite authors are Kim Harrison, Patricia Briggs, Vicki Pettersson, Jeaniene Frost, Charlaine Harris, and MaryJanice Davidson. Have you ever heard of any of them?" I ask, wondering if he even *knows* what urban fantasy is.

"Are you kidding?" he says, "One of my favorite authors is Kim Harrison as well! My sister gave me a copy of *Dead Witch Walking* several years ago and I couldn't put it down! I've read every book in The Hollows series so far. And believe it or not, Vicki Pettersson's book, *The Scent of Shadows,* is next on my reading list."

"Ooh, you'll like it too!" I say, remembering how much I enjoyed reading it.

We talk for a while about our favorite Kim Harrison characters, and about how much we both love urban fantasy books. Then our food arrives.

We eat in comfortable silence until the food is gone.

"I didn't realize how hungry I was!" Brendan says.

"Me too!" I say, trying to stifle a burp. When I get control of my bodily functions, I ask, "So how did you end up in the Houston area?"

"Well, I always liked plants and flowers. I know it's weird for a man to admit, but the shapes and smells, and how plants can completely change a space, have always intrigued me. Out here in Sedona, it's mostly desert, so when a friend of mine from college said he was moving back home to Houston, I thought, *Why not give Houston a shot?* It's not the desert, and it looks lush and green in all the pictures I've seen.

I had been saving up to start a business of my own for a long time, and so I moved to Houston where I could work with flowers instead of cactus."

A man who loves flowers! I sit there and catch myself staring dreamily at him.

"Wow. That's so brave to move to a new city and start fresh," I say when my brain starts working again.

"I wasn't brave. I had a goal of working with plants, and so I moved to where my creativity could be free to roam."

"Wow . . ." I say. I catch myself staring at him again.

He smiles, stands up, extends his hand, and asks, "Would you care to dance?"

I stare up at him. I should say no.

"It would be my pleasure," I say, taking his hand.

I stand up and start to panic.

*Oh no! Please don't squirt water, or a CHUD, or worse. Relax, breathe. He puts his pants on one leg at a time just like everybody else. Shit! Don't picture him naked!*

He leads me to the dance floor, puts his hand on the small of my back, and we start dancing like we've been partners for life! It feels wonderful to be dancing again! He, who will not be named tonight, and I used to swing dance at least twice a month back in our happier times.

"Where did you learn to dance like this?" I shout near his ear.

"My mother thought that dance lessons would make me a well-rounded gentleman!" he shouts back.

After our third song, it changes to a slow one. He smiles and twirls me, and when my body comes back to meet with his body, I almost faint. He is so strong and hard . . . *Ahem!* And such a wonderful dancer.

*Good save there. Don't need to think about things like that when you're this close to him.*

We dance for hours with just a few breaks here and there to get a drink and catch our breaths.

He has since taken off his sports jacket, and the color of his white shirt against the color of his hair and skin is enough to make me gulp. I notice that I'm not the only one who is appreciating his dreaminess. Several girls glance his way while we dance, but he only has eyes for me.

Around one thirty, Brendan and I are resting for a bit, but when the band makes the announcement that it is the last song of the night, he looks at me, I look at him, and we make our way back out to the dance floor.

We are dancing cheek to cheek to a slow song, and when he twirls me out this time, I tell myself that I'm not going to think about how hard his body is. When he brings me back to him, our bodies meet, and our eyes lock.

"My god, you are so beautiful," he says. Then, without warning, he dips me, and now he's kissing me!

*Oh, my god! Oh, my god! Oh, my god! He's kissing me, and it's just like in my dream! (Except for the princess trapped in the castle tower thing.)*

*What do I do?*

*You kiss him back, dummy.*

*No, you don't, you dirty old woman! Step away, and take your lips off of the boy!*

Where did that *other* voice come from?! It's getting confusing in my head!

*Ooh . . . It feels so good.*

*Come on! Kiss him back! You know you want to!*

The new voice—we'll call it the *evil* voice—wins out, so I wrap my arms around him and give him *everything* I have. I kiss him back with every ounce of passion that has been lying dormant in me for at least a decade.

The kiss goes on forever. Nothing in the world exists but the two of us. People have devoted pages and pages in romance novels to this kind of kiss! Whole movies have revolved around a kiss like this! After what seems like hours, I feel the end of the kiss coming. *Damn!* Then he brings me back up from the dip and holds me up in front of him. (My legs are wobbly, and I think I would fall if it weren't for him holding me.)

He looks at me for a second or two and says softly, "Wow!"

"Me too," I say, touching my hand to my lips. *Did that just happen?!*

Suddenly it's as if the world around us reappears, and I realize that the music has stopped playing. He must've just noticed this too, because we both look around us at the same time and find that we are standing in the middle of the dance floor. All eyes are on us.

When the crowd sees us looking, they all break into loud applause. How embarrassing! What do we do now?

I look at him, he looks at me, and it's as if we are psychically connected, because he turns to the crowd and bows and I do a curtsy at the same time.

"Come back tomorrow night for our next performance!" Brendan shouts, and then he grabs my hand. We dash to our booth to get my cardigan and his jacket (I had my Louis on me while we were dancing) and then we head to the exit as fast as humanly possible.

# Earth to Ella. Come in, Ella

THE VALET BRINGS THE CAR around. We jump into the car and speed away into the night

"My friend Darren, who owns the club, is never gonna let me live this down!" Brendan says with a laugh.

*"Uh huh..."* I say, not really paying attention. My mind is still back at that club, out on that dance floor, receiving the *best* kiss of my life.

"Are you okay?" Brendan asks.

*"Uh huh..."* I say.

"Ella?" Brendan pulls the car over to the side of the road. "Did I upset you by kissing you? I'm so sorry. I knew I shouldn't have done it, but you looked so beautiful, and we were having so much fun, and I just got caught up in the moment! Please forgive me for not behaving in a more gentlemanly manner," he says seriously.

I snap out of my stupor and realize that he thinks that I'm upset about the kiss.

"Don't apologize! I really... I *uh*... I really enjoyed it very much," I say, feeling my face turn red. I'm glad that it's dark in here.

Brendan exhales deeply and says, "Thank goodness! I thought for sure that I messed up and stepped out of bounds with you. It's just that we were having so much fun, and you looked so pretty..."

*"Uhhh . . .* I'm okay. It's okay. Everything's okay," I say, mainly to myself.

Never in a million years would I ever think that I would be in a situation like the one that I'm in right now.

"What do you say we go and get a cup of coffee? I know of an all-night diner that serves good coffee and great dessert," he says, smiling at me.

"Okay," I say, against my better judgment. I don't want this evening to end! I know that this will be the last time I will ever see him and I wish at that moment that I had the ability to slow down time.

# Cake Fixes Everything! (I Hope)

We enter the diner and find an empty booth. He sits across from me, thank goodness, because I don't think I can keep my hands to myself if he were right beside me. As soon as we are settled in, our waitress comes to take our orders. I order a piece of chocolate malted cake and a glass of milk.

Comfort food.

"What? No coffee?" Brendan asks.

"Doesn't really go with chocolate cake," I say, concentrating on my napkin in my lap. I can't seem to find the nerve to look him in the face right now. I'm afraid that he will see how much of an effect he has on me.

He chuckles and orders a cup of coffee, and two cake doughnuts.

When the waitress leaves, he leans forward and says, "Ella, are you sure you're okay?"

"No, I'm fine," I say.

"If you're so fine, then why won't you look me in the face?"

"*Ummm . . . ahhh . . .* I don't know," I say, knowing full well why I won't.

"Ella?"

I guess that kiss was my undoing, because all a sudden, I actually say what I am thinking. "I can't look at you because you are so charming, and so sweet, and so funny, and so handsome, and so very, very sexy, and I don't want to think this way about you!"

*Oh,* bleep*! What did you do?! Take it back! Take it back! Maybe he didn't hear you.*

*Of course, he heard you. Everyone in this diner heard you. Aaaahhhh!*

My eyes are closed. It's so quiet that I can hear crickets chirping. I slowly open my eyes and look up at him. I expect to see a look of horror on his face. Instead, I see a huge smile. To be more exact, I see a huge grin.

The conversation in the diner that had stopped dead during my outburst has resumed somewhat, but I can still hear a few snickers here and there.

"Can we pretend that I didn't just make a huge ass out of myself in front of you and everyone else in here?" I implore.

He shakes his head and says, "Nope! I'm going to remember every word you said for as long as I live!"

I put my face in my hands and drop my head. I am so embarrassed and ashamed by how I acted that I can't even hold my head up. I guess that's where the saying, "Hold your head down in shame," comes from.

I feel something touch my cheek and I jump a little. I remove my hands from my face and see that it's Brendan's hand.

"I'm sorry. I shouldn't have teased you. Why don't you eat your cake and see how you feel after?"

In my craziness, I didn't see the waitress put our food and drinks on the table in front of us. *Mmmm . . . chocolate cake . . . chocolate* malted *cake.*

I polish off the cake and milk in record time.

"Feel better?" Brendan asks.

I nod my head and give him a small smile.

"Good. Are you ready to go now?"

I nod my head yes again.

We arrive at my hotel fifteen minutes later. (Blissfully there was no conversation along the way.) We pull up at the front entrance, and Brendan gets out first. He goes around and opens my door.

When I take his hand for assistance, I take it and hold on tightly. This is where we say good-bye. This is where I end this before things blow up in our faces. My eyes fill with tears.

*Wow! I'm actually on the verge of tears at the thought of saying good-bye to this wonderful young man!*

"Well, I thought it was a great evening . . ." Brendan says, looking down at me with eyes that I could live in.

"I liked all of the first part, and the cake in the second part," I say honestly.

He laughs. "You are *so* refreshingly adorable!"

"Thank you?" I say.

He laughs again.

*Okay, here it comes . . . Be brave, and do it fast, so you can get it over with. Tell him good-bye!*

"Well, it was really nice meeting you, Brendan. I hope that you have a wonderful life," I say awkwardly while extending my hand.

He looks confused. "I don't understand."

"Well, you're leaving day after tomorrow, and I'm staying here for a few more weeks, and we both have our own lives to get back to."

"But you said . . . I thought we had something between us?"

"We do . . . er . . . We did . . . But this is just a vacation fling as the kids call it, right?"

"No. This isn't a fling. I don't make it a habit of going around picking up girls in airports," he says, sounding slightly off-put.

"What I mean is: how can this be anything more than a fling?" I ask, wishing that I had the balls to just run away from him and lock myself in my hotel room. "What do you see in me?" I ask, wondering why he's making this so hard. I thought all men liked to have no strings attached.

"What do I see in you?" he says, and then he puts his hand softly under my chin and tilts my face up to him. "I see a smart, beautiful, funny, sweet girl who has a lot going for her," he says softly.

I can't take it anymore! Those eyes, those hands, those lips! I pull him to me by his shirt and give him a continuation of the kiss in the club.

*Stop!*

I stop kissing him and push him away from me.

He looks confused.

"I'm sorry, but I have to go!" I say as I run away from him, and my feelings.

I don't stop running until I make it to the elevator in the hotel lobby.

When I get to my room, I head straight to the bathroom where I can jump into a cold shower. I stand under the running water until I'm pruney and force myself to move. I brush my teeth, but I don't bother removing my makeup.

I put on one of the cute sleep shirts that I purchased during my shop-a-thon, pull back the covers, and plop down on the bed. I reach over and turn on the bedside radio to try to drown out my thoughts with music.

A few minutes later, I realize that the music isn't helping. I can't get him out of my head. What is wrong with me? I can't control my body or my thoughts anymore. My mind starts to drift back to our first kiss, and then our second one.

*"Ahhh!"* I say in frustration as I put a pillow over my face. I have to get to sleep and end this mix of a wonderful and terrible day.

A little while passes; I still can't relax. I'm like a tiger lying in waiting for its prey.

Ring!

*Huh?*

Ring!

*What is that? Oh, it's my cell phone.* I grab it from the nightstand.

"Hello?"

"Ella?"

*It's him!*

"Brendan?"

"What's your room number?"

"Three zero seven," I say without thinking.

"I'm coming up," he says.

*Click.*

He's coming up? . . . He's coming up! I should stop him! A million reasons why I should call him and tell him *not* to come up, race through my mind. I'm still thinking about those reasons when I hear a knock on my door. My heart is racing. I break into a cold sweat.

*Ella, no! This is going to end badly. Please don't do this to yourself,* or *to him,*

I pull the sheets over my head. I hear another knock. I can't very well just let him stand out there in the hallway knocking when he knows I'm in here. That's rude.

I'll just answer the door and tell him that it's late, and that I need to get back to bed. There! That sounds good.

I get out of bed and go stand by the door. When I get there, I freeze. What am I doing? I can't open that door. I won't be able to stop myself from grabbing him and pulling him to the bed and having my way with him. Turn around and go back to bed.

Surely he'll take the hint and go away.

A third knock.

*Shit!*

I take a deep breath, and . . . I . . . slowly open the door.

Well, wouldn't you?!

## ?!?!?!?!?!

Our eyes meet and *KAPOW!* He grabs me, I grab him, his lips find mine, and all thoughts of telling him to go away fly out the window!

We kiss at the doorway for what seems like forever. Then he reaches down and picks me up. Somehow, the door gets closed and we are in my hotel room!

He carries me to the bed and gently lays me on it, and then he lies down beside me. He's lying there on his side, propped up on his elbow. Then he leans over and says, "I have wanted you since the moment I first saw you!"

*Are you freaking kidding me?! This is my dream come true!*

He starts kissing my neck and shoulders, and then I feel his hand running slowly up my inner thigh. All of the yummy feelings from my dream come crashing over me. They add to what I'm feeling in this moment, and I say to him, "Oh yes! Take me now!"

Somewhere in the background, I hear the song "Sweetest Sin" playing on the radio—again! This time, instead of getting embarrassed, I just smile . . .

## A Lady Doesn't Kiss and Tell

Apparently, I'm no lady, because I *have* kissed and told, but I say a *real* lady doesn't you-know-what and tell, so I'm going to skip over this bit. I *will* say, though, that it is the best you-know-what in my life, and I plan to do you-know-what all night long!

# How Ella Got Her Groove Back

I DON'T REMEMBER FALLING ASLEEP, BUT I awaken feeling all tingly and full of energy. I stretch my body, and I think back on the amazing dream that I had last night.

(Insert the sound of a needle scratching a record.) It wasn't a dream!

Oh shit! It wasn't a dream!

I stop in midstretch and look to my right, only to find an empty pillow. I sit up, look around the room, and find that I'm the only one here.

I turn to grab the pillow that Brendan had laid his head on, and see that there is a note on top of it. I must've missed it in my panic.

I pick it up.

> Dear Ella,
> I didn't want to wake you since you were sleeping so peacefully. I had to get up bright and early in order to help my sister with my mom's birthday party today. Last night was amazing! Call me when you wake up.
> 
> B

All of the great feelings quickly disappear. I drop the note, flop back down on the bed, and pull the covers over my head.

What have I done?

I screwed things up royally—that's what I've done! Why can't he be like all the other men out there and be satisfied with a one-night stand?

*Because he obviously has feelings for you, and you have feelings for him, and it would crush you if he was like all the other men!*

I catch myself just then and realize that I'm thinking of him as a man, not a *young* man. Who could think of him as a young man after he played my body like a concert cellist last night!

Wait! Feelings? Does he have feelings for *me*?

*Stranger things have happened!*

Do I have feelings for *him*?

Sadly, the answer is yes from all of the voices in my head.

I decide that I can't handle this on my own anymore. I call the one person who will tell me what I should do and be brutally honest about it.

Ring!

"Hello?"

"Hi, Mary. It's Ella."

"Well, how the hell are you, Facelift Barbie?" she jokes.

"Well, a lot has happened in the past few days since we last spoke." (I had called Mary before running off to Sedona, and when I told her that I was going to get a little work done, she said, "Why the *bleep* would you go and do a *bleep*ing stupid thing like that? Your face is *bleep*ing fine the way it is."

"Have you had all those surgeries you were gonna get?" Mary asks.

"No, not yet. I kind of got sidetracked."

*That's an understatement.*

"What's going on El? You've got that tone in your voice like you've gone and done something wrong."

Damn, she's good.

"So . . . *uh* . . ."

"What the hell has gotten you all a twitter? You know I won't let up until you tell me!"

"Well, I *uh* . . . *I uh* . . . met a really young man on the plane ride out here, and then we had coffee, and then we . . . danced. And then we kissed, and then we had dessert, and then we had sex!" I blurt this last part out.

"You had sex? You had sex! Well, it's about damn time! I was beginning to think that your hootenanny was gonna shrivel up and fall out from lack of use," she says happily.

*Cringe!*

I choose to ignore that she ever made reference to my "hootenanny." Instead of telling her that she has forever messed with my head and that from this moment on I won't be able to get the gross picture she painted of my "hootenanny" out of my head, I say, "But he's younger than me!"

"How much younger?" Mary asks.

"I don't know for sure, but he looks like he can't be much older than Maggie."

Silence.

*"Ha ha ha!* This is awesome! You cougar you! I have to think of some way that I can work this news into a conversation with my brother the next time I see him. This is the best news I've heard all year."

Pause.

"So how was it?"

"This is awful."

"It was awful?" Mary asks.

"No! *This* is awful! Having slept with a young man that's old enough to be my son is awful," I say on the verge of tears.

"Shit, Ella, men our age chase girls young enough to be their daughters all the time. And when they sleep with them, they are known as heroes in the male world. It's about damn time that the tables were turned! So you never told me how it was . . ."

"I hate to admit it, but it was amazing. I don't want this feeling to end, but it has to!" I say, feeling defeated.

"Wait—feeling? You have feelings?"

"Well, kind of. And I'm pretty sure he has feelings for me too."

"Well, that's all fine and good, but this is just a vacation romp. You'll come back to Houston and leave him behind in Sedona. No muss, no fuss."

"But he works in *Clear Lake*."

"Oh shit! Does he know that you live there?"

"No, just the Houston area."

"Well, you just need to tell him that it was fine while it lasted but your life is too busy for romance right now. He's young. He'll get over it," she says, sounding sure of herself.

"But don't you think that it's awesome that I slept with him?" I say, feeling confused.

"It *is* awesome that you slept with him."

"Then why are you so keen on me ending things with him?"

"Because he's so *young*!" Mary says. "What could you possibly have in common?"

I think for a minute. "We both like dancing, and we both like Kim Harrison," I say hopefully.

"You can only dance for so long, and Kim Harrison doesn't have a magical wand that she can whip out and use to help you when you're sixty and he's forty and you start looking like an old lady to him. Even if she did, she wouldn't waste any of her magic on *you*. She'd tell you you're as *bleep*ing crazy as *I* think you are. *Then* she would tell you to go get your head examined. See! That's why men are so *bleep*ing stupid! They get with a younger woman in hopes that *they* will feel that young again. It lasts for a while, until they discover that they have nothing to talk about. I think they are genuinely surprised when it doesn't work out. And yes, I'm using Pete as an example. You need to break all contact with this young boy. Don't see him, don't call him, don't text him, nothing. Just end it before someone gets hurt."

When her verbal tirade ends, I say, "But that sounds so mean! How can I *not* give him some kind of explanation after all that we've shared? And by the way, I think Kim Harrison would be proud of me for being brave enough to follow my heart!" I say, feeling miffed that she could even *think* that Kim Harrison would turn her back on two people in lov—I mean *like!*

"Do you honestly think that there's a future for the two of you?

"Well, no. I wish there could be, but no."

"Then don't you think you need to do the smart thing and end it while it's on an upswing, instead of having things turning sour a few years down the road?"

She has a point.

"Okay. I'll end it. I'll call him and end it," I say, with a sinking feeling in the pit of my stomach.

"Can you really dump him and mean it? No backsies?" Mary asks, sounding very serious.

"Yes, I can. You're right. Who am I kidding? I've known this was a bad idea from the start, but my hormones took over, and then my heart joined in. I just feel so happy when I'm with him," I say wistfully.

"Well, you can be happy with a vibrator and a big piece of chocolate cake, so go on and make that call before he's ready for round two!"

Leave it to Mary to be bluntly crass yet loving, all at the same time.

"Okay, Mary. I will call him right now, and I will call you right after," I say sadly.

"You know, you're my best friend, El. I just don't want to see another bastard splatter your heart across the big state of Texas again."

"I know, Mary. I know your heart's in the right place, even when your mouth isn't," I say, trying to lighten the mood.

"Okay then, I don't want this to turn into a mushy-gushy fest, so I'm going to hang up now. Make that call!" *Click!*

# Breaking Up Is Hard to Do

For a minute, I stare at my phone lying innocently in my hand.

*Just do it, Ella. Do the right thing and end things with Brendan now.*

I dial his number. It's ringing!

"Hi, Ella!" Brendan answers so cheerfully. Little does he know that I'm about to become the bitch that dumped him after sleeping with him for the first time.

"Hi, Brendan. Do you have a minute?"

"For you, I have all day. What's up? How are you feeling today after our busy night?"

*I'm still feeling the afterglow of mind-blowing you-know-what mixed with feeling super shitty for what I'm about to say.*

"Here's the thing. I thought that I was ready for a physical kind of relationship, or whatever this is, but I'm not. Don't get me wrong. You made my dreams come true last night"—*literally!*—"but I just can't do it again. I'm sorry."

Brendan was quiet for a few seconds. "No, *I'm* sorry. I shouldn't have rushed things. It's just that when we kissed, it seemed like you wanted it as much as I did."

"But I did," I said, not wanting to be having this conversation over the phone. He is too good of a person to do this in such a cold, impersonal manner. But if I saw him right now, I couldn't do it.

"I understand. You just need some time. I can wait," he says with what sounds like a small smile.

*I'm about to wipe that smile off your face.*

"Listen, Brendan, I really like you, but I just can't do any of this right now. I'm still dealing with my ex-hu— boyfriend—and all of the bad feelings about that. *Plus*, I'm trying to start a new business. My head's just not in a good place right now. I'm sorry if I led you on."

"You didn't lead me on. I should've known better than to push things with you, after you got so emotional at the coffee house. I always want to swoop in and 'rescue' damsels in distress. I guess I need to learn to leave them alone and let them save themselves," he says, the last part mostly to himself.

"If you change your mind, you know how to reach me. Good-bye, Ella. I know this will sound corny, but it was nice knowing you."

A gentleman even when he's being dumped. Oh, this is horrible!

I hope I haven't changed him into a bad guy for the next woman who comes along. For every bad guy out there, there is usually some terrible girl who ripped his heart out of his chest and ate it while he watched.

"Good-bye, Brendan. It was really nice knowing you too."

*Click!*

He hangs up first. I'm still holding my phone, not wanting to let go just yet. I give my head a shake, trying to get rid of this bad feeling, but it doesn't work.

"I did it. It's over," I tell Mary when she answers her phone.

"Good," she says. "How do you feel?"

"Like shit," I say.

"It'll pass," she says. Then I hear her stifle a laugh.

*Really?! She's making potty humor jokes at a time like this?!*

"Wow, you must really feel bad, if you can't even laugh at a joke," Mary says.

"Yeah, well, I do, but thank you for trying to make me laugh."

"Any time, El. Well, my work here is done. If you don't need any more advice, I'm gonna go. I have to make a call to the *bleep*ing cable company. I tell you, I'm almost ready to go down to that cable office and put my foot up someone's butt! 'We'll be there sometime between the hours of nine and five.' What kind of bullshit is that?"

"Good-bye, Mary," I say, wanting to end this conversation that is now going nowhere, so I can crawl back into bed.

"Good-bye, Ella." *Click.*

## Tell Yourself It Was Just a Dream

I WAKE FROM A RESTLESS SLEEP to hear my cell phone ringing. I groan and reach for it just in case it's my kids. It's not. It's my mom.

"Hello, Mom."

"Hello, Ella. How are you today?"

I'm never going to tell her about Brendan and how I behaved. "I'm okay, just a little sleepy. What time is it?"

"It's almost eleven o'clock. Your father has gone off with some of his buddies to go practice for tomorrow night's gig. How would you like to come over?"

"That would be wonderful," I say, thinking that being in my parents' home that is so full of love will be just what I need to pull myself out of my funk.

I shower—quickly. I don't want to have time to think about last night.

I pull up in front of my parents' house, and out of the blue, I start to cry. Why am I turning into such an emotional train wreck?! I tell myself to snap out of it and finally get my emotions in check.

I wipe the tears from my face, get out of the car, and walk up to the front door. I am *so* happy to see my mother standing there smiling and holding the door open for me.

"Hello, sweetheart! Come on in!" she says, closing the door after us.

Inside, the smell of cinnamon rolls and coffee greet me warmly like old friends.

"Have a seat, Ella," my mom says, pulling out a chair for me. "Have some coffee and some fresh cinnamon rolls. I wasn't sure if you had already eaten by now, but I know you always have room for sweets," she says while pouring me a cup of coffee and placing a big, beautiful roll on a plate in front of me. I say thank-you and start eating. I haven't eaten today, and I realize that I'm starving.

"So Ella, dear, how was your evening? Did you have a good dinner?"

That was all it took. I start bawling like a little baby. Then, everything comes out at once. I tell her about meeting Brendan on the plane and then about our lunch, and then our dancing, and our kiss, and I *even* tell her about sleeping with him. During this emotional meltdown, I notice that she must have developed some kind of tic, because every once in a while, her head jerks to the left and to the right.

"And I had to call him this morning and end it with him, and he was such a gentleman!" I start hiccupping and have to stop to catch my breath. I look at my mother, and she is now sitting perfectly still. She sits like this for almost a minute, looking lost in thought. I wait for the look of disapproval, but it never comes. Instead, she gets up from her chair, comes over to me, and bends down to hug me.

"It sounds like your hormones are all over the place, sweetheart. I went through that same thing with your father. Fortunately, we were married at the time." She chuckles ever so slightly. "Your poor father didn't know what hit him."

What?! Did my mother just talk about her sex life with my father? Then (I couldn't help myself) an image of my mother wearing a black leather bustier, carrying a whip, and chasing my father around the breakfast table catches me as funny, and my hiccups turn to laughter. My mother starts laughing, not realizing that I had taken the word *hit* and run with it to the farthest reaches of my imagination.

Just about the time we are settling down, and the laughter has turned to chuckles, we hear a voice that says, "I *thought* I heard laughter in here."

It is my father, and we are so busted!

# Sorry, Pop

"Sorry, ladies, I didn't mean to interrupt. I forgot to take my sheet music with me to practice," my father says while passing through the kitchen on his way to the study. During this time, my mother and I are just sitting there like statues, too scared to move for fear of attracting his attention.

"Found it!" he says, returning to the kitchen with sheet music in hand. When he gets to us, he stops short with a strange expression on his face. He stands there staring at me like he's trying to get something straight in his mind. He says, "You know, you bear an uncanny resemblance to my daughter, Ella."

When he says my name, I jump from my chair and run to the guest bathroom. I don't know why I'm doing this, because I have all but admitted guilt by fleeing the scene of the crime.

I hear muffled voices on the other side of the door. I can make out my father's voice saying, "Looks just like Ella." Then my mother says, "Slight resemblance." Then my father again quite clearly says, "You've been acting mighty suspicious for the past few days, my darling Jade. What aren't you telling me?" He pauses. "Aha! I think that's Ella hiding in the bathroom. It is, isn't it?!"

It sounds like he's right outside the door!

*Knock! Knock! Knock!*

"Ella, honey, is that you?"

"No, it's not me. *Er* . . . I mean, I'm not Ella."

*You suck under pressure.*

*Can you blame me in this situation?*

*Good luck digging yourself out of* this *hole.*

"I know it's you. Please come on out and talk to me," my father says nicely. "I need to be able to put my eyes on you for a minute, because right now, I'm very confused." He sounds so off-kilter that I have to go out.

I open the door slowly—just a crack. "Mom, can you move Pop to his easy chair and sit him down on it, please? I don't want to cause another parent to go to the hospital," I say while trying to compose myself.

I have to go out, and I hope that he will believe me when I tell him the "got some work done" story.

"Is he in his chair?" I yell through the crack of the door.

"Yes, Ella, I'm in my chair, although I have no idea why you two are treating me like an invalid."

"Okay, I'm coming out!" I yell.

I walk down the hall to the living room. I stop at the doorway and say to him, "Now, I've had a little work done, as you have probably already guessed. The doctor did a really good job—in fact, too good. I look like I did when I was in my thirties!" I say, slowly approaching my pop in his easy chair.

I sit down on the edge of the coffee table, so that he can get a good look. My mother is sitting on the couch with her legs crossed. The top leg is twitching from nervous energy, and she is chewing on her bottom lip.

"Doesn't she look good, Tom? There's hardly any swelling," my mother says expectantly.

My father looks from my mother to me and says, "Do you two ladies think that I'm senile? If you think that I'm going to believe that there is a doctor out there who can shave twenty years off your age, with no swelling or bruising or scarring, in under three weeks, then you don't know me very well. What's really going on? Did aliens abduct you? Did they make you drink from the fountain of youth? I'd believe *that* more than the "had some work done" story. What happened? Tell me the truth, Ella, because I always know when you're lying." My father says this last part with a surprisingly calm voice.

I look to my mother.

"I think you should tell him, Ella," she says.

I look at my father who is waiting for the truth.

*He can't* handle *the truth!*

I take a deep breath and tell him about how I took a long nap in my recliner, and when I woke up, I looked like I do now. There! I have told him.

My father sits quietly for a moment and says, "Huh. I guess this must be like what your mother was dealing with around *her* special lady time change thing, except she could shoot water from her armpit. I'll never forget the day I saw *that* happen!" He chuckles softly.

*"You knew?!"* my mother and I say in unison.

"Of course, I knew. You can't keep secrets when you live in the same house," my father says matter-of-factly.

"Why didn't you ever tell me you knew?" my mother asks him.

"I figured that it was your story to tell, and when you were ready to tell me, you would. It's been interesting over the years, because I never knew what to expect with you. I will have to say though, the time when I woke up early one morning, and found you . . ."

"You saw that?!" my mom interrupts him. "I haven't told her about that yet. I don't want to scare her."

"Scare her? Well, I think it's pretty neat, and I would want to know if it were me, but I guess I will have to honor your wishes. My lips are sealed." He looks intently at my mother. He stands up, looks at his watch, and says, "Now, I have to get on to practice. I want you both to promise me that when I come home after, I get a full explanation of what exactly is going on with you two."

My mother and I stand as well. I think that we are both in shock.

My father, however, seems unaffected. He walks over to my mother and gives her a hug and a kiss on the cheek.

"I'll see you in about an hour," he tells her.

She's a statue in his arms—shock I guess. He comes to me and gives me a big hug too.

"I love you, Ella Bella. It's going to take some time, but I think that I could get used to you looking like this. After all, I've seen you look like this before, only it was twenty years ago!" He chuckles a bit, pats me on the back, and leaves the room, whistling a tune as if he didn't have a care in the world.

My mother and I turn and look at each other.

"What just happened?" she asks.

"I don't know. He's *your* husband," I say, wondering how he could be so calm about everything. "I thought you said that he couldn't deal with change," I say.

"Apparently, I don't know my husband as much as I thought I did," she says, looking bewildered.

"Looks like you've got a lot of explaining to do," I say, standing up.

"Looks like . . ." My mother looks a little green around the gills.

She stands up and we head back to the kitchen. When we go to sit in our chairs at the table, I notice that there are weird things, that look strangely familiar, sticking in the wall behind where my mom has been sitting.

"What is all that?" I say, pointing to the things in the wall.

"Oh. Those are your CHUD, dear. I should probably remove them," she says, getting up.

"Did I do that?!" I ask getting up and going over to where she's standing.

"Yes, you did this when you were telling me about your friend, dear."

I think back to our earlier conversation, before Pop came home.

"Oh! *That's* why you were jerking around in your seat. I thought you were having some sort of nervous tic because of the subject matter!" This gave us both a good laugh. I tell her to please sit down, and I start pulling the CHUD out of the wall.

"I guess I lost all control when I was talking about Brendan. I'm sorry I nearly shot you again!"

"That's all right, dear. You were very upset."

"Yes, I was," I say wistfully.

Suddenly, the smell of pot roast flirts with my nose. I realize that I am still starving.

"Is that pot roast? If so, is it going to be ready anytime soon?" I ask with a watering mouth.

An hour later, my father comes home, and my mother loads our plates with meat, potatoes, and vegetables.

To our surprise, she brings out a big plate of chocolate chip cookies. *How did my nose miss those?*

After all of us have finished with our lunch, my father turns to my mother and says, "It's time to spill the beans, woman!"

For the next hour or so, my mother and I take turns telling him about what has been going on with The Change.

When I tell him about how I can have heat waves and fire come from my hands, he says, "Now I've got to see *that!*"

"I will need a picture of Pete. Do you have one?" I ask.

My mother says, "Yes. We still have pictures of Pete. Let me go get one." She heads off toward the back of the house.

"Why do you need a picture of Pete?" my father asks.

"Apparently, I have to become very angry in order to acquire the full heat wave thing in my hands, but if I see his face, I reach full force flames immediately."

"Oh," he says, looking so excited that he can't sit still.

"I found one," my mother says cheerfully when returning to the kitchen.

"Don't let me see it," I say, closing my eyes.

"I forgot. Sorry, dear."

"I think that we should go to the garage in case this gets out of hand. Do you have a fire extinguisher?"

When I open my eyes, I see that my pop already has one in his hands.

# The Amazing Ella

THE THREE OF US GET to the garage, and while my father is moving the cars to the outside, my mother and I work to clear a space for my performance.

There are a few folded up-paper grocery bags that that will come in handy, and we find a metal bucket.

"I forgot about the water," I say. I take the bucket inside to fill with water.

We all gather around. I tear off two pieces of paper and scrunch them up a bit to form two balls. I put a ball in each hand palm up, and say, "Stand back. Okay, Mom, show me the picture!"

My mom holds his stupid, grinning face up in front of mine, and *poof!* The paper balls burst into flames.

"Wow!" my parents say in unison. I drop the flaming paper into the bucket.

"That was something," my pop says.

"What else can you do?" he asks excitedly.

"Mom, would you kindly attach that picture to a wall that you don't mind getting a few holes in please?" I ask, closing my eyes.

My mother digs around in a toolbox and finds a thumbtack. She attaches the picture to the wall and steps back. I open my eyes and close my fists so that I can concentrate on shooting CHUD instead of fire. I look at that turd face butt licker and let 'em fly! I give him pointy evil eyebrows, a Hitler mustache, and a goatee.

When I'm done, my parents and I look at the picture and burst into gales of laughter.

"That's got to be the funniest thing I've ever seen! No, seeing your mother put out a small kitchen fire with her armpit was the funniest, but this is a close second." My father doubles over with laughter.

My mother stops laughing and turns to my father in shock.

"You saw that *too*?!" she asks him.

"Sure did," he says in-between chuckles.

When his laughter dies down and he can speak again, my father asks, "So looking at Pete's face is the fastest way that you can get your hands to do that, right?"

"Right," I say.

"And you have saved people twice by using your, what did you call it again?"

"Her CHUD, dear," my mother says.

"CHUD?" he asks.

"Chin Hair Urticating Defense. Michael named it."

"Well, okay then," he says, "you have helped people using your CHUD, but have you ever thought about how you can help someone with your flaming hands? I'm sure that neat little trick could come in handy."

"*Hand*y," I say, giggling. Once again, my self-defense mechanism of laughter kicks in. This day has been incredibly stressful and very weird.

"They can come in handy heating up leftovers," I say, waiting for a hearty laugh from him.

Nothing. I guess he doesn't find it as funny as my mother and I did when I said it before.

"Seriously, Ella, these Gifts, as you call them, can be a good thing. Think of the two people that you helped. Because of you, their lives turned out better than they would if you hadn't been there." My father is serious.

My mother and I think this over.

"Tom, I wish that I had been open with you from the very beginning. I was so afraid to tell anyone because of what happened to my mother . . ." my mother says tearfully.

My father hugs her and says, "I understand. You were scared."

Suddenly, he looks to be deep in thought, and then he snaps his fingers.

"I got it!" he says. "Jade, do we have another picture of Pete, but only smaller than the other one?"

"I'm sure we do, but why?" she asks.

"You'll find out," my father says with a smile.

"I'm going to my workshop for awhile. Would you mind helping me find a picture, honey buns?"

"Anything for you, Tom," my mother says, looking at him as if he were her whole world.

My parents go off in search of pictures. I go to the living room, sit down, and turn on the TV. I always get tired after using my Gifts, so I'm just going to relax for a few minutes. I shut my eyes.

I'm dreaming that I'm back in the castle tower, but I know that Brendan won't be there to rescue me this time.

"Ella? Ella, dear, wake up. Your father has something for you."

"Huh?" I groggily open my eyes. *Where am I?*

I see my parents' faces hovering above mine.

"Here, Ella. I made this for you," my father says, and he picks up my left wrist.

I'm fully awake now. "What's going on?!" I ask, feeling slightly cranky.

"Look," says my pop, and he holds out a beautiful bracelet in front of him.

"Pretty!" I say, and I give him my wrist.

The bracelet has black leather straps, and a beautiful round, green jade charm in the center.

"This is beautiful, Pop! Thank you, but why—"

"Turn it over," he says.

"Turn what over?"

"The jade. It's got something on the back for you." I look at the stone and see that it's on a setting that can spin. I turn the jade over and see a small picture of Pete smiling up at me.

*Poof!* My hands go up in flames. I instantly move my other hand from off of the arm of the chair, so that I don't burn it. Unfortunately, I have left a small black mark.

"That's okay, dear. You can barely notice it," my mother says when she sees what I've done.

"So I thought that you should have a way to harness your Gift of fire. I was thinking that you need to have a way to carry Pete's picture around with you, in case you need to use your hot hands for fighting crime, or roasting marshmallows," he says with a wink.

*Now* he has a sense of humor about my hands.

"I chose black leather so that if you got any burn marks on it, you wouldn't be able to tell."

"It's perfect," I say, flipping the dreaded picture over, so that I can gaze at the pretty stone. I look up and find my parents standing next to each other with my father's arm around my mother's waist.

They are standing there smiling at me, happy that I like it.

I have the best parents in the world!

I decide to stay at my parents' house for a few more hours. We seem to have reached an unspoken understanding that there is to be no more Gift talk for the rest of the day.

My father's gig is tonight, so I decide to head back to my hotel room to shower and change. Now that he knows that I'm in town, I'm invited to watch him play.

On my way out the door, my father says, "I'm really proud of you, Ella. You seem to be handling this Change thing with dignity and grace."

My mother and I look at each other, each trying to stifle a giggle. If he only knew! I don't want to wipe that smile off of his face, so I say, "Thank you, Pop. That means a lot to me."

I give them both big hugs, and after getting directions to the concert tonight, I leave.

# It Happened at the Lodge

After showering, I go to the closet to see what cute things I will wear tonight. I choose jeans, a black tank top with a black matching cardigan, and a pair of black heels. I finish the outfit off with a pair of diamond stud earrings, the bracelet Pop made me, and my favorite bag. It's an LV Damier Azur Canvas Speedy 25. It's cute, has plenty of room inside, and goes well with jeans.

I smile at myself in the mirror, and then I leave my hotel for the second time today.

I pull into the lodge parking lot and find a parking space. As I'm getting out of the car, my tummy growls. The pot roast kept me full for several hours, but now it's six thirty and I am hungry *again*. I'm so glad that they serve dinner at the lodge. It's only hamburgers and french fries, but that will do just fine.

I go inside, pay the entry fee, and find that my mother has secured a table on the left side of the dance floor and we are very close to the stage. I give her a quick hug and take a seat.

"Wow, I am starving," I say.

"It must be from expending all of that energy when you use your Gifts," my mother says quietly, so that no one can hear but us.

*Now why didn't I ever come to that conclusion?*

My mother and I get in line to order our food and drinks. I am pleased to find out that they are selling desserts to benefit the lodge's local charity. I buy a plate of chocolate chip cookies, a yummy-looking chocolate cake, and a tray of fudge.

My mother looks at the pile of sugar that I have just bought and smiles at me.

"I don't plan on eating it all tonight, for goodness' sake. I can always take it back to my hotel room to snack on later. Besides, it's for charity," I say, feeling a little defensive. I can't help myself—it's chocolate!

I look at her tray. I see a coconut cream pie on and a plate of sugar cookies. I look up at her and say, "It takes one to know one!"

We're still laughing when we get back to our table (I have to make two trips) and settle in to eat. Pop and his band are onstage warming up.

A thought suddenly hits me. I am *so* happy right now. My kids and my cat are okay. I called them earlier to check in on them. My spa is coming along nicely. Javier sent me pictures of the changes that have taken place since the last time I saw the space, and we spoke on the phone for a few minutes. Before ending the conversation, Javier said, *"Uh, Pablo asked me to tell you hello and that he hopes that you have a safe trip."*

My parents are fine, and I'm having fun getting to spend time with both of them.

Life is good, and if I keep thinking positive thoughts, then eventually I will forget that I ever met Brendan. Thank goodness, he's leaving Sedona in the morning, and thank goodness, I have lots of chocolate!

My mother and I are finishing our food when the band begins to play.

My pop is on fire! (Not literally!) He can still play that violin like a pro, and he has the stage presence of a superstar. There's a group of women, who are around my mom's age, standing right in front of the stage. My pop notices them and his eyes get that sparkle. He walks across the stage to stand in front of them and gives them all a big grin. I look over at my mother, and she's got a smile on her face. She knows that my father only has eyes for her. He's just a big, harmless flirt.

The first song ends. The next one is just getting started when I excuse myself and go off looking for the restroom. I find it on the other side of the room, down a hall from the front entrance.

As I'm washing my hands, I realize that the music has stopped. "That was a short song," I say out loud. I'm by myself, so I don't expect a reply from anyone.

After checking myself in the mirror, I put my hand on the handle of the door to open it, when all of the sudden, I hear screaming.

*Wow! The ladies here sure are frisky tonight. You'd think that Elvis was onstage!*

I open the door and step into the dark hallway. I stop in my tracks. There, by the front door, not fifteen feet from where I'm standing, looks to be a big man wearing a ski mask, and he's holding a rifle! *Holy shit!* I immediately press myself back against the wall, hoping to blend in. I am *so* glad that I chose to wear the black shirt tonight. When my eyes adjust better to the darkness, I can see the big man more clearly. He's facing the other way toward the stage, which means he hasn't seen or heard me yet.

I look past the big man and see that the musicians onstage, including my pop, are standing with their hands in the air. The people in the audience have their hands up in the air as well.

I count two other men in masks who are carrying handguns, but I hear loud, mean voices coming from the other side of the room. Women are screaming, so I'm betting that there are more than just three gunmen.

My mind tries to take in what is happening. This is a robbery!

9-1-1! I'll call the police. I reach for my phone but remember that it's in my bag back at the table. *Shit!*

*Think, Ella, think. How can you help these people? Create a distraction and then take out the gunman by the door, grab his gun, and shoot the rest of the bad guys.*

I'm a pretty good shot, but the odds are at least five against one that I'm bound to get shot. Then I'll be useless. Am I really thinking I can take Big Man's gun away from him?!

I'm still thinking of my next move when a loud male voice says. "Rick, why don't you go check around and make sure there's no one back in those restrooms?"

I hear a man's voice from off to the other side of the room say, "I'm on it."

*Shit!* Thankfully, it turns out that Rick isn't Big Man with the rifle by the front door, because he doesn't move an inch. His back remains to me.

I quietly go back into the restroom and quickly scan the room for something that I can use as a weapon.

I don't know what they're doing to make those women scream, but I'm not going down that way. I look up to ask for a miracle.

Then I see one. It's a fire sprinkler! Is there a smoke detector in here?

Yes! Over by the sink.

I can start a fire thanks to the bracelet my pop gave me, set off the alarm, and hopefully the police or fire department will show up soon.

I run toward the sink and grab a handful of paper towels in my left hand, because that's the one the bracelet is on. Without looking, I use my right hand to flip the jade charm over on my bracelet. I raise my left hand toward the smoke detector, look at the picture of Pete, and *whoosh!* Beautiful flames shoot out and ignite the paper.

Just then, Rick opens the door to the restroom. I'm standing there holding the flaming paper towels, praying that the alarm and sprinklers go off soon!

"What the hell are you doing over there?" Rick yells in a muffled voice. He's wearing a ski mask.

"Put your hand down now, or I'm gonna shoot you!" He raises his gun and points it straight at me, when all of the sudden, the alarm goes off loudly and the sprinklers kick on!

"What the—" Rick looks up at the sprinkler and then uses the arm with the gun to cover his head. I almost laugh, because his ski mask is soaking wet and starting to sag.

Yet he's still trying to keep his head dry with his arm— his gun arm!

*Aha! This is your chance, Ella, go get him!*

I shoot my CHUD at his face and arms with as much force that I can possible use. I've only got one chance to get out of this situation without leaving on a gurney.

*"Ahhh!"* he screams, and he drops the gun while clawing at his hand and face.

I grab the gun and hit him over the head as hard as I can. *Thump!* He goes down like a sack of potatoes. I kick him hard in the stomach (I was aiming for his crotch!) just to make sure he's really out.

He is.

I look down at the handgun I'm holding. It's a weapon I hope I don't have to use. I stick the handgun in the back waistband of my jeans.

*One down and hopefully only four to go.*

I run down to the end of the hall and see the chaos that is taking place. People are going nuts trying to get out of a building that they think is on fire.

I look around for my parents, but I don't see them anywhere.

I am *pissed*! Who the hell do these assholes think they *are* coming in here and robbing these people at gunpoint?!

I look at Big Man close to me by the front door. I see him surrounded by frantic people who are trying to get past him to escape. He is pushing people and even hitting a few with his rifle.

*Oh, hell no!* I see red, and the next thing I know, I've pushed my way through the mob of people and I'm standing nose to belly with him. I look up at his face, and he manages to look down at me. *Ffftt . . . fffttt . . . fffttt!* I blast him with CHUD!

"My eye!" he screams, and starts clawing at his eye. (*Ewww!* I was aiming for his throat!) I shoot him with a few more strategically placed CHUD lower down his body. Judging by where he's grabbing at himself, I think I missed hitting his family jewels.

*Damn! I've got to work on my aim!*

He falls to the floor crying, and I use this opportunity to grab his rifle.

*Oh no! He's blocking the door!*

"Help me move him!" I yell at a man to my left who looks able bodied.

He nods as though in a dream, and we pull Big Man out of the way.

When I open the front door, at least twenty-five people make it out of the building. The man who helped me stays behind.

"What can I do to help?" he asks me.

"Get out of here, so I don't have to worry about you," I say, looking around for more gunmen.

"No way am I leaving without helping!"

*Might as well accept the help, Ella.*

"Okay, fine," I say. "Do you know how to use one of these?" I ask, holding out the rifle.

"I sure do," he says, reaching for it.

"I've got a gunman down in the restroom, and this knucklehead here. Make sure they don't come after me. Oh, and don't shoot anyone unless you have to," I say while turning around and scanning the room for my parents.

I spot them over by the left side of the stage. They're in a group of people huddled together—held at gunpoint by a tall, thin gunman.

*Mom! Pop!*

I look around the room and notice that there aren't any bad guys other than the gunman, Big Man, and Rick. *Where did the other ones go?*

Who cares? All I care about is that there is a gunman who is standing there pointing a gun at my parents.

I make my way quietly across the room toward my parents and the gunman. The sprinklers are still spraying water, but it has gotten a lot quieter now that the group of screaming people has gotten out. All who are left are as quiet as can be, in hopes of not getting shot.

I get to about fifteen feet behind, and to the left of the gunman, when I see my pop's face. He's standing protectively in front of my mother with a look of pure anger on his face that I hope I never see again. Suddenly, my pop sees me. The angry look goes away and is replaced with a small smile.

"What's that over there?" my pop shouts as he points to the gunman's right.

The gunman turns quickly to his right, and I start running at the gunman from his left. In the movies, they always show this part in slow motion, following a battle cry from the person who is doing the attacking.

I don't utter a sound, because I want the element of surprise on my side. Also, everything is happening super fast, not slow.

I tackle the bad guy from his left side. He drops his gun and we both land on the floor with me on top.

"*Ahhh!* It burns!" the gunman screams.

In my anger, my hands have heated up nice and hot. So much so that his clothes are smoking where my hands are grabbing on to him! Anger builds inside of me, and I sit up and start hitting him repeatedly. I feel myself start to zone out a little bit.

When my brain starts working properly again, I say, "You *bleep*ing *bleep*er! Point a gun at *my* parents! Take *this,* you rotten piece of donkey turd!" then I glance at Pete's picture and grab the guy between the legs.

"*Ahhhhhh!*" he screams as his pants begin to smoke.

At least I got *one* of the bad guys in the balls!

I remove my hand, and he stays on the ground writhing in pain. I stand up to look for my parents. I see that my pop has the bad guy's gun in his hand and is directing people to the exit.

My mom runs to me and grabs a hold of me. "Ella, you saved us!"

This snaps me out of my rampage. I stop, step back from her, and look around the room.

Tables and chairs are tipped over. Food is on the floor. Water is everywhere!

I also see two bad guys on the floor, and vaguely remember a third one lying unconscious in the bathroom.

"I did?" I ask.

"Yes, you did! Let's get you outside," she says, leading me to the exit door.

Just then, police cars, an ambulance, and a fire truck show up.

My pop makes his way over to us, and they both hug me.

"When the gunmen came and I couldn't find you, I was scared to death! But I knew that you would stay safe and think of a way to save us. It was you who set off the fire alarm and sprinklers, wasn't it?" my mother asks.

"*Uh,* yeah," I say, suddenly feeling very tired.

"There she is!" The man who helped me move Big Man is pointing to me and talking to a policeman.

"There's the woman who saved us!"

The policeman walks over to me. "Hello, I'm Sergeant Carl Ray. Is what this man said true?" he asks.

"Well, I had some help from him (indicating the man who helped me) and my pop," I say wearily.

I see several policemen with guns raised enter the building. Then I remember.

"Tell the men to look out! There are at least three bad guys still in there! One that I knocked out was in the ladies room. The two other are awake but injured. One was by the entrance and the other was by the stage. And there were a few other bad guys that I never saw, only heard."

Sergeant Ray gets on his radio and says, "Be on the lookout for three suspects. One was last seen in the ladies room, one by the entrance, and another by the stage."

Sergeant Ray says to me, "About twenty minutes ago, a van ran a red light a few blocks from here. It was involved in a high-speed chase for a few minutes, until it crashed into a light pole. The van turned out to be stolen, and the two men inside it were soaked to the skin and in possession of guns and three garbage bags full of purses and wallets. Judging from witnesses, there were five gunmen. So with the three you got, and the two we picked up, I'd say they are all accounted for."

Just then, a policeman emerges from the building.

"We've apprehended three suspects, and they all need medical attention."

Sergeant Ray looks at me.

"*Uh,* I hit one over the head with his own gun after I set off the sprinklers and alarm. Here you go," I say, handing him the gun from the back of my pants. He takes it from me with an amazed look on his face.

"I stabbed the second one in the eyeball with a safety pin."

A look of *Ewwww!* flashes across his face.

"I was actually aiming for his throat," I say, trying to prove to him that I'm not an evil monster. *"Ummm* . . . and I burned the third one with my lighter when I tackled him."

*You're getting better at thinking on your feet, Ella.*
*Why thank you!*

The man who helped me says, "I was wondering what you got him in the eye with. You were so fast! I never saw your hand move."

Everyone turns and looks at me. Suddenly, my legs get wobbly and I feel myself falling. Sergeant Ray catches me. He motions to someone near the ambulance and says,

"She needs medical attention over here."

"No, I'm fine. All I need is a shower and some sleep," I say woozily. *I'm so sleepy.* All I want to do is find a quiet place to lie down.

"Do you need her right now, sergeant, or can we take our daughter home?" my pop asks.

"For now, I just need her name and contact information. I have written down what she has told me so far, and if I need more information, I will get in touch with her in the morning," he says, handing my pop his business card. "I have enough witness accounts backing up most of her story now, anyway."

My pop gives the sergeant his and my mother's information. I try to make my mouth work to tell him my name, but all that comes out of it is, "Choco."

My mom laughs and says, "Ella, dear, when you wake up, you can have all the chocolate that you want!"

That's the last thing I remember hearing.

## Did I Do That?

Yawn. Huh?

*Where am I?* I sit up and look around at my surroundings.

I realize that I am in the bed in my parents' guest room.

I look down at myself and see that I'm wearing what looks to be one of my mother's floral pajama sets. *I don't remember putting this on. I don't remember getting here. What do I remember? I remember . . . Oh, wow!*

Everything that happened at the lodge comes flooding back to me. I can't believe that I did all that *and* that it all worked out!

It's daytime, so I guess that I should get out of bed. I drag myself up and out of the room to look for my parents.

I find them in the kitchen drinking coffee.

"Ella, you're up," says my pop.

"Barely," I say.

"I just remembered what happened last night and feel like I should go back to bed. Boy, am I tired," I say, having a seat at the table.

Meanwhile, my parents are exchanging glances like something's up.

"What's going on with the looks?" I ask.

"Well, dear, those things didn't happen last night. They happened a few nights ago."

"Huh?" I say.

"You slept for two days, Ella Bella," my pop chimes in.

"I did?"

"Well, technically you slept. A few times, I caught you sleepwalking. I know from your childhood that that means you have to potty. So I would lead you to the restroom, you would potty, and then I would help you find your way back to bed," my mother says, smiling.

"I also woke you up a few times just to get you to drink a little bit of water. I didn't want you to become dehydrated. Hence, your need to potty," she continues.

*How embarrassing. It's like I'm a little kid again!*

"Are you hungry?" she asks getting up from the table.

My stomach growls in answer.

"Yes, I would say that you *are* hungry," she says, opening up the refrigerator.

I yawn and stretch, and notice two things: one is that my arms are covered in bruises, and two is that my bracelet is missing.

"My bracelet!" I say, starting to panic. I love that bracelet.

"It's okay. I have your bracelet. Let me go get it for you," my pop says.

He leaves the room and comes back with it in his hand.

"This thing was covered in food and filth, so I cleaned it up for you." He puts it on the table in front of me. I touch it lovingly.

"Thanks, Pop!"

"Why don't you go take a shower and get cleaned up? When you're done, I'll have breakfast waiting for you," my mom says while pulling out a frying pan.

"Okay," I say, feeling even more like a little kid. *I'm an adult. I think I know when I need to take a shower.* But I humor my mother and go to the restroom.

I turn on the light, and *aaahhhhh!* What happened to my hair? My hair is sticking up here and there in clumps! On closer inspection, I see what looks to be bits of bread and something unidentifiable in among the mess. Yuck! *Sorry, Mom, you were right!*

I shower and shampoo quickly because my stomach is growling more aggressively. When I step out of the shower, I find a nice, soft, fleece robe hanging on the back of the bathroom door and I put it on. I put my hair up in a towel turban, brush my teeth with the new toothbrush that I find in its box, and go back to the kitchen.

Yum! I smell eggs, bacon, pancakes, and syrup. I also pick up the faint smell of something in the oven. I sit at the table and my mom puts in front of me a plate that is stacked sky high with two fried eggs, four pieces of bacon, and four pancakes covered in butter and maple syrup.

I barely get the words *thank you* out of my mouth when I start tearing into my food. I can't seem to get it in my mouth fast enough! I guess this is what not eating for two days does to a person.

To my delight, I discover that the smell from the oven is homemade biscuits. I eat two right away with my eggs and save two to eat with strawberry jam after I'm finished with my meal.

"Make room for doughnuts," my father says, coming through the back door. He's carrying two brown paper bags.

I didn't even notice that he'd been gone.

After seeing what is inside of the bags, I decide to save my biscuits and jam for later on. There are chocolate-covered doughnuts—cake and glazed. Bear claws, chocolate chip muffins, apple Danish, and even a few doughnut holes.

I love my parents!

Between bites, I ask, "So how are you two doing today? Are you okay after everything that happened?"

"We're fine. We wouldn't be if it weren't for you though. In fact, a lot of people owe you their gratitude," my mom says.

I look up at her.

"When the police arrested those gunmen, they ran their fingerprints and IDs. They found out that the two of them who were trying to escape in the van were wanted in Nevada for armed robbery and aggravated assault."

"What?!" I say, nearly choking on a piece of bacon.

"That's right, Ella. Those men were bad news," my pop says seriously.

"What about the three men that I took down?" I ask, almost not wanting to know the answer.

"The one in the restroom was out on parole for assault with a deadly weapon, and the hooligan you tackled in front of us was out on parole for rape," Pop says.

*I'm glad that I roasted his nuts. Karma will get you every time!*

"What about the big man by the door?" I ask.

My parents look at each other.

"I need to know," I say, looking at them both.

"He is wanted for murder," my pop says, not looking me in the face.

Thank goodness I'm sitting down because the room starts spinning.

"Apparently, these yahoos started in Nevada and have been hitting small cafés and venues like the lodge along the way. I guess they thought that there would only be old men like me in there so it would be an easy holdup job. Little did they know that our Ella would be there waiting to kick some bad guy butt!"

Suddenly, I feel sick. I get up, run to the restroom, and promptly throw up everything that I've just eaten.

"Ella, are you all right in there?" my mom asks through the door.

"I'm fine mom. Almost finished," I say.

A few minutes later, when I think I'm finished, I brush my teeth, gargle with mouthwash, and go out to the hall toward the guest bedroom.

Along the way, I glance out a window.

"What the—?" I say, going to the window and moving the curtain back for a better look.

There on the lawn, I see people—lots and lots of people. I also see several vans parked at the curb. *News* vans to be exact!

"Mom? Pop? What are all these news vans doing here?"

My parents walk up behind me, and each puts a hand on my shoulders. "They're here for you, dear," my mom says.

# Headline Blues

"Why? What did I do that was newsworthy?" I ask, feeling annoyed that strangers are camped out on my parents' yard.

"Well, Ella, you managed to help ensure the safety of forty-seven people, and you single-handedly took down three very dangerous criminals. You're a hero," my father says proudly.

"Oh," I say.

We all step away from the window, and go to the living room. I choose to curl up on the couch, and my parents sit down in their matching recliners.

My father gets up again and leaves the room for a minute. He comes back in a few minutes carrying a newspaper. In big bold letters, it reads, "Ella Malone—Hero."

I start reading the article, which includes interview after interview with people who are grateful for my "quick thinking and bravery."

They interviewed the man who helped me move Big Man. He told them about how I was the one who set off the sprinklers as a distraction. He also said that I had asked him to make sure that the guy in the bathroom that I knocked out, and the big man that I knocked down, didn't get back up and hurt someone.

My father was quoted as saying, "I knew that she would do something great with her Gifts!"

They listed his first and last name. So that's probably how they all found me, and now are trampling the grass out front.

"So Pop, how were you able to go out and get those doughnuts earlier? It looks like a news van is blocking the driveway."

"I just called Mr. Vance next door. He brought his ladder, and I brought mine, and we met at the fence between our yards. I climbed over, and then he let me borrow his scooter. Nobody recognized me in the helmet."

*"Ahh ha ha ha ha ha!* Pops, you *are* a sly old fox, aren't you?!" I say, appreciating the laugh. "Now, about those doughnuts . . ."

My mom leaves the room. A few minutes later, she returns with the bags of sweets and a glass of milk.

I feel safe and cozy while I eat my goodies.

"Oh, I almost forgot. We were on the evening news," he says, turning on the TV.

"I record the news every evening with the DVR. Here, look at us," my pop says, pointing to the screen.

"Tom, don't show her that," my mom says loudly.

"But it's *funny*," he says with that twinkle in his eye.

The camera shows the lodge at night. There are wet and dirty people wandering around. The camera zooms in on a news reporter who says, "Tonight, an attempted robbery was foiled by one lone woman. This is Dusty Goodman reporting to you from the Elks Lodge on the west side of town. Witnesses claim that she single-handedly detained three suspects in this attempted crime. I'm sure our viewers out there would love to know what was going through her mind at the time."

He turns to his left, and there's the man who helped me move Big Man. He sure has managed to get in front of a lot of reporters.

"I witnessed her in action! First, she stabbed the big man in the eye, then I helped her move his body away from the exit door so that people could escape. She was awesome! She even gave me a gun to use. When she handed it to me, she told me, 'Don't shoot anyone unless you have to.' She sounded like Dirty Harry or somebody like that!"

"Sir, can you point her out to me?" the reporter asks.

"Sure. She's right over there." He points directly at me.

I'm leaning against a police car and my mom is holding me. My father is speaking with a policeman.

When the policeman leaves, the reporter approaches. My father steps in front of him, blocking him from getting to me.

"Hello, sir. And what's your name?" the reporter asks, shoving a microphone in my father's face.

"My name is Tom Borrelli. I was here tonight playing a gig with my band. We are the Screaming Strings, if anyone's interested in hearing us play next week at the Knights of Columbus Hall." He gives a big smile.

"So what is your relationship to the hero of the evening?" the reporter asks, all smiles.

"I'm proud to say that she's my daughter," Pop says, smiling back at him.

"I would really love to have a word with her right now," the reporter says, turning toward my mother and me.

"I'm afraid that you'll have to wait to talk to her until another time. She's pretty beat up right now and needs to get home," my father says, putting a hand on the reporter's chest.

Just then, my mother and I get up, and she is helping me walk.

The reporter sees us move and lunges at me with the microphone. "Tell me how it feels to be a hero."

I look horrible! My hair is wet and sticking up in clumps, I've got something that's reddish brown smeared across my face, and I look completely out of it! I cover my face with my hand to shield me from the bright lights being aimed at me. My father is trying hard to shield us, and my mother is trying to move me along.

The reporter is persistent. "Have you had any military training?" He's trying to shove past my father, but he's no match for Pop.

My mother and I manage to get past him, and then, over my mother's head, I see my raised arm, and *ta-da!* There goes my middle finger. Oh no!

*"Ha ha ha!* That's my girl!" my pop says, slapping his knee with his hand.

# The Finger Seen 'Round the World

I CAN'T BELIEVE THAT I FLIPPED the newscaster off! *I've never flipped* anyone *off!* It's very disconcerting to see yourself doing things that you have no memory of doing.

The newscaster turns to the camera with a huge fake smile on his face. He says, "There you have it, folks. That is one crime fighter who believes that actions really *do* speak louder than words. This is Dusty Goodman for Channel 2 News. Frank, back to you."

"I am *so* embarrassed!" I say, putting my face in my hands.

My pop stops the horrifying video and says, "I think it's the funniest darn thing I've ever seen! That Dusty Goodman is a pushy SOB and I think it's about *time* someone showed him up. Did you see the look on his face when your finger flew?! I thought that my interview went quite well. I got to talk about my band on TV, so maybe we can get a few more gigs out of this."

My mind has been rolling around an idea from the moment I saw myself on that report. "I think that I should say something."

"What's that, dear?" my mother asks.

"I think that I should say something to those people out there. The last thing I want to do is talk to a bunch of reporters, but I don't want them to have the wrong idea about me. I've seen how celebrities are treated. Granted,

I am no celebrity, but judging how celebrities are treated, the ones who cooperate with the news crews and offer up interviews are treated with a little more respect than the ones who shy away from the reporters. I would rather people hear my side of the story than have the media make up stories that make me look like I'm some kind of uncouth loony tune."

"She's got a point," my pop says.

"*And*," I say, "If I give them an interview, maybe they will go away and leave us alone. It gives me the creeps knowing that they're out there lurking."

"I have to give them credit," my pops says. "They've been pretty quiet since I squirted them with the garden hose."

"Pops, you didn't!" I say, laughing.

"I sure did! You were so exhausted that night and probably in shock from all that happened. When we left the lodge to take you home, we found that when we got you here, Dusty and his crew had followed us. They camped out over night and were relatively quiet, but the next morning was a different story. Word must've traveled that you were here, because the noise from outside woke us up. When we looked out the window to see what was going on, we saw that the yard and street were packed with news vans and people everywhere. I walked out on the front porch to tell them to go away, and they swarmed me. Your mother had to come to my rescue and shoo them away with a broom. She held them off long enough for me to get back inside."

I look at my mother and say, "Look at you, Mom! Being Pop's hero!"

My pop continues. "I called the police, but all that happened was the reporters were told to stay off the lawn. The people moved to the street until the policeman left, and then they were right back where they were before. I could tolerate them being on the street, but being in my yard and making so much noise was just too much. I went and pulled out the high-pressure attachment for my garden hose. It's the one that I use to wash the tires of my cars with, and it packs some pressure! Anyway, I went out the back door and came around the side of the house. I told those reporters that they had to the count of three to get off my lawn and pipe down, or else I was gonna ruin their cameras with my hose. I guess they didn't believe that I would do it, because they didn't leave. At the count of three, I started shooting! You should've seen 'em. Screaming and covering their heads—even the men. But it worked! Not a single person was on my property after that. I told them that I would keep shooting them until they respected my family and me. They better stay off the lawn, and shut their darn mouths."

"Stop! I can't breathe!" I say during the laughter that started when he told about my mom shooing the reporters away with her broom. When I finally get control of myself, I manage to say, "You two are worth your weight in gold!"

"I made the news all on my own because of that. Look here," he says, turning the TV back on and pushing a few buttons on the remote.

There, on the midday report, is a video of my father in all his glory, shooting news people with his garden hose. Then the camera is on Dusty Goodman. He smiles and says, "This is Dusty Goodman. We have learned that the unidentified woman's name from last night is Ella Malone, and what you just saw was Ms. Malone's father shooting hardworking news people with a high-pressured garden hose. What kind of family did Ella grow up in? How was she able to single-handedly take down three dangerous criminals? Well, if her father is any indication of her childhood, it was one filled with violence and anger. This is Dusty Goodman signing off, and hoping to stay dry."

"Now that I see this again, it's not so funny. I stopped watching after they showed me in action, and I never heard what he said after. I'm gonna go give that Dusty a piece of my mind!" my pop says, getting up from his chair.

My hands are heating up from the anger that is dripping off of me after seeing that report.

"Wait, Pop! They'll just twist your words and make it worse than it already is. Let me see if I can handle things, and if I can't, feel free to bring out the hose."

*Damn the media! Who the hell do they think they are making my sweet pop out to be the bad guy?! If I could get that Dusty alone in a back alley, I sure would like to give him a piece of* my *mind!*

I stand up from the couch. "I'm going to go make myself presentable for television. I can't believe I was on the evening news looking the way that I did. I'll be back in a minute," I say on my way to the guest room.

I realize along the way that I don't know where my clothes are.

*I can't very well wear a robe while I'm being interviewed. They'll probably start calling me crazy and say that I'm obsessed with Hugh Hefner or something as equally ridiculous!*

I head back to the living room.

"Did my clothes survive the other night?" I ask, hoping that I had something to wear.

"Yes, dear, they did. They are clean and hanging in the laundry room. Do you think that you should wear the same clothes that they showed you wearing the other night?" my mother asks.

"Probably not," I say. "But what can I wear?"

"Why don't you go put on your clean jeans and under things and let me see if I can find something of mine you can wear."

She goes to her bedroom, and I go to the laundry room. I find my clothes and go to the guest room to change. I'm just pulling up my jeans when there is a knock on the door.

"It's Mom."

"Come on in," I say.

She walks in and stops. She's staring at my chest.

I look down at my bra. "What?" I ask her.

"It truly is amazing what The Change has done for you," she says as she smiles. I smile back. Having gravity reversed on *any* part of your body is a miracle that *any* woman can appreciate!

"I think that this would look good on you," she says. She is holding up a beautiful, white, long-sleeved peasant blouse.

"White will make people think of innocence when they look at you," she says.

"I hope so, because this is really getting out of hand. I hate what they implied about the two of you, and I want them to eat their words. I hope I don't make things worse." I say, pulling the blouse over my head.

"You'll do fine, dear."

I go to look at myself in the restroom mirror and realize that I don't have any makeup!

"Makeup! I can't go on TV without makeup!"

"Do you have any in your purse?" my mother asks from the other room.

My Louis! Where is it? Did it get ruined? Did the bad guys take it? I can feel the tears welling up in my eyes. "I don't have my purse! The last time I saw it, it was resting safely on my seat, next to you, at our table at the lodge!" Then I remember that besides bronzer and lip-gloss, my ID, some cash, a credit card, and my cell phone were in it! "Oh no!"

My mom appears at the doorway. "Don't cry, dear! I have your purse." She leaves and comes back a few minutes later carrying my cute little Louis.

"It's a miracle that it survived the night," she says, handing it to me.

"It *is* a miracle," I say, taking it from her and hugging it to my chest.

"Sergeant Ray called and said that they were getting people's stolen possessions back to them. He said that your purse, my purse, and your father's wallet were among the items found in the thieves' van. He sent them over the next morning with the officer who came when your father complained about the reporters."

"That was so thoughtful of him," I say, still hugging my bag.

"Yes, it was. However, he questioned us about your birth date on your ID during his phone call. We told him that you've had a little bit of work done, and he seemed to accept that," she says.

"I'm going to go check on your father. I don't want him doing anything crazy to that reporter!"

"Okay, Mom. Thank you," I say.

"You're welcome, dear," she says as she gives me a pat on the shoulder. Then she heads off toward the living room.

I inspect my little Speedy from every angle. Not a mark on it!

Assured that my bag is okay, I turn to the mirror to see what I have to work with. My hair has since air dried, so it's all big and wavy. It actually looks pretty good with the blouse I'm wearing. As far as makeup goes, luckily, my eyelashes are naturally dark, so I can get away with not wearing mascara. After a bit of bronzer and lip-gloss, I am presentable enough to meet the press.

# I'm Ready for My Close-Up

I WALK TO THE LIVING ROOM.

"Well, I'm as ready now as I'm ever going to be."

My parents rise from their chairs and we head toward the front door. My father wants to go out first, so that he can make sure that it's safe enough for my mother and me to come out. As soon as he walks outside, we hear a collective gasp from the crowd.

"Don't worry. I come unarmed." My father tells them.

This gets some laughs from the crowd.

"I would like to invite you all to come closer to the house. It's not a setup. My daughter would like to come out and answer a few of your questions. Please know that if you rush at her like wild animals, I *will* get the hose!"

This gets another laugh.

My father opens the front door and pokes his head in. "Okay, girls, are you ready?"

My mother and I both take deep breaths and put our shoulders back.

"We're ready," we say in unison.

My mother walks out first and holds the door open for me. I walk out onto the porch. The reporters all step forward and start yelling questions at me. My father steps forward as well and shakes his finger at them. The noise level immediately lowers.

*You go, Pops!*

"Hello, everyone," I say, but my voice can't be heard over the noise of so many people. Someone walks up and hands me a microphone. "Thank you," I say, speaking into it. I haven't prepared anything to say, because I find that it stresses me out trying to remember a planned speech, so I just wing it.

"Hello, everyone. I'm Ella Malone. *Er* . . . Thank you for letting me speak. Before I begin answering your questions, I want to comment on something that needs to be addressed. Dusty Goodman made some horrible innuendos about my parents that are incredibly distasteful and very much untrue. I was raised by loving, supportive parents who are the sweetest people that you will ever meet. My father acted upon his paternal instincts when he used the garden hose on y'all. I was hurt and tired and had been through a very stressful event, and he wanted to protect me from a mob of people—you!" I point at the crowd.

"If any of you are parents, I'm sure that you can understand why he did what he did to get y'all to back off and quiet down."

People in the crowd start looking at each other.

"Dusty Goodman was just ticked off that I wouldn't talk to him that evening and should be ashamed of himself for taking it out on my parents! *Ummm* . . . Now I would like to address another issue that is very embarrassing to me. I apologize for flipping off Mr. Goodman and the viewers watching the other night. I had been through a very trying ordeal. Quite frankly, I have no recollection of anything that I said or did after I walked out of that building. I was mortified when I found out what I did! I have never flipped someone off. I wasn't raised that way. So again, I apologize. Okay, *now* I'm ready for your questions." I try to smile like a normal person instead of a weirdo.

Everyone starts talking all at once. My anger level shoots up.

"I can't hear anything if you all speak at the same time! If you have a question, raise your hand!" I shout.

Dozens of hand shoot up in front of me. I scan the faces for a friendly one. *Aha!* There's a nice older gentleman with white hair and a white shirt. *Perfect.*

"Yes, you with the white hai—*er,* shirt," I say, pointing at him.

He steps forward and says, "Bill Powers, Channel 27."

"Hello, Bill Powers Channel 27," I say with a smile, hoping to break the ice with humor. That got a few chuckles from the audience. But apparently, Bill Powers Channel 27 doesn't find it funny.

He clears his throat. "Is it true that you nearly bludgeoned one of the criminals to death, maliciously blinded a second one, and then set the last one's testicles on fire?"

I hear a few gasps come from the crowd, and I even see a few men reach down and cover themselves down *there*, as if to protect it from me. This makes me smile.

*Wow! I sound like a badass.*

*Yes, but now is not the time to smile.*

"Uh . . . err . . . It's *nearly* true. When the gunman came into the bathroom where I was hiding, he put a gun in my face. As soon as I got the sprinklers to go off and he was distracted, I got the gun away from him. I hit him *once* in the back of the head. I knew that there were other bad guys in the building who needed to be detained. The only way that I could insure that he wouldn't follow me out of there and shoot me, was to knock him out. I was pleasantly surprised that I had enough strength to do it with the first blow.

"The second guy was a very big man, but when I saw him hit several people with his gun as they were trying to escape the building, I knew that I had to play dirty. I used a safety pin that, luckily, was in my pocket, along with a lighter. I jumped at him when he was distracted by the mob of people around him. I was actually trying to stick him in the throat, because it was the only exposed part of his body close to me. I felt bad when I realized that I got him in the eye, but at least it made him go down. Then people could get past him and out of the building. The last guy, well, he was pointing a gun at my parents. You don't point a gun at my parents and walk away unharmed!

"My dad saw me sneaking up behind the bad guy. Pop distracted him, so that I could knock him down and get the gun away from him. I pictured my parents' faces when he had his gun pointed at them, and I couldn't help myself. The safety pin was stuck in the other guy's eye, and all I had on me was the lighter. We were scuffling on the floor. I wanted to hurt him and make sure that he didn't get back up, so I burned him with my lighter in the crotch. In my defense, the sprinklers were still going off at that time, so I knew that his pants wouldn't burn for long."

This part got a big laugh from the crowd.

Bill Powers Channel 27 seemed to accept my answer and backed away while turning off his recorder.

"Next question?" I ask.

Hands go up, and I pick a woman this time. I point to her, and she steps forward.

"Hello, I'm Gail Weathers."

"Hello, Gail Weathers," I say, smiling at her.

She returns my smile and says, "You seem to hate men. Are you a lesbian?"

*What?!*

"*Ummm* . . . Excuse me, but did you just imply that I hate men and ask me if I'm a lesbian?"

"Yes, I did," she says, staring at me intently.

"No, I don't hate men, and I'm not a lesbian." I'm so confused!

*I save a few people, take out a few bad guys, and suddenly I'm a lesbian? . . . Not that there's anything wrong with that!*

"Oh, so you *hate* lesbians," Gail Weathers says.

"What?! No! I didn't say that at *all*. I *don't* hate men, I *don't* hate lesbians, and I am *not* a lesbian," I say, getting really ticked off. These people can make up a lie and then just throw it out there for people to grab onto and run with.

She opens her mouth again, and I say loudly, "Next question!"

I look around and a cute handbag catches my attention. I look at the woman holding it and she gives me a big smile. I smile back and point to her. She steps forward and says, "Hello, Ella, I'm Lisa Johnson."

*Please be nice to me Lisa Johnson!*

"Hello, Lisa. What's your question?" I notice that she's not carrying a camera, or a recorder.

"Well, I've realized that nobody here has thanked you for your incredible act of heroism the other night. How does it feel to be a hero?"

*"Ummm . . . I'm not a hero. I just did what needed to be done in order to save all of those people from the gunmen. Soldiers, police officers, firefighters, nurses, doctors, and teachers are heroes, not me,"* I say, feeling embarrassed.

"That's exactly what a hero would say. My parents were there the other night, and I want to personally thank you for saving their lives." She smiles again.

I smile back with what feels like my DMV smile.

*Don't just stand there smiling like a dingbat! Do something Ella!*

"Uhhh . . . please come on up here Lisa," I say, motioning her to the porch.

She climbs the stairs and stands next to me. We shake hands, and everyone takes our picture.

"Thank you so much for your bravery and quick thinking," she says and gives me a big hug.

I awkwardly say, "I'm just glad I could help."

She releases me and steps back down from the porch.

*Let's change the subject please, because being called a hero in public has knocked me for a loop.*

"You," I say as I point to a young man in a brown sports jacket.

He steps forward and is about to speak when, out of nowhere, Dusty Goodman steps forward and interrupts. "Good morning, Ella. You're looking a lot better than you were the other night. You really look good for your *age*," he says with a smirk.

"*Uh*, thank you?"

"Yes, you look remarkable for someone who just turned fifty this year!" The crowd goes wild. People start rushing the porch, and my parents step in front of me to protect me. I move them away from me and back out of harm's way.

"Stop!" I yell into the microphone. The people who were trying to get to me actually stop their advancement.

*Shit! Looks like the cat's out of the bag, Ella.*

I look at my parents for guidance. My mom mouths, "Lie."

"Yes. It's true. I'm fifty years old. I *ummm* . . . had a lot of work done."

"Who's your doctor? How much did it cost?" Everyone is clamoring for an answer.

"*Er* . . . My doctor retired and moved away. The cost was quite a bit. But wasn't it worth it?" I ask, striking a model-type pose. I'm hoping that humor will diffuse the situation.

Instead, I hear a few whistles and catcalls. That damn Dusty! I hope this nips this subject in the bud, because I could die of embarrassment right this very minute. I'm not like my pop. I don't like to be the center of attention.

"So Ella, if you're not a lesbian, then is there a special man in your life right now?" a man shouts from the crowd. I can't see who it is, and he's breaking protocol by not waiting for his turn, but I'm just happy for a change of subject.

"Yes . . . I mean no . . . I mean there was, and then we danced, but things got complicated . . ."

*Shut up! You're babbling like an idiot! Snap out of it!*

I can feel my face turning red. "No! No, there is *not* a special man in my life right now."

*"Mrrrftt."*

"What was that? I'm sorry, I can't hear you. Can you step forward please?" I say.

I look to my right and see the crowd part. Then I see a tall, young man with brown hair walking toward me. He looks oddly familiar . . .

*Wait a minute!* "Brendan?!" I say, tripping over a cable of some sort that has magically appeared at this exact moment, just to humiliate me.

"Who's Brendan?" the young man asks as he's getting closer.

I guess that it was a mirage or something, because this young man looks nothing like Brendan, other than his hair color.

"Who's Brendan?" he asks again when he gets in front of the porch.

*"Uh,* he's a friend of mine," I say, praying that he won't say his name again.

"Good," the young man says, "because you are one hot cougar, and I want to ask you out!" He starts high-fiving men around him and yelling "Hell, yeah!" with every slap.

Everyone is laughing and egging him on.

"Kiss her!" I hear someone yell.

I close my eyes. I silently ask that a giant hole open up beneath me, so that I can escape the nightmare that is unfolding before me.

My father takes the microphone from my death-gripped hand and yells, "Settle down now! That's enough! You!" He points to the young man who is headed our way. "You!" he repeats. "You owe my daughter an apology! That was very disrespectful! Didn't your parents ever teach you manners?"

The young idiot stops his high-fiving and looks at my father with a blank look on his face.

Pops looks around and then shouts, "All right, no more questions! My daughter has been kind enough to come out here and face you all. Now have some respect for her, and kindly leave the premises. Thank you, and have a good day."

He puts the microphone down on the porch floor and ushers my mother and me back inside the house.

# Out of the Slimelight

"That was horrible!" I say, when we all get back inside the safety of my parents' house. My mother nods her head. (I think she might be in shock).

My father says, "But you handled it with style, and I don't even think anyone noticed that you tripped over that cable."

My stomach grumbles just then and tells me that I need to eat again.

"Do you have any leftovers?" I ask. This seems to snap my mother out of her self-induced, walking coma.

She says, "I'll see what I can put together."

We all go back to our family meeting place, a.k.a. the kitchen, and my father and I take our seats.

"My kids!" I suddenly remember that I have two kids back home and that I haven't checked in with them in days.

"The kids are fine," my mother says as she opens the refrigerator.

"We spoke with them yesterday. They both called saying that they were worried about you because of the tube. I don't know what the tube is, but I told them all about what happened, and it didn't involve a tube!" my father says happily.

"The tube?" I say.

After a delicious plate of leftover goodness, I excuse myself from the table and go to the living room to call Maggie. It goes to voicemail, so I leave a message.

"Hello, Maggie. It's your mom. I'm fine. Everyone is fine. I hope you and Monkey are doing well. I love you!"

Then I call Michael. He picks up on the first ring. "Mom, I'm glad it's you! Listen, have you been on the Internet lately?"

"No, I haven't been on the Internet since I left Texas."

"So you haven't seen the video that someone posted of you on YouTube?"

"YouTube! That must be what your grandfather was talking about. He called it 'the tube'! Wait! *What!?* Someone posted a video of me?"

"Yes. Yesterday, a friend of mine sent me the link; luckily, he didn't know it was you. When I watched it for the first time, I couldn't believe my eyes! You looked like an action hero. Grandpa told me how you saved all those people and it blew my mind! It's an amazing video. And it's gone *virrrf.*" He mumbles the last word.

"It's gone what? I ask.

"It's gone viral," he says meekly.

"Viral? What do you mean by viral?" I ask, fearing the worst.

"It means that a lot of people are watching it and then sharing it with their friends. You've had over two hundred thousand people watch it so far."

"What is the video about?" I ask, feeling the horror start to work its way through my body.

"Well, it shows you tackling some guy and then sitting on top of him and calling him every dirty word in the book while you're hitting him. It's kind of like the scene in *A Christmas Story* where Ralphie suddenly snaps after being constantly bullied and then beats up the mean kid while he's cussing the whole time. Then the video becomes blurry. I think the person recording you has his finger partly over the lens, because there's no video after that, but you can hear the man start screaming like he's being tortured. What did you do to him to make him scream like that?"

"I was cussing? I don't remember cussing. I remember tackling him and then burning his . . . nu . . . *er* . . . crotch."

*"Ah ha ha ha!* Grandpa told me you got someone in the package. He just didn't say *who*. He also said that guy had been arrested for rape before this, so it looks like the punishment fit the crime. Right on, Mom!" he says proudly.

"I think I need to go now, son. Suddenly I need to lie down."

"Are you okay? Did I upset you by telling you?" he asks sounding worried.

"No, Michael, I'm glad that you told me. It's just been a long couple of days, and this isn't news I wanted to hear, but it's news I *needed* to hear, so thank you."

*"Um,* you're welcome?" Michael says.

"I'll call you tomorrow," I say, fantasizing about running away and changing my identity until things cool down.

"Okay, Mom. *Er* . . . I sent you a link to the video already, but you don't need to watch it. Just delete it," he says, sounding as ready as I am to be finished with this subject.

"Okay, Michael, honey. Thank you again for telling me. I love you!"

"I love you too, Mom." *Click.*

As soon as we hang up, I bring up Michael's e-mail on my phone. I click on the link and it takes me to YouTube. Thank goodness, my phone survived that night.

The caption for the video reads, "Foul-Mouthed Female Tackles Armed Robber."

*Oh dear Lord.*

I watch the video with a mixture of amazement and humiliation. I'm amazed that I was actually able to tackle him to the floor and that I didn't get me, or anyone else, shot. I'm humiliated by the fact that I was saying the most foul-mouthed cuss words ever uttered by a human being, and that I am on display doing this for the whole world to see, with just the click of a button.

# I've Gone Viral! Someone Call a Doctor!

I WALK BACK TO THE KITCHEN and take my seat at the table. I put my phone on the table and my head in my hands. "When will it end?!" I say in frustration.

"When will *what* end, dear?" my mother asks as she tentatively touches my shoulder.

"The humiliation," I say, looking up at my parents' concerned faces.

"You know the tube that you thought that Michael was talking about, Pops? Well, it turns out that he was talking about YouTube, and I'm on it!"

"YouTube? Is that the Internet channel with all those funny cat videos on them?" my father asks me.

"Yes, it is, but not all of the videos are funny. Someone at the lodge the other night recorded me, I'm assuming with a cell phone, when I tackled that bad guy who was holding you at gunpoint." I put my head in my hands again.

"I have to see that!" my father says. "It would be great to get to see you tackle that chump again and then beat the heck out of him, and *then* set his family jewels on fire. I wonder if it's as good to watch from a different vantage point from the one I had. I got to see the look on his face when you knocked him down. Priceless!"

"Here," I say, handing him the phone without taking my head out of my hand. "It's still on the video, so all you have to do is press play."

"The screen is black. This phone is just too complicated for me. Here, you pull it up. I'm dying to see it," he says, handing me back the phone.

I bring the video back up, turn down the volume (don't want to have to hear those words come out of my mouth again), hit play, and hand it to him. My mother comes around behind him. She looks at it over his shoulder.

"There's that SOB! He was a tall, skinny one, wasn't he? Oh, there goes Ella! Wham! Down they go. Look at her. She's really beating on him pretty good. I guess they didn't get the sound on this. She was letting the cuss words fly. Some of those words I've never even heard before."

I cringe.

He continues. "Judging from the angle, the person filming this must have been on the floor, and probably under a table or something. Oh darn! We didn't get to see you roast some nuts on the fire."

"Tom!" my mother says shocked.

"What?" he asks innocently.

"You mean to tell me that it doesn't give your heart joy seeing Ella tear into that man who had a gun pointing at our faces? Well, it sure does mine. I don't condone violence. I'm a peaceful man, but when someone threatens the life of me or mine, the gloves are coming off!"

I've never seen this side of my father. Of course, we've never had anything like this happen to us as a family. No violence ever, thankfully.

Now that I think about it, Pops *was* in the war many years ago. I guess that way of thinking is what helped save *his* life along with the lives of several soldiers in his company.

I give myself a mental shake. God bless our troops, but I don't want to think about war right now. All I want to do is crawl into bed and stay there until my life is back to normal.

"I'm going to go watch that video again on my computer, so I can see it in more detail. Ella, honey, would you mind telling me how I can find the video on the YouTube?" my father asks.

I close my eyes and say, "Go to YouTube dot com, and in the search bar, type in 'foul-mouthed female tackles armed robber.'"

*"Hee hee!* That's a good one!" he says as he goes down the hall toward his study.

"Ella, dear," my mom says, "it's really not as bad as you think it is. Why, in a few days, you will be old news when some silly celebrity gets arrested for drunk driving or some such nonsense! You'll have your life back soon."

"Thank you, Mom, for trying to make me feel better," I say, smiling at her.

"Well, sure, sweetie. Any time. I can't stand seeing you upset! In fact, today at the press conference, I could barely keep myself from running out into the crowd and slapping a few of those horrible reporters in the face! And that Dusty Goodman! His name should be Crusty *Bad*man. He is just a horrible *bad man*. How dare he try to embarrass you in front of all those people! But you sure did handle things smoothly. I was so proud of you," she says while leaning over and giving me a hug.

Meanwhile, I'm trying not to laugh. Tears are welling up in my eyes, and my shoulders are shaking.

"Oh, don't cry, Ella. Everything is going to be all right," she says, looking concerned.

"*Bwaa haa haa ha!* Crusty Badman. That's funny!" I say, barely able to get the words out between snorts.

When I can speak coherently, I say, "I'm sorry, it just caught me off guard when you called him that. I didn't want to be rude and interrupt you with laughter."

"*Hee hee!* It *is* a funny name, isn't it?!" she says, sounding proud of herself.

Just then, we hear laughter coming from the study. Pop must've just watched the video on his big computer.

## Missed Calls

After my mother and I settle down, I glance at my phone and see that Maggie's number is showing up. She's calling me right now, but there's no sound.

"Maggie?" I answer.

"Mom? I'm so glad you finally answered! I've been trying to reach you since yesterday. I was happy to hear your voice message a little while ago, because I was really worried about you. Grandpa told Michael and me what happened the other night, and I even saw the vid . . ." She stops herself.

"It's okay, Maggie, I know about the video on YouTube. I've even watched it. In fact, your grandfather is back in his study, right now, playing it over and over."

"So you're okay with it?" she asks.

"Well, no, of course, I'm not. But at least they didn't film me using my CHUD or shooting flames from my hands. I would have to be going into hiding right now for fear of dissection!" I say, feeling my old and trusty sense of humor coming back.

"It's good to know that you still have your sense of humor, Mom!" Maggie says laughing softly.

"Well, without it, I would probably be locked in a loony bin somewhere right now!" I say, feeling better after hearing her laugh.

"So how are you and Monkey doing right now?" I ask, changing the subject.

"We're doing fine," she says, and I can hear the smile in her voice. "Monkey is a little devil, but she's so easy to love. She and I play every morning before I go into work. When I come home from work in the evening, after she squawks at me and tells me how she doesn't like me leaving her all day, we play again," she says happily.

"Well, good, I'm glad. I miss that little crusty cat, and I miss you too!" I say, with a touch of homesickness.

"Everyone is good here, Mom, so no need to worry. Have you talked to Michael yet?" she asks.

"Yes. Just a little while ago. He's the one who told me about YouTube," I say.

"I sure wish he would've told me that he spoke with you. I was so worried! Anyway, I'm very curious to know what you did to that guy to make him scream the way he did." Maggie says.

I tell her the details and she says, "Way to go, Mom!"

We chat for a few minutes, and then we say our I-love-yous.

"Good night, Maggie."

"Good night, Mom."

*Click.*

# You Have Nine Messages

After ending my call with Maggie, I do some investigating on my phone. *Why isn't it ringing?*

I look around and discover that the ringer is turned off. When did I—oh, I must've turned it off before Pop went onstage.

I see that I have some voicemails. I have nine to be exact. Four are from the kids calling me after seeing the YouTube video. You can tell that they are worried about me. One is from Javier telling me that the tile that I had picked out for the salt spa is on back order. He asks if I want to wait a week or pick a new tile.

Two messages are from Mary.

The first one says. "Hi, Ella, it's Mary. I hope that you're having fun out there in the desert. Hey. I just saw this video of a woman who beat the *shit* out of some armed gunman, and I'll be damned if she doesn't look like she could be your daughter. And I could've sworn that I saw someone in a group of people that looked just like your dad. Crazy, huh? If you get a chance, look for the video titled, "Foul-Mouthed Female Tackles Armed Gunman" on YouTube. It is freaking funny as hell! Well, anyway, have fun, and I'll talk to you later."

The next message is from Mary again. "PS, You'd better be staying away from the young stud!" *Click.*

The eighth message starts. "Ella, this is Brendan."

*Brendan!* Why is he calling me?

I hang up the phone and tell my mother that I need to go to the bathroom.

"Be right back," I say, pocketing my phone.

When I close the restroom door, I call my voicemail again. "Ella, this is Brendan. Oh my god! I just called my mom to let her know that I had made it back home to Houston safely, and she told me about the attempted robbery at the Elks Lodge! Wasn't that where you said your dad was playing? I hope that it didn't happen the night that you were there. I know that you don't want to be in contact with me anymore, but could you at least send me a text, or something, so that I know that you're okay? Good-bye, Ella." *Click.*

The ninth message says, "Ella, this is Brendan again. I just wanted to let you know that I saw the YouTube video of you beating the heck out of that gunman. I was wrong! You're not a damsel in distress at all! I didn't see how the video ended. I could only hear what I think is the bad guy screaming. I also went online and read about what happened. It said that the hero of the evening—you—was okay and that you didn't need medical attention. I'm glad you're okay, Ella. Take care of yourself." *Click.*

*Brendan! I want to call him. I miss him. Ohhh! Why does he have to be so damn caring and adorable?! I should call him. It's the polite thing to do!*

*Don't you dare call him, Ella! You did the right thing and ended it with that young man. Don't make things worse.*

*Why would it make things worse if I call and thank him for calling to see how I was doing?*

*You're on your own!*

I look up his number in contacts and am about to dial, when I catch myself. I can't do this to myself, or him. Instead of calling him, I'll just text him. Yes, I'll text him. A text is impersonal, so I can tell him that I'm okay and he won't get the wrong idea.

"Dear Brendan."

*Don't put* Dear *in there! It'll sound like you still care.*

"Hi, Brendan."

*That's better.*

"I'm sorry that I haven't gotten back to you sooner. I was asleep for two whole days after the incident. I'm fine. Still amazed that I did what I did and lived through it. I discovered that I'm tougher than I thought, and that I don't like reporters at all. Well, anyway, thank you for checking up on me. Take care, Ella."

*That's good. Now hit send.*

*But I want to add that I miss him, and that I think about him all the time, and that he's so gorgeous, and that I want him in my bed again . . .*

*Hit send, damn it.*

I hit send and put down the phone. I feel sad because that text was the last time I will ever communicate with him. I can't make myself erase his two messages. It's all I have left of him.

I go back to the kitchen.

"Are you all right, dear? Did you vomit again?" she asks, sounding concerned.

"No. I'm fine."

I wish that were true.

# Mary Needs the Scoop

After a few minutes, I excuse myself again and tell my mom that I need to call Mary, and then I'm going to take a nap.

When I get to the guest room, I plop down on my back on the bed and call Mary's number. I figure if she ever finds out that it was me in the video, and I haven't 'fessed up, she would kick my hiney!

"Did you see that video I told you about?" she asks.

"Yes, I did. *Ummm* . . . Mary . . . you know how I came out here to have some work done?"

"Yeah, did you do it?" Mary asks.

"Yes, and *ahhh* . . . That woman in the video is me," I say, waiting for the cuss words.

"What the *bleep*? Are you *bleep*ing kidding me? How the hell . . . What the hell?!" she says, being at a loss for words for only maybe the second time I've known her.

"Well, my doctor has perfected this surgery so much, that the recovery time is just days instead of weeks." I hope she buys this.

"That doctor is a freaking miracle worker! But shit, Ella, how the hell did you get yourself in that situation?"

I tell her about being there that night to watch my pop and his band perform. I tell her about going to the restroom and how the gunman came in the restroom when I was in there. I fib and tell her that I lit the paper towel with a lighter that I found on the restroom counter, and that I stabbed the big man with a safety pin. Then I lit the tall skinny guy's pants on fire with the lighter.

"So when the video gets blurry, and all you can hear are sounds, is that when you set his crotch rocket on fire?" she asks expectantly.

"Yes, that's when I set his crotch rocket on fire," I say, smiling.

"Nice!" she says.

I tell her about the reporters and all of the craziness that's been going on. When I get to the part about Dusty Goodman telling the world my true age, Mary says. "That dirty bastard!"

I tell her about the woman calling me a hero and how embarrassed I was.

"I didn't know how to act. I'm not a hero! I was just lucky!"

"Shit, Ella. You're the most nonviolent person I know. If I hadn't seen the video, I would have a hard time believing that you really did all that. Were you scared?" she asks.

"Of course, I was scared, but they had guns pointed at people, including my parents. I saw the big man guarding the front door hit people with the butt of his gun, so I knew that these guys were loose cannons. All it had to take was one person with an itchy trigger finger, and then someone could've been dead," I say, thinking back on how it felt to be looking down the barrel of a gun. I never told my parents about that part.

"That was so funny hearing those cuss words come out of your mouth. I think you invented a few new ones that I might just add to my repertoire. And holy shit! Your face and your body! I can't believe how *bleep*ing young you look. The video was kinda blurry, but from the looks of it, you could pass for Maggie's age. I wonder if your doctor is the same one who worked on Demi Moore. That broad looks amazing. I think she made a deal with the devil. For her to be that hot, and that talented—please!"

We chat for a little while longer, and then I tell her that I really need to take a nap.

"Oh sure, I understand. Shit! You've been through the ringer, so you should get lots of rest. Take care, lady, and I will talk to you another time."

"Good-bye for now, Mary." *Click.*

I put my phone down for a minute, and then I pick it up again. I call my voicemail and listen to Brendan's voice again.

# Finally, They're Gone

I DIDN'T REALIZE THAT I HAD fallen asleep, until I wake up to a quiet house. I stretch and hop out of bed. I walk out into the hall and notice again how quiet it is. I walk into the kitchen but can't find my parents. I look all over the house, and thank goodness, they're not behind a closed bedroom door.

I step out on to the back porch, but I don't see them. I go take a look out in the workshop, but still no parents. I look in the garage and start to feel panic when I see that both of their cars are there. I haven't checked out front yet. Maybe they're out there shooing away reporters.

I open the front door and see both of my parents in the front yard, carrying around big trash bags.

"Where is everybody, and what are y'all doing out here?" I ask.

"Some local politician was caught cheating on his wife, so everyone left to go stalk him and his family. Those darn vultures left water bottles and soda cans all over the yard. I've even found a few half-eaten burgers and tacos! Those people have no respect!" my father says while bending down to pick up a soda can.

"Here, let me do this. I'm the reason they were here, so I should do the cleaning," I say, trying to take the garbage bag from my mom's hand.

"No, Ella, you need to rest. We're almost done," she says while picking up an empty bag of potato chips.

"At least let me help!" I say.

My dad points to a box of garbage bags by my foot.

"If you insist, there you go!"

I rush back inside to change out of the white blouse and into my black tank top. I also grab a pair of Mom's flip-flops because I can't very well do yard work in heels.

We get the yard back to looking like itself again in just a half an hour.

Darn vultures!

# Time to Get Out of Their Hair

WE PUT THE TRASH BAGS at the curb and go back inside. We all go wash our hands and meet up back at the kitchen table. Mom makes a pitcher of sweet tea and a big plate of sandwiches.

"Thank you, Mom." I say, putting a roast beef sandwich on my plate.

"Thank you, honey," my pop says while taking a turkey sandwich.

"You're welcome," Mom says while taking a ham sandwich.

I think that my mom has a secret grocery store hidden below the house, because she seems to have a never-ending supply of food to choose from. When I start eating, I notice that I'm starving. I think back on the day and realize that I haven't eaten very much at all today. We finish eating in silence (I think we were *all* starving) and sit for a minute.

"This sure has been an interesting couple of days," my pop says.

"*That's* an understatement!" I say. "How are the two of you doing by the way? Your lives went from nice and peaceful to nonstop action almost overnight."

"I love it!" Pop says. "Of course, being held at gun point wasn't enjoyable, but seeing you spring into action as a superhero was amazing to behold. I wish that I could've seen you nail those other two bad guys."

"I feel the same way, Ella. It's certainly been an adventure," Mom says.

"Granted, the night at the lodge was scary, and even though I knew that you could take care of yourself, it was still hard watching my little girl fight with an armed robber. I didn't care for all of the news people camped out in front of our house, but it was wonderful seeing you handle yourself in front of them," my mom says, smiling.

"You certainly have used your Gifts well. Except for your water ability," she says.

"My what?" I ask.

"You know . . . your water ability," she says, pointing to her armpit. "I've been meaning to help teach you how to control it, because it's a little bit tricky."

"Oh! You know, I haven't felt that lump since the first time it happened on the airplane. Maybe it was a one-off and it will never happen again."

"Did you have a few days after your first time it happened that you didn't have the lump?" I ask my mom.

"No, it was there from then on," she says.

"Well, then I guess it just didn't take. It would come in handy in case I ever accidentally catch something on fire with my hands, but oh well . . ." I say wistfully.

"I think that the Gifts you have now are pretty darn good, Ella. As long as you're careful with your hands, you'll be okay. However, you might want to think about buying a few of those small fire extinguishers. You should keep one in the kitchen and the other ones stored in several rooms around your house. Oh, and always keep one in your car," Pop says, happy that he still gets to offer me fatherly advice.

"Thanks. I will buy some as soon as I get back to Texas."

"Okay, good," he says, smiling.

"Well, I think that I should probably get out of y'alls hair and go back to my hotel. I'm paid up until the end of the week. Just in case, if any of those vultures want to come snooping around again, you can honestly tell them that I'm not here," I say, clearing our dirty dishes from the table.

"But we've loved having you here, sweetheart," my mom says, looking at me with her big eyes.

"And I've loved being here, but I think that I need to get out of your house before I bring any more drama to it. I think I'm going to head back home at the end of the week anyway. I need to see how things are going at the spa. There is an issue with the tile, and I really don't want to hold up the building process by not being there to make a decision. I've got a few days left, so why don't y'all come visit me at the hotel," I say.

"By the way, what hotel it is that you were planning on hiding from me all this time?" my dad says with a wink.

I tell him the name.

"That's a good one. I hear that they have a really nice pool," my pop says hopefully.

"Why don't y'all stop by tomorrow afternoon? We can relax by the pool and have some lunch."

"That would be nice," Mom says.

"Sounds great," Pop says.

I go get the rest of my clothes and my precious Louis bag, find the keys to my rental car, and hug them both good-bye for now.

# Alone at Last

I OPEN THE DOOR TO MY hotel room and feel the peace and tranquility wash over me. It's so nice to be alone. I love my parents, and I enjoy spending time with them, but with everything that has happened in the past few days, I just want to be alone right now.

I immediately take off the clothes that I've been wearing, because they are sweaty and smelly from being out in the yard, cleaning. I walk to the bathroom and turn on the water for the tub. I haven't taken advantage of the Jacuzzi yet, so I think it's about time.

I sit in my underwear on the edge of the tub, watching it fill as though I am mesmerized.

"Wow! This has been a long day," I say to the empty room. When the tub finally fills up, I sink down into it and let out an *ahh* . . .

My mind drifts to the press conference and how I had thought that that crazy kid was Brendan. I vow to myself that I will never contact him again. When I answered his message with my text, I felt like the lines of communication were open. I have to harden my heart. *Hmmm . . . Isn't there a song called that?* "I've gotta harden my heart, I've gotta swallow my tears, I've gotta turn . . . and . . . see-ee you-oo leave!" I sing out loud. Something like that.

Anyway, that's my theme song for right now. A theme song always helps, and tomorrow I'm going to look it up and download it on my iPod.

I turn on the jets and try to clear my mind.

Forty minutes later, when I'm good and pruney, I turn off the tub and drain it. I then step into the shower so that I can wash my body and my hair. I've never felt quite clean after taking a bath. I don't see how rinsing yourself off with dirty bath water, filled with soap residue and shampoo, can leave you clean. Anyway . . .

When I'm done, I wrap my body in a towel and put my hair up in a towel turban. Then I go back into the room and sit down on one of the comfortable chairs. The evil clock says that it's twelve minutes after seven. What's on TV on a Tuesday night? I turn on the TV to find out. To my delight, the movie *Red* is just starting. I love this movie.

Around eight o'clock, my stomach interrupts Bruce Willis with a big grumble. I can't be hungry again. I just had a big sandwich at my parents' house only a few hours ago.

I pick up the room service menu and see what jumps out at me. For some reason, I'm craving pasta. I know that I shouldn't be eating such bad things, but I figure that a few more calorie and fat-ridden meals won't kill me. In fact, I decide that I can eat whatever I want while I'm in Arizona, but as soon as I get back to Texas, the healthy eating begins!

I call room service and order a plate of spaghetti and meatballs, French garlic bread, and a glass of red wine—I hardly ever drink, but after the mess I've been through lately, I need one. I can't have a meal without dessert, so I order tiramisu. I should probably have a little green with my meal, so I add a Caesar salad.

Bruce Willis, Helen Mirrin, and John Malkovich are kicking butt when my food arrives. I finish the movie and my meal and decide to make it an early night, because I'm sleepy. I guess Mom was right when she said that I expend so much energy using my Gifts and that my body needs to rest so it can repair itself.

I change into my nightgown, brush, wash, and climb into bed by nine thirty.

# Another Crazy Dream

I'M DREAMING THAT I'M STANDING by a tall stone tower. It looks to be at least ten stories high. Suddenly, I hear a male voice shouting, "Help me! Someone, please help me! I am an injured prince trapped in a tower!" That voice sounds familiar. Wait a minute. I look up and see a man leaning out a window. It's Brendan!

"I'll save you, Brendan!" I yell at the top of my lungs.

Now, how am I going to get up there? I look around and see a bow and arrow with a rope attached to it. The arrow is made of metal and has big spikes on the tip. *Aha!* This must be what he used to rescue *me* in the other dream.

"Stand back from the window, for I am coming up!" I yell.

I've never shot a bow and arrow before, but apparently my dream self has, because on my first try I get the arrow in the window. I tug on the rope to see if it's secure.

Feels good.

I start climbing. For the first few feet, I feel great. I'm easily scaling this castle wall, but then I hear a noise to my right. I look over and see a blonde twentysomething, with big boobs, climbing a rope too!

"I'm coming, Prince Brendan! I will save you!" she shouts.

Damn it! What's *she* doing here? Well, I'm not going to let her get to Brendan first. *I'm* going to rescue him.

I start climbing faster, when all of the sudden, what looks and smells like maple syrup starts streaming down the castle wall right at me. It covers me completely. I can hardly see, and I'm having a hard time holding on to the rope. I look to my right. I see that the buxom blonde hasn't even been touched by the syrup, and she is gaining ground.

"I have a broken heart and cannot escape this tower. Please save me!" Brendan yells out the window.

I stop my struggle. Doesn't he see us down here?

I can't bear to see him in agony, so I use all of my strength to start climbing again. I start moving to the right, so I can follow in Blondie's clear path, when again, I'm covered in goo. This time, however, it's tomato sauce. "Oh, *come* on!" I say in frustration.

Just then, I hear Brendan say, "You've saved me!"

I wipe my eyes, look up, and see the beautiful young maiden and Brendan embraced in a passionate kiss.

"Well, shit," I say. Then a bird comes swooping by and lands on my head! He's eating the food off of me.

"Help!" I scream.

I try to shoo him away, but my hands are so slippery that I can't risk letting go of the rope. Then two more birds come along and start snacking on me.

"Help me! Somebody, help me please!" I say, crying.

The bird sitting on my head leans over and starts poking his beak in my ear. *Ewww!* I can't stand for my ears to be messed with. Without thinking, I reach up with my left hand to swat at him, and then I lose hold with my right hand.

I'm falling!

I wake up shaking and clawing at my head. This time, I'm glad that it *was* just a dream.

# It's a Beautiful Morning

THE NEXT MORNING, I WAKE at eight o'clock feeling surprisingly refreshed. My stomach is growling—again—so I get washed and dressed and go down to the hotel restaurant. I treat myself to a Denver omelet and pastry plate. After I finish my breakfast, I go back up to my room and call Javier. I had forgotten to call him back regarding the tile.

"This is Javier," he answers.

"Hello, Javier. It's Ella Malone."

"Hi, Ms. Malone. I'm glad that you called. Did you get my message about the tile?" he asks.

"I did, and I'm so sorry that's it's taken me so long to get back to you. I've been really busy lately," I explain.

"Busy fighting crime?" he asks.

"What do you mean?" I ask, fearing that I know exactly what he means.

"I saw a woman in a YouTube video that looks just like you, tackling an armed robber!" he says. "Was that you?"

I consider lying but choose to be honest. "Yes, it's me."

"Hold on just a minute. Hey, guys, it *was* her in the video! I'm sorry, but a few of us had a running bet that it was you and I had to let them know. Wow, Ms. Malone, that was pretty incredible. You really knocked him around."

I interrupt him. "So I'm calling regarding the tile. My plans have changed, and I'm coming home on Sunday of this week instead of next week, so I can pick another tile."

"Okay, sounds good," he says.

"Oh, and Javier? Please call me Ella," I say nicely. "I'm not married anymore, and I don't want to have any reminders." I would change my name, but I want to have the same last name as my kids.

"I'm sorry, I keep forgetting," he says. *"Ummm . . .* Ms. Ella?"

"Yes, Javier?"

"What exactly did you do to that guy to make him scream like a girl?"

I tell him the edited version, and I can actually hear him covering his private bits with his hand.

"I'm going to go now," I say. "Good-bye, Javier."

"Good-bye, Ms. Ella." *Click.*

I feel full of excess energy, so I decide to go for a run. I load up my fanny pack with the essentials from the vending machines and decide to take a washcloth this time. When you get really hot, a wet washcloth on your head or back of your neck really helps cool you down. I got a little overheated on my last run, so I want to be proactive this time.

I have downloaded "Harden My Heart" on my iPod and am singing along as I run out of the hotel.

I stop after an hour and drink a bottle of water. This dry heat sure does zap your moisture.

When I get back to my room and pull my phone out of my fanny pack, I see that I have missed a call from my parents. I listen to the voice message.

"Hi, Ella. Your father and I were wondering if we could come by today around eleven o'clock. Call us. Love you."

I call them back. "Hi, Mom. Eleven is fine."

"Okay, we will see you then."

It's almost ten, so I quickly shower and wash my hair. I'm going to let my hair air dry again today. In this dry climate, it doesn't take long.

I don't put on any makeup because we're going to be by the pool. I'm not going swimming because I don't really care for the water. I like to look at it, and I like to be on it in a boat, but I'm a little nervous to be *in* it.

I just finish putting on a tank top and shorts, and at eleven o'clock on the dot, I hear my pop's familiar shave-and-a-haircut knock on the door.

"Hi, Mom. Hi, Pop. Come on in," I say, opening the door.

"This sure is a nice room," my father says, walking around the room. He gets to the sliding glass door. "Really nice," he says, opening it.

We all step out onto the balcony to enjoy the view.

"I never get tired of looking at them," my father says, referring to the red rocks.

We stand there for a few minutes, and then my father smacks his hands together. "Who's ready for a swim?"

# Marco! Polo!

We get to the pool area and find three lounge chairs together. My mother and I pick the ones that are shaded by a big umbrella, and my father takes the unshaded one, since he plans on spending most of the time in the pool.

We spread our towels out on the chairs, and then my father says, "Excuse me, ladies, but the pool is calling me." He takes off his shirt, walks over to the deep end, and dives in.

"Pop sure does love the water. Why haven't you ever gotten a pool put in your backyard?" I ask my mother.

"It's because the workshop is so big and takes up so much of the yard that there isn't room for a proper pool. Your father likes to swim laps, so he just uses the pool at the YMCA. He says that he would rather go there and use their big pool than to have a tiny little pool in the backyard that's only good for sitting in. Besides, you know how much your father likes to entertain. He likes having enough room in the yard for extra seating when we do our barbecues."

"Oh," I say.

We both go silent.

It's so relaxing out here. There aren't too many people around, so we almost have the pool area to ourselves.

After about twenty minutes, my father gets out of the pool and lies down on his lounge chair. He's Italian, so he's not afraid of the sun. Since my mother is Irish with red hair, she avoids the sun like the plague.

I inherited a combination of their skin types. I don't burn, and I can get a nice tan, but I freckle if I get too much sun at once. Since I have a do-over with my skin, I want to treat it kindly and not cook it in the sun on purpose.

The three of us are resting peacefully when we hear a woman's panicked voice yell, "Christine! Where are you, honey?"

A woman and a man come up to us hurriedly. "Have you seen this girl?" she asks, shoving her phone in our faces.

The girl looks to be in her teens and has long, straight, dark hair.

We all look at the picture and shake our heads no.

"Our daughter's boyfriend chose to break up with her over the phone today during breakfast. She became hysterical and ran from the restaurant crying. We thought that she went back to the room, but when we got there, she was nowhere to be found. We've been looking for her for the past twenty minutes but can't seem to find her. We can't call her because she threw her phone on the floor and stomped on it before she left," the man says, trying to sound calm.

Just then, a man in a suit with a nametag comes over.

"Excuse me, Mr. and Mrs. Martin, but I was just told that a couple of hotel guests who were out on the hiking trails saw a distraught young girl matching your daughter's description. She ran past them on the trail. They followed her, but when they got close, she picked up a handful of rocks and threw them at them. She told them to leave her alone, and then she ran off," he says, sounding like he doesn't like having to be the one to deliver this news.

"Well, at least we know where to look for her," Mr. Martin says.

His wife starts crying, "My poor Christine!"

I sit there being grateful that I only went back to my thirties instead of my teens. You couldn't pay me a million dollars to relive that time in my life. Hormones rule teenagers and make them crazy.

My father puts his hand on my shoulder and says, "My daughter, Ella, here, is very good at helping people. If anyone can find her, she can."

He looks to me and asks, "Ella, are you up for some search and rescue?"

*Thanks for putting me on the spot, Pops. She'll probably scream and cry until she realizes that she's tired and scared and then come back to the hotel. I can think of other things to do than chase a rock-throwing crazy teenager, but if she were my daughter . . .*

I stand up and say, "I'll help. Let me run to my room, and I'll be right back."

My parents also offer to help, so they follow me to the room. Mr. and Mrs. Martin say that they will wait for us by the pool.

Along the way, we stop by the vending machines, and we each get two bottles of water, four granola bars, and two bags of dried fruit. We go to the gift shop and purchase more suntan lotion, two first-aid kits, and a small backpack for my pop. My father suggests that we each get a few bandanas. "Because they really come in handy."

We get to my room and regroup. My pop heads to the bathroom to change, while my mother and I load up our bags.

When my father gets out of the bathroom, we all slather on suntan lotion and then put the lotion tubes in our bags. I put on my running shoes, and my shades, and we all head to the door. On the way out, I grab Pop's bracelet—just in case.

# The Hunt for Teen Christine

We find Mr. and Mrs. Martin by the pool where we left them.

We divide ourselves into teams. The hikers who last saw Christine are one team; my pop and Mr. Martin are another; and then there's Team Me. It's decided that Mom and Mrs. Martin will stay behind in case Christine makes it back to the hotel by herself.

We all follow the joggers to the last place they saw her.

"I guess that we should spread out. Let's make sure that we have each other's phone numbers, so that if one team finds her, then they can let the other teams know," says my pop, taking charge.

We exchange numbers, make sure that everyone has a map of the trails, and head toward the last place that she was seen. When we get there, we decide to fan out in case she went off the path. The hikers agree to run on ahead and see if she stayed on the trail. My pop and Mr. Martin angle off to the right, and I go left. It's agreed that we will check in with each other every fifteen minutes.

This time, I don't have Britney Spears singing in my ears. I need to have all of my senses available to find this little girl.

I walk along for about twenty minutes, keeping track of where I am on the map, when I think I hear a noise. I stop walking and listen. There it is again. I can't tell if it's a person or an animal, so I decide that I should investigate. I walk another fifty feet, and then I hear it clearly.

Someone is crying! I walk in that direction and find a girl sitting on a rock, crying. She has long, straight, dark hair just like in her picture. I look down at my map to see where we are. I look up, and when she looks up and sees me standing there, she gets up and starts running away from me.

"Get away from me! I want to be left alone!" she yells over her shoulder.

# The Race Is On!

"**O**H, *HELL* NO," I SAY as I chase after her. "Christine, come back! I'm not going to hurt you. Your parents are worried about you," I say while jumping over rocks and dead tree branches. I look for cairns along the way but don't see any. We are *way* off the beaten path.

We run for what feels like forever and get to a big outcropping of red rocks.

"Leave me alone! I just want to die!" she yells. She starts climbing the biggest rock.

"Come back here, you crazy girl!" I shout as I start climbing after her.

We keep climbing higher and higher, and I make the mistake of looking down. *Holy shit! We're really high up.*

We get to the top of the rock, and it's fairly flat and long up here, so she starts running.

"Don't do that!" I scream at her. "You crazy little fool!" I say under my breath.

We are running along at a fairly fast pace, when suddenly, she disappears from sight.

"Christine!" I scream. I run to where she was. I look down and see that she has fallen into a big crack in the rock—a crevasse!

The top of her head is about two feet below the surface and she's struggling to get out, but she can't.

*Ahhh! I can't believe this is happening! Okay, keep her calm, because there is about a thirty-foot drop below her. Don't sound scared, because she will freak out. Don't be warm and fuzzy—keep her anger up so the fear won't come. That always works for me.*

"Well, there you go," I say. "You got your wish, because there is no way you can get yourself out this situation."

She quits struggling, looks up at me, and says, "Fine! Just go away! Maybe this will make Billy feel guilty for breaking up with me for Erica!" She looks scared but is trying to come off as cocky.

"Are you kidding me?!" I say down to her. "This will make life *easy* for Billy. First of all, everyone will feel so sorry for him, because his last girlfriend died. Then, Erica will look like a sweet and kind girl for helping him get through his loss. Everyone will think that they are such a brave couple." I say, hoping that my plan works.

She's quiet for a minute. "Do you really think that would happen?" she asks.

"Yes, I do. Christine, the best way that you can get back at them is by living a great life, so that every time Billy passes you in the halls at school, he will kick himself for letting a great girl like you get away," I say.

"Maybe he would even want me back," she says hopefully.

"Do you really want someone who's capable of cheating on you? Let me tell you: once a cheater, always a cheater! I've seen *way* too many women who are married to cheaters get their hearts broken time and time again."

She looks up at me with a conflicted look on her face.

"Those women end up wasting a lot of their good years on those cheaters, and in the end, they usually put on about twenty extra pounds from stress eating," I say, staring down at her intently.

*That ought to do it.*

"Well, I don't want to get *fat*!" she wails.

"Well then, don't trust a *cheater!* Pick a nice boy who is honest, opens doors for you, and holds your hand."

Silence.

"I want out of here," she whimpers. "Please, will you help me?"

"I sure will, but only if you promise me that you will never want to kill yourself over a stupid cheating boy," I say seriously.

"I promise," she says.

"Okay, then give me your hands," I say, reaching down to her.

She lifts her arms. I grab her hands and pull.

*"Owwww!* My foot!" she says.

I get on my stomach and hang my body from the waist down in there with her. I survey the situation. It looks as if one of her feet is caught in a smaller crack below.

I look at her and say, "Don't worry. I have my phone, so I can call for help."

I pull my torso out of the crevasse, stand up, and look around.

*Oh no. I don't know where we are.* I look for my map and realize that I must've dropped it.

*Okay, Ella, get a hold of yourself. Don't panic and cause Christine to freak out and fall to her death.*

I reach in my fanny pack, and pull out a bandana and a bottle of water. I pour a little water on the bandana. "Here you go," I say, handing them down to her. "You can use the bandana to wipe your face, and then you can wrap it around your neck to keep you cool. Drink some water slowly, so you don't get sick to your stomach. I'm going to call for help now. You okay?"

"For now," she says as she takes a sip of water.

I walk away from her, so she can't hear me say that we're lost.

I call Pop.

"I found her," I tell him when he answers.

"Are you both okay?" he asks.

"I'm fine, but Christine . . ."

"Hold on, Ella, Mr. Martin wants to talk to you."

"You found Christine? That's wonderful! Is she okay? Where was she?" he says in a rush.

"First of all, she's okay, but we will need some help. Her foot's stuck in a crack, and I can't pull her out." I didn't tell him about her being stuck in an actual *crevasse*.

I figure one hysterical Martin is enough.

"My little girl! Is she in pain? Let me talk to her."

"I don't think she's in pain, and I'll let you talk to her in just a minute, but I need to speak with my father first, please," I say, trying to sound polite. I'm a little angry that he hijacked Pop's phone.

"What's going on?" Pop asks when he gets back on the line.

"Here's the thing. I don't want to alarm Mr. Martin, but his daughter fell into a crevasse. I can reach her hands, but her foot is stuck and I can't pull her out. Now that I think about it, it's probably a good thing that her foot stopped her, because we're up pretty high."

"Where are you?" he asks.

"I don't know! I lost my map when I started chasing after her. I can't find any cairns, so I know that we're lost. We're on top of a big red rock. That's all I can tell you," I say, trying not to cry.

"Don't you have a map thing on your fancy phone?" he asks.

"I forgot about that!" I say, and push the app button. Nothing. I try again, but it doesn't work.

"It won't work!" I say, feeling a tear fall.

"Calm down and look around you. Do you see anything that stands out, like an odd shaped tree, a big rock that looks like a face, or something? Anything that could be seen from a distance?" he asks, sounding worried.

"No! I chased her all over the place, and I can't get my sense of direction out here. Everything looks the same!" I say, walking farther away from Christine.

"Ella, I need you to focus. If there's nothing for us to look for, then you will need to *make* something for us to look for that can be seen from far away. What do you think that might be?"

I think for a minute.

"I don't know," I say, frustrated and scared. I don't want to let this little girl down, so I pull myself together.

"Okay, I need something that can be seen from far away. *Hmmm . . .*"

"Ella, you need to make a fire," he says.

"That's a good idea! But wait a minute. I don't have a lighter," I say, frustrated.

"Ella, yes, you do. You have two lighters. Remember?"

*Duh! I can't believe that I forgot about* that *Gift!*

"Thanks, Pop. You always know what to do," I say, feeling much better.

"Just remember to make a circle of stones around the fire, so you don't burn everything down."

"Okay, Pop, thank you. If you want to pass the phone to Christine's dad, I'll let him talk to her. I love you, Pops," I say, teary eyed.

"I love you too, Ella Bella. I'll call the authorities and tell them what you have told me. With all of us looking, we'll find you," he says.

Mr. Martin gets on the line, and I walk over to Christine.

"It's your dad," I say, handing her the phone.

"Is he mad at me?" she asks.

"No, just worried about you."

She puts the phone to her ear. "Hi, Daddy. I'm so sorry for acting like a spoiled brat! . . . I'm fine; it's just that I'm stuck in a crack . . . No, I'm not in any real pain. My foot hurts a little, but I'm okay. Daddy, are you coming to get me? . . . Good! Okay, I love you! Tell Mommy I love her too!"

She hangs up, gives me the phone, and wipes her face with the handkerchief.

"Are you hungry?" I ask her.

"Yes, I kinda am. That jerk Billy called me right before I got to eat my breakfast," she says, sounding less scared and more feisty.

"Here, I've got a granola bar and some dried fruit. I have to go look for something to make a fire with, so that someone can find us. I won't be gone long. Will you be okay?" I ask.

"It's not like I have a choice, but yeah, I'll be okay. Thank you for following me when I ran from you. I'd probably die up here if I was by myself," she says seriously.

I decide not to tell her that she's right.

# Smoke Signal

It takes me awhile to gather what I need for the fire because I have to climb back down from the rock to find anything useful. I build the fire about thirty feet away from the crevasse, so that Christine and I don't get too hot from the flames.

After I set the last stone in place in the circle around the fire pit, I look at my wrist, flip over the jade pendant, see that stupid face, and *woosh!*

We have a fire! Once I get it burning strong, I go over to Christine and sit down.

"You still okay?" I ask.

"Yes. Just uncomfortable," she replies.

"Yes, I imagine you *would* be," I say. "How 'bout you tell me about your friends? Do you have a best friend? Do you get into all sorts of trouble together?" I ask, hoping that if I can get her talking, it can lower the chances of another freak out. I worry that if she moves around too much, she might unwedge her foot and fall farther down.

She can't really see what's below her because of a little ledge, but I can see, and it's not good.

"I have a best friend, Wendy," she says. "We don't get in any trouble, but we do a lot of crazy things together! This one time . . ."

I'm sorry, but I tune her out. I'm thinking about how each of us has only a half bottle of water to drink. I tried to conserve it, but I had to take a big drink after lighting the fire. I wish that I would have brought more, but I didn't think that I'd be out here so long. I honestly thought that a few minutes after searching, we'd all get called and told that she had returned to the hotel unharmed.

"And then one time, Wendy and I . . ." She's going on and on. "Have you ever done that?" she asks me.

*Oh shit! What did she just ask me? Did she ask if I took algebra in school or if I ever went to a slumber party? Or what if she asked me if I had sex before marriage?! I don't know how to answer!*

"Umm . . . I don't remember," I say vaguely.

"You don't remember if you ever got your ears pierced?" she asks.

"Oh! Yes, I'm sorry. Yes, I had my ears pierced," I say.

Suddenly, I hear a loud noise. It sounds like it's coming from the sky. I stand up and look in the direction of the sound. It's a helicopter!

I yell down to Christine, "They found us! I see a helicopter!"

"Yay!" she yells back.

I start waving both my arms for help. If you wave one arm, it means you're fine and don't need help. This is a tip that my pop gave me when we went camping in the mountains one summer.

The helicopter circles and finds a wide enough area to land on the rock, which is about fifty feet away from us. When it touches down, three men get out of the helicopter. One of them is carrying a first-aid kit and a cooler. He walks toward to me.

"You must be Ella, I'm Robert," he says and shakes my hand.

"Hi Robert, let me take you to Christine." I lead the three of them over to her, and they gather around the opening.

"Thank goodness, you're here! Can you get me out of this?" Christine asks when she looks up and sees them.

"We will get you out of here soon," Robert tells her confidently.

"We'll go get the gear," one of the other rescuers says. He and the other man head back to the helicopter.

Robert opens the cooler and pulls out two bottles of water.

"Here you go," he says, handing Christine a bottle.

"Thank you," she says, taking it from him.

"Drink it slowly," he tells her.

"I know," she says, looking up at me.

"Would you like a bottle?" he asks me.

"Yes, please." I finish off my old bottle and then take a few sips of the cold water. *Ahh!*

The other two men return from the helicopter with their gear. I step back and walk away, so that they can do their job, and I can call my pop.

"We're both okay. A helicopter just got here," I say when he answers.

"Great. Just hang tight, Ella Bella. I'm going to call everyone who's still looking for you and let them know that you've been found."

"Okay, Pop, and I'll call Mom to let her know that I'm okay. Love you!"

"Love *you,* my brave girl."

I call my mom.

"Ella, thank goodness! I was so worried!"

I decide not to tell my mom about Christine, so as not to panic Mrs. Martin.

"We're both fine. Please tell Mrs. Martin that a helicopter just landed and I think that we will be out of here soon," I say, watching a bird fly across the sky. "Mom, I should get back to Christine. I love you!"

"I love you too! See you soon," my mom says cheerfully.

I walk back and see Robert and one of the other men sitting on the edge of the crevasse. They take a harness that is connected to a rope and manage to get it secured around Christine's body.

"Are you ready to get out of here?" Robert asks Christine.

"I'm ready," she says, trying to sound brave.

The other man, who helped with the harness, puts on a harness of his own and lowers his torso down into the crevasse. Robert leans over and hands him a hammer, a block of foam the size of a small throw pillow, and a long metal pole with a chiseled end. The third man takes a rope that is attached to Christine's harness, and ties it around a big rock on one side of the crevasse. He goes to the other side and wraps another harness rope around a thick rock and then his waist. He grabs onto the rope with both hands and yells, "Ready!"

*Clank, clank, clank!* I'm standing close enough that I can see the top of Christine's head. *Clank, clank, clank!* Suddenly, her head drops from sight! I rush forward and see her safely dangling by the harness.

"*Ahhh!* Get me out of here!" she screams. When she looks down and sees the long drop below her, she starts screaming and flailing her arms and legs.

"Christine, calm down or they're gonna drop you!" I yell.

The men look at me like I'm crazy for telling her that.

Sure enough, the cold, hard truth settles her down. She lets out a whimper and puts a death grip on the harness.

"Okay, I'm calm," she says quietly.

They manage to pull her up and out safely.

"Yay!" I shout when she comes up.

"Yay!" she says weakly.

They gently set her on a rock, and Robert inspects her foot.

"Can you move it?" he asks her.

"I think so," she says. "Ouch!" she says when it moves.

"I don't think anything is broken, but just in case, I'm going to wrap it up to support it. You could've gotten hurt a lot worse. You are a *very* lucky girl," he tells her.

She looks at me and says, "I know."

As he wraps her foot, he looks at me and says, "That was smart thinking starting that fire. We were unable to track your phone, so the fire is what helped us find you."

"It was my father's idea," I tell him.

"Smart man," he says.

I nod in agreement.

He finishes with her foot, and then inspects her from head to toe. He cleans and bandages her cuts and scrapes, and says, "That should do it." He turns to me and asks, "Do you have any injuries?"

"Nothing that a cold shower and a long nap won't heal," I tell him.

Just then, the two other men appear next to us holding a long, narrow board with straps. I didn't even notice that they had been gone.

"Christine, we're going to have to put you on this board," Robert says.

"What do you mean?" she asks, sounding worried. "Are you gonna carry me by a rope dangling under the helicopter like I see in the movies?" She frantically tries to stand up.

He stops her. "No, you'll travel *inside* the helicopter, but we need to use the board because we can't risk trying to carry you without support on this uneven terrain. It will be best if you stay on it until we can get you to the hospital, because it will make it a lot easier to get you in and out of the helicopter without injuring you further."

Christine's looks like she wants to cry and run away. "It looks so scary! I just want to go home!" she wails. Apparently, the stress of the day has just caught up with her.

"You can do this, Christine. You'll be inside the helicopter with me. Think about what a cool story this will be to tell your friends at school," I say to her smiling.

She stops crying. "I guess if there's no other way . . . ," she says quietly.

The men get her strapped onto the board, and then carry her to the helicopter.

I stay by her side, so that she can see me. After they get her safely loaded into the helicopter, I climb in. I look down at Christine lying on the board. She smiles at me and gives me a thumb's up. I smile back. The helicopter engine starts and I feel my heart speed up. I've never ridden in a helicopter before, so I'm really excited to get this chance.

# Up, Up, and Away

*T*HIS IS AMAZING! *I* FEEL *like a bird! Why haven't I done this before?*

We fly across the desert, and along the way, I look down at the amazing scenery.

A little while later, we land on top of a hospital. "It's protocol," Robert tells me as we get out of the helicopter.

Two paramedics from the hospital come out to meet us. They transfer Christine to a gurney, and wheel her away.

Robert climbs back into the helicopter.

"Wait!" I shout, and follow him in.

"Thank you for saving us," I say to all three of them.

"We're just glad we could help," they say in unison.

*Hey, that's my line!*

I smile and climb out of the helicopter. I walk a safe distance away and watch them take off.

"We should get going now." I turn around and find a friendly-looking nurse standing behind me.

"They've already taken your daughter, so we should probably go catch up with them," she says, putting her hand on my lower back.

"She's not my daughter. She's . . . a friend," I tell her as we start walking.

She leads me through a door and into an elevator. When the elevator reaches the first floor, the doors open and my parents are standing right in front of me.

"Oh Ella!" my mom says, grabbing me and hugging me.

My father comes over and hugs both of us.

"A doctor will need to examine you now," the nurse says.

"I'm fine," I say to her.

"You should really have yourself examined just in case," she says while looking at my mother.

"Really, I'm fine," I say to both of them.

"Well, we can't force you, so if you can come with me, I will have you sign some forms that say that you are refusing treatment."

"Okay," I say, and then I follow her to an office. I sign the forms and have just made it back to my parents when Mr. Martin comes over to us.

"Thank you so much for saving my daughter," he says, smiling at me.

"The helicopter men saved her, not me," I say, embarrassed.

"Christine told me how you followed her up that rock, and how you made the fire, so *you* saved her. You saved my Christine," he says with finality.

I look to my parents and see them smiling at me proudly.

# You Again?!

My parents and I get to the front doors of the hospital and stop short.

"You've gotta be freakin' kidding me," I say.

Standing about fifty feet from the exit doors is a swarm of reporters.

"Darn vultures!" my pop says.

We immediately turn around and regroup. We find a waiting area out of the line of sight of the doors and sit down.

"They are definitely here about Christine," I say. "A little girl having to be rescued by helicopter is a pretty big deal. I doubt that they have released her name because she's a minor, and chances are that it's too soon for them to have my name yet. Just in case though, we should probably use a different exit, because they all know us and that could cause a stir. I don't want to create a circus for that poor girl when she's ready to go home."

We go back toward the emergency room and use that exit. Pop snaps his fingers. "Darn it! We parked around front. Maybe we can sneak out behind them," he says.

My mom says, "We can only hope."

We all put on our sunglasses and wish for the ability to become invisible. *That would be a cool Gift!*

We come around the corner and see the vultures. Here we go!

*We are not the people you are looking for. Don't mind us, we're just passing through.*

It never hurts to try the Jedi mind trick, because you never know when it might work. Unfortunately, this is not one of those times.

A few newscasters spot us. Someone points to us, and the next thing I know, there's a stampede heading straight for us! We make a run for it and manage to get to the car. Pop scrambles in his pocket for his keys.

"Come on, Pops! They're almost here!" I say, feeling my anxiety level hit maximum capacity.

"Please hurry, Tom!" my mom says sounding panicked.

"Got 'em!" he says, and he hits the unlock button on the remote.

The locks click open, and we jump inside the car, just as they descend upon us like a swarm of locusts.

They're shoving cameras at the windows and shouting at us.

"Ella! What are you and your family doing at the hospital?"

"Did you see the people who were rescued earlier today?"

"Are they any relation to you?"

Good. They haven't put two and two together yet.

My pop starts the car, but they won't move. He honks the horn a few times, but it doesn't seem to help.

I roll down the window and shout, "Please get out of the way! We're trying to leave!"

"Ella! Did you see the people who were brought in by helicopter?" a faceless voice asks.

Here's my chance to throw them off the track! "No, I didn't. We were just here to visit a friend. Now if you don't mind, we would really like to get home."

I look around at the faces that are staring at us. Finally they start to back away from the car.

As we back out of the parking spot, I see Dusty Goodman step forward. He locks eyes with me . . . and smiles.

*Damn that Crusty Badman!*

# That Was a Close One!

We all breathe a sigh of relief as we pull out of the hospital parking lot.

"Please take me to the hotel. I don't want them harassing you again," I say, referring to the reporters.

"But Ella, dear, you've been through an ordeal. You should really stay with us, so that we can take care of you. You've got a nasty sunburn. By this evening, you will be *very* uncomfortable," my mom says, turning in her seat to look back at me.

"I'm fine. I'll use my first-aid kit," I say, sinking into the back seat.

"You need to put some aloe vera on, or you're going to blister. Our house is on the way. We can stop and I will grab one of my potted aloe vera plants for you. How does that sound?"

No matter how old you are, you are always your parents' child.

"That sounds good, Mom. Thank you for caring about me," I say with a sleepy smile.

I spend the rest of the car ride in a stupor. That adventure today sure did make me aware of every little muscle in my body! I can only imagine how I'd be feeling right now if I had done that with my fifty-year-old body. Yikes!

We stop at my parents' house for a few minutes, so my mother can get the aloe vera plant.

I can barely keep my eyes open by the time we get to the hotel. When we get to my room, my mom leads me to the bathroom. She helps me undress and get in the shower. I stand for a few minutes before I start the painful process of washing myself.

When I get out, my mom rubs aloe vera gel all over the burned parts of my body. *Ahhh! This feels nice.* She brings me a robe, and then we both go back to the room and find Pop asleep in a chair. He's had a long day too.

We decide to let him sleep. I could really use some sleep too, so I lie down on the bed. My mom pulls out a book from her bag and settles into the chair next to Pop. Within minutes, all I see are the insides of my eyelids.

A ringing phone awakens me. I look around, and see that it's my phone. I reach out to get it off of the bedside table and answer before checking caller ID.

"Hello," I say groggily.

# It's the Five Oh!

"Is this Ella Malone?" a male voice asks.

"Who is *this*?" I ask.

"This is Sergeant Ray from the other night. Is this Ella?" he asks.

"Oh yes. I'm sorry Sergeant Ray. Yes, it's me," I say, wondering why he's calling me.

"The reason I'm calling you is that a minor was involved in an incident today, and your name came up as the woman who came to her rescue," he says.

"Yes, I was there, but it was the helicopter crew who saved both of us," I say, hoping to end this conversation quickly. I'm very uncomfortable talking about anything that might make me slip up and talk about my Gifts.

"Christine Martin told me how you chased after her and climbed those rocks trying to get to her. She also told me how you stayed with her and kept her calm, even after she was such an, and I quote, 'a-hole' to you," he says, chuckling softly. "Anyway, I just wanted to thank you for what you did, and to tell you that it might not be a bad idea to put the cape away for awhile. You need to get some rest, Wonder Woman!" he says.

I laugh and say, "You know, that's not a bad idea. This vacation is certainly anything but."

"Well, you sound sleepy, so I'm going to go now. Have a good evening," he says.

"You too, Sergeant Ray," I say. *Click.*

After I hang up, my parents, who are wide-awake, look at me expectantly.

"Everything is fine. He just wanted to check up on me and tell me that maybe I should hang up my cape for a while and get some rest. He called me Wonder Woman," I say, slightly embarrassed.

"How about that?! A policeman calling my daughter Wonder Woman!" my pop says, beaming.

I frown.

"What's wrong, Ella?" my mom asks.

"I'd like to let people know how it was Pop's idea to start the fire. After all, that was what helped them find us," I say, feeling frustrated.

"Don't worry about that, Ella Bella. I think that we need to lie low for now. I don't relish the thought of having that circus in my front yard again. I hope that it takes at least a *few* days before the news gets wind that it was *you* up there on that rock," Pop says.

"Me too!" Mom and I say in unison.

My parents get up to leave.

"Are you sure you're going to be all right?" Pop asks.

"Yes. I've got my ointments and gels. I will just order up some room service and then go back to bed," I say sleepily.

My mom has a worried look on her face. I pick up the extra room key that was sitting on a table and hand it to her.

"Here you go. If I ever *don't* answer the phone, you can get in here any time you need to check up on me," I say with a smile.

I get a smile back from her.

# It Burns!

My parents leave and I order room service. I want cool food, because I feel warm from my sunburn. I order a chicken salad, iced tea, and a piece of chocolate cream pie.

I finish my meal, get washed up, and climb wearily back into bed.

I'm dreaming that I'm in a burning building. The flames are everywhere, and I can't find a way out. It's so hot! Help me!

I wake to discover that I *am* on fire! I feel like I'm burning up! Oh no! Did I burn the bed like last time? I turn on the bedside lamp and pull back the covers. Nothing. Huh? And then it hits me—sunburn!

I ease out of bed and make it to the bathroom. I turn on the light.

*"Ahh!"* I yelp, when I look in the mirror. I look like a lobster. I guess my suntan lotion was no match for hours trapped in the desert. *"Ouchee!"* I say when I touch my shoulder.

Well, thank goodness, I didn't burn the bed. That would be really hard to explain.

I apply more aloe vera from Mom's plant, drink half a glass of water, take off my clothes, and get back into bed.

When I wake up the next morning, I feel like I've visited hell in my sleep. I feel sick. I want my mom!

I tough it out and manage to pull on a lightweight shirt and some sweatpants. I call room service and order cold cereal, a blueberry muffin, and some fruit. Then I call my mom.

"Hello, Ella. How do you feel today?" she asks first thing.

"Mom, I feel sick. *Ummm* . . . Would you be able to maybe stop by sometime today and help me get the aloe vera rubbed on my back, please?" I don't like asking for help.

"Of course, dear. I can be there in about twenty minutes. Is that good for you?" she asks.

"That's great for me," I say, feeling better already.

# Yay, Mom!

My mom shows up just as the food arrives. She takes it upon herself to bring the food in. She places it on the bedside table, so that I don't have to move much to get to it. I slowly eat my breakfast while my mom sits on the edge of her seat, waiting to jump in and assist me if I need help. I feel like such a baby.

When I eat the last bite of muffin, I realize that I never offered her anything to eat. "I'm sorry, Mom. Did you want some breakfast?"

"Oh no, thank you. I've already eaten. Why don't we get some gel rubbed on your poor little burned body, and then I'll put you back to bed?" she says while cleaning up the mess that I've created in bed.

"Okay," I say, and I carefully get out of bed.

She slathers me with aloe vera gel and then I get right back into bed.

My mom leans over and kisses me on the top of my head. "I'm going to let you sleep. Please call me if you need me again. I love you," she says with a smile.

"I love you too, Mom, and thank you for coming to my rescue," I say, feeling my eyelids droop.

I wake up four hours later, feeling slightly better. I turn on the TV and surf for a while until I find something that catches my interest.

# Hello, Friend

I'M WATCHING A REPEAT OF *Everybody Loves Raymond* when my phone rings. Caller ID shows that it's Tammy. Tammy is a great friend of mine. I have known her since childhood. Everybody who knows her calls her, "Dude," because her favorite movie is *The Big Lebowski*. She reminds me of the main character, "The Dude," because she has such a laid-back attitude.

One time she matter-of-factly told me about how she tripped and fell into her large outdoor trashcan.

I asked her how horrible it must've been, and she said, "It wasn't so bad. It was better than when I tripped over my grandson's toy in the bathroom and broke my nose on the edge of the tub. It was kind of a bummer going to the hospital."

Tammy could take any situation and diffuse it with her calm. I need to carry her around with me in my pocket!

"Hi, Dude," I say, answering the phone.

She laughs. "Hey, Ella. How's it going with you?"

*Where do I even begin?!*

"It's going okay," I say. "How are you?"

"Not too bad," she says. "I was calling to see if you would like to come up and visit me in November. Bring Mary too if she wants to come. The lake house should be done by then, and it is so beautiful that time of year," she says, sounding chipper.

"I would love to, and I'm sure that she would too," I say happily.

Tammy lives in Fryeburg, Maine, and has been building her dream house by Lovewell Pond over the last two years. Nothing sounds more appealing to me right now than to be in the snow. I would throw myself naked in it right now if I could.

"Cool," Tammy says. "Well, I've got to go feed the kids," she says, referring to the alpacas that she raises.

She has been raising alpacas for almost fifteen years now. She uses their fur to make clothing and blankets that she sells at the local fairs and online. She raises goats too and makes soap from their milk.

I could never imagine her being in the corporate world again.

After graduating from college, she went on to law school to be an environmental attorney. Unfortunately, there is so much red tape and butt kissing involved that she quit her job after three years to practice on her own. Now she represents farmers only.

"No corporate allowed," she says.

Pretty cool, huh?!

"Okay, Tammy. Just let me know when the house is ready, and I will be there with bells on!"

"Sounds good. Take it easy." *Click.*

*Yep! Just like The Dude.*

I lean back and smile. I haven't seen Tammy in almost three years, so I'm really looking forward to this trip.

I have a lot of things to look forward to. I've got two wonderful kids and a semi-lovable cat waiting for me back home. I've got a crazy friend who has a bigger heart than she will ever admit to, and I've got a new business that I can't wait to open.

My mood has dramatically improved since I woke up today.

## Mood Breaker

I'M SMILING WHEN THE HOTEL phone rings. "Hello?" I answer.

"Ella Malone, this is Dusty Goodman."

"How the hell? Are you stalking me?! I have better things to do than to be talking to you! Good-bye!" I say, starting to hang up the phone.

"Don't hang up," I hear him say as the receiver gets to the cradle.

Almost there. All I have to do is move the phone two more inches, and I won't have to talk to him.

"Please wait," he says.

Damn! I'm just too nice of a person to hang up on someone who says please.

"What?! What do you want? Do you want to talk to me, so you can take my words and twist them around? Do you want to badmouth my parents again? What?! What is it?" I ask, trying to keep myself from cussing him out.

"I want to thank you," he says.

*Huh?!*

"I'm sorry. What did you say?" I ask feeling very sure that I heard him wrong.

"Sarah Martin is my sister. She told me how you were the one who saved my niece," he says.

"Huh?" I say, feeling totally lost.

"Christine Martin, who you helped save yesterday, is my niece," he says, sounding slightly irritated.

My mind finally wraps around what he is saying.

*Really? Christine is his niece? What are the odds? Wait a minute. It's a trap! He's lying and trying to get me to confess that I was there yesterday!*

"I have no idea what you're talking about," I say.

"Look. I'm not lying. I want to protect my niece, so this is one story that I am opting out of reporting on. The Martins are in town visiting *me*. I was at the hospital with Sarah and her husband when Christine was brought in. I only went outside and joined the group so that I could see if anyone had found out about her," he says.

*He sounds really convincing, but I'm not falling for it.*

"Once again, I have no idea what you're talking about. Actually, when I was walking by the nurses station on the way to my friend's room, I heard them talking about a little *boy* who had been rescued." *There. That ought to do it.*

"I appreciate the fact that you want Christine's identity out of the spotlight as much as I do. Just know that you have earned my respect. I will leave you and your family alone from now on, unless you do something remarkable again and feel like giving me an exclusive interview," he says. I think that I can actually hear him wink and smile.

"Um . . . okay. If I ever feel like being interviewed, I will give you a call," I say, feeling very confused.

"Well, I will be signing off for now. Thank you, and good night," he says. *Click.*

I stare at the phone in my hand for a minute before I hang it up.

I don't know if he was really telling the truth or not, but hopefully for now, my parents and I will be safe from at least one vulture with the name Dusty.

# Preparing to Leave

THE REST OF THE DAY goes by without any surprises. I call my parents around six to let them know that I'm still alive.

"Hello, Ella. How's my little lobster feeling?" my pop asks cheerfully.

"I'm feeling much better, thank you. How are you doing? You were out in that desert for as long as I was," I say, walking over to the balcony.

"You know me—I don't burn. I'm feeling just fine," my pop says. He's always the optimist.

"That's good. I was calling to see if I could spend the day with y'all tomorrow and then take you out to dinner. Since I'll be leaving the next day, I want to be able to spend as much time with you two as possible before I leave," I say, missing them already.

"Why don't you come on over when you wake up, and we will cook a big breakfast for you? I also want to check your bracelet, to see how it's holding up," Pop says.

"I will see you tomorrow then. Is nine okay?" I ask.

"Nine is fine," he says as he chuckles. "I'm a poet, and didn't know it!"

"You are so silly, Pop. Love you!" I say, smiling.

"Love you too, Ella Bella. Good night." *Click.*

## Best Parents Ever

THE NEXT MORNING, I AM up at 7:30 and leave the hotel at eight thirty. As I'm driving to my parents' house, I think about how much I've learned about them during this trip. How funny is it that my mother never told my father about The Change because she didn't think that he could handle it? But my father knew about my mother's armpit Gift all these years and never questioned her about it. They also are so much stronger than I ever imagined they could be. I've always been so proud of them both with how they have lived their lives. They have always been good people and such amazing parents.

I pull into the driveway and feel a lump form in my throat. I'm really going to miss them. I talk to them on the phone often, but it's just not the same as seeing them in person.

*Hold it together, Ella. Make this a happy visit, not a sappy visit.*

I get to the front door and am greeted by them both.

"Hello, dear," my mom says, giving me a big hug.

"Hi, there," my pop says, hugging both of us.

After a few seconds, we all start laughing. We realize how silly we must look, all huddled together at the front door.

I enter the home, and the wonderful aroma of eggs, bacon, hash browns, pancakes, and muffins hits me. *Mmmmm . . .*

We all sit down at the breakfast table and look at each other.

"What would you like to do today since it's your last day?" Pop asks.

"I was thinking maybe we could take it easy and just chat, play some cards, and look at old pictures," I say, feeling sad but trying not to look it.

"That sounds nice, dear," Mom says.

Pop snaps his fingers. "I almost forgot. I made you something, Ella. Actually, I've made a few things. I'll be right back," he says as he heads out back.

A few minutes later, he appears with four small pouches. He sits down and puts them down on the table in front of me.

"What are they?" I ask.

"Open them," Pop says.

I open the first pouch. It's a bracelet in the same style as the first one he had made me with a black band; only this one has a rose quartz charm. I open the next pouch, and it's another bracelet. This one has a brown band and a turquoise charm. The third pouch surprises me with a necklace. It has a long, silver chain, and a rose quartz charm.

Pop picks up the fourth pouch and says, "This is for the first bracelet I made you."

"These are so pretty Pop. Thank you!" I say, admiring the necklace.

"Well, I know how you ladies like to have a variety of jewelry to choose from. This way, hopefully, you will always have something that matches what you're wearing," he says, smiling.

"How very thoughtful," I say, getting up and giving him a hug.

"I had no idea that he was making these for you," Mom says, looking at him adoringly.

"After we finish eating, don't let me forget to check your first bracelet. I need to see if it needs any repair after the desert adventure," he says.

"Okay," I say, looking at the pretty things lying before me.

I try on each new bracelet, so we can all admire them. When I'm finished, I put them in my Louis for safekeeping.

When we finish eating, I give Pop my bracelet, and he heads off to the workshop.

"I don't know why he doesn't make more jewelry than he does. He's really good," I say.

"Your father's big love is music. He likes making jewelry, but he has more fun when the two of us go out rock hunting. He likes to move around, and I think that it's really hard for him to sit still long enough to finish a piece," Mom says.

"Yes, I can see how that would be hard for him," I say, looking in the direction of the workshop.

A few minutes later, Pop comes back inside and puts my bracelet back on my wrist.

"It held up pretty good," he says. "I just had to clean it up a bit."

# The Rest of the Day

WE SPEND THE REST OF the day talking, laughing, playing cards, and looking at old photos. The time goes by quickly. Before we know it, it's time for dinner. I brought a change of clothes with me, so that I didn't have to spend any time apart from them on this day.

We have reservations at their favorite restaurant, so they are both excited. We have great food and great company to look forward to. I drive us to the restaurant, so we can chat going and coming.

We have a wonderful dinner, with lots of laughter, but when time comes to leave, the mood changes. On the car ride back to their house after dinner, we are all very quiet.

When we get to their house, we go inside and have a seat at the kitchen table for one last time.

Mom makes some coffee and produces a coffee cake. Yum!

We chat for a while, and then the time comes to say good-bye.

"I'm really going to miss you," I say, feeling my eyes begin to tear.

"We're going to miss you too, dear. It's been so wonderful having you here," my mother says.

My father nods in agreement.

"I promise that I will come visit more often. Next time, I'll bring the kids," I say, trying to sound cheerful.

I look at them and get so sad. I always get sad when we say good-bye. I worry about them because they're getting older. They don't *act* like they're getting any older. They stay busy and seem to be really happy and healthy, but I still can't stop worrying about them. They're my parents!

"We would love to see the kids again," Pop says, smiling.

"Well, I guess I should get going. I've got an early flight," I say, forcing myself to leave.

We all get up, and after I've collected my Louis, they walk me out to the car.

"I love you, Mom. Thank you so much for everything. Your support, guidance, and tender loving care have helped me more than you will ever know," I say, hugging her tightly.

"I love you too, Ella," she says, sounding a little choked up.

"And Pop, thank you for *your* help! I don't know if I could've tackled that gunman at the lodge without you distracting him. I also don't think that Christine and I would have survived if you hadn't calmed me down and told me to light a fire. I love you," I say, giving him a big hug.

"I love you too, Ella Bella. It was fun being your sidekick," he says, trying to lighten the mood.

It works, and we all laugh.

I get in my car, wave, and drive away.

In the car, I let the tears fall.

When I get to my room. I pack, brush, wash, and go to sleep.

# Texas Bound

THE NEXT DAY, MY FLIGHT goes off without a hitch. No squirting armpits, no cute young men. Just smooth sailing. Er, flying.

The plane touches down at Hobby Airport, and I finally start to feel the sadness of leaving my parents go away. In its place is the happiness of seeing my kids and my cat.

I call Maggie and arrange to meet her so I can pick up Monkey.

I get to Maggie's house, and she greets me at the front door with a hug. "Hi, Mom. Welcome back!" she says, flinching. I don't know if she'll ever get used to me looking like I could be her sister.

"Hi, Maggie! I've missed you so much! It's good to be back," I say happily.

When I walk through the front door, I see Monkey sitting on top of the climbing post in the living room.

"Monkey!" I say, running over to her so I can pick her up.

She jumps down and runs from me. She does this every time I have to leave her for more than a day. She gets so angry with me. She makes me chase her, even though all she wants is for me to take her home.

I play along for a few minutes and then finally catch her and put her in her carrier.

"Hey, Mom, Michael and I thought that it'd be a good idea if we all have dinner tonight. We already called Mary and asked her if she would like to come too. She's really anxious to talk to you about fighting those men. She has called Michael and me several times in the past few days, to see if we had any new news," Maggie says, laughing.

I laugh.

"That sounds great," I say. "I'm going to be so busy in the next few days going over things with Javier. I need to get construction back on track. I'm glad that you planned this dinner."

*My kids are so wonderful!*

Monkey and I head home. Along the way, I call my parents to let them know that I landed safely. I also call Michael and Mary to tell them that I'm looking forward to dinner tonight.

When I pull into my driveway, I get misty eyed.

So much has happened since I've been gone, that it feels like I've been gone for years.

After I get Monkey and my luggage inside, I unpack and turn on the shower.

I'm just getting undressed when I'm hit with a major power surge! I switch the water all the way over to cool and jump inside.

*"Ahh!* That feels good!"

Suddenly, I get déjà vu! I shake my head and laugh it off.

A few minutes later, when I'm finished washing and shampooing, I step out to start getting ready.

I choose the white top that my mother gave to me the day of the press conference, (she insisted that I take it home with me), my dressy jeans, a pair of black sandals, silver hoop earrings, my new necklace from Pop, and my LV

Indian Rose Vernis Alma BB bag. (I want to let my little Speedy 25 rest a few days after the incident at the lodge, and my White Pochette reminds me of my date with Brendan, so I have to pick a bag that didn't go with me on my trip. Never again will I let my beautiful bags go to waste by being hidden in my closet.)

# Hello, Family

WHEN I WALK INTO THE restaurant, I see my son's smiling face. "Hi, Michael, honey. I've missed you!" I say, hugging him.

"I've missed you too," he says, sounding slightly uncomfortable.

Since he was a teenager, Michael has always gotten embarrassed when I hug him in public. I've always wished that he would grow out of it. Just as I back away from him, Maggie walks in and we give each other a big hug.

Mary arrives, and now it's a party!

The evening is a blast. Mary makes me tell, in detail, how I beat up each of those three gunmen. She loves it when I get to the part about burning the guy's crotch! (Of course I have to give her the version of the story that I gave to the police.)

"I sure wish the person who was filming you wouldn't have *bleep*ed it up and put a finger over the lens when you did that," Mary says.

Michael and Maggie give me looks that say, "Thank goodness for that person's finger!" We finish dinner, then dessert, and I suggest we all go to my house for coffee and more dessert.

We all form a caravan and head to my house. Along the way, we make a quick pit stop at the grocery store. I run in to pick up some coffee cake and cream for our coffee.

On my way out, I glance over at the side of the store where I had my first taste of what I could do with my Gifts. To this day, I still smile when I think about how I handled that jerk! I have to remember to get signed up for kickboxing again.

# A Perfect Ending

WE ALL MAKE IT TO my house, and I pull into the driveway, followed by Maggie. Then Mary parks beside me, and Michael pulls in behind her. We all get out and make our way toward the front door.

"Hello, Ella," I voice says from behind us.

We all jump and turn around.

It's Pete! Oh, my hell. It's Pete! I feel my hands start to burn, so I quickly hand everything I'm holding to Michael. I make fists to try to stop the flames.

"What the hell are you doing here?" Mary asks Pete angrily.

I just stand there in angered shock.

"Well, you told me that you were going to dinner with Ella tonight, and I thought I would come over and say hi. I've just been over there, waiting for you," he says, slurring his words and pointing to a car parked across the street.

Mary says to me, "He called me earlier today, and it slipped out that I was having dinner with you tonight. Sorry."

"Are you drunk?! Let me take you home, so you can sleep it off," Mary says to Pete, taking him by the arm and trying to lead him to her car.

"But I *miss* her!" he says loudly to Mary while trying to shake off her hand.

"Well, she doesn't miss *you!*" Mary shouts.

Pete turns around and looks at me. He wobbles slightly but catches himself.

"You don't miss me, Ella?" he asks, sounding like a drunken fool.

All of the sudden, I feel such a wave of anger that I almost fall over. It is so powerful that I feel like I'm going to explode.

I'm not in angered shock anymore. I'm just downright pissed, and I lose all control of myself.

"You mean to tell me that you're honestly confused at the thought that I *wouldn't* miss you? You miserable *bleep*ing jackass! You leave me after all these years for someone young enough to be your daughter, and you really think that I would *miss* you?! Let me tell you how I feel about you," I say, walking toward him. I start cussing him up one side and down the other. I'm not aware of Mary or the kids at this point. I'm just focused on *him*.

Suddenly, I see Pete's eyes grow incredibly wide, and he starts to shake. He also seems to be getting shorter. *What the—?!*

Then I hear Maggie say, "Mom! Oh my god!"

I try to turn around to look at her and discover that I can't, because I'm floating in the air about three feet up from the ground!

"What's going on?!" I ask Mary, hoping she can tell me.

"Holy shit!" she says, letting go of Pete. Pete mumbles something and then passes out.

Maggie and Michael walk around in front of me and stare up at me in shock.

I'm still really ticked off because of Pete, but *now* I'm ticked off because I'm up in the air and no one is doing anything to help me!

"Well, don't just stand there staring! Somebody get me down!"

To be continued . . .

Julie Ray created Ella Malone (Hott Flash) in 2007 as a way to use humor to help her mother deal with "The Change". She lives with her boyfriend and her photogenic cat in Texas.

For further information please visit: www.julieray.us

CPSIA information can be obtained at www.ICGtesting.com
Printed in the USA
LVOW08s0052081113

360486LV00005B/265/P